SHAKE OFF

ALSO BY MISCHA HILLER

Sabra Zoo

Mischa Hiller

SHAKE OFF

TELEGRAM

I would like to thank those who gave this book verisimilitude.
And thanks Fran, for making things better.

The Kahlil Gibran quotation is from *Kahlil Gibran: The Collected Works*,
(Everyman's Library, 2007, p. 165).

ISBN: 978-1-84659-088-7

This first edition published in 2011 by Telegram

A full CIP record for this book is available from the British Library.
A full CIP record for this book is available from the Library of Congress.

TELEGRAM
26 Westbourne Grove, London W2 5RH
www.telegrambooks.com

Printed and bound by CPI Mackays, Chatham, ME5 8TD

For my parents

intifada

/ɪntəˈfadə/

noun.

[ORIGIN: Arabic *intifāḍa* lit., a shaking off, der. of *fāḍa* to shake off]

An uprising by Palestinians to protest against Israel's occupation of the West Bank and the Gaza Strip.

ONE

Nobody was there to meet me. Not openly, anyway. I scanned the people waiting behind the barrier as I emerged into the arrivals hall at Heathrow, looking for familiar faces, gaits, physiques, anything that might indicate someone I'd seen before or might see again. I was travelling on a Swiss passport, with $75,000 in thousand-dollar bills taped inside a copy of *The Sunday Times* I'd bought at Tegel Airport before leaving West Berlin. The front-page headline read: 'Kremlin in Crisis as Gorbachev Fights to Keep Control.' Newspapers are my preferred way of carrying money or documents; they are easy to ditch, and you can carry one under your arm even as your bags are being searched. This is detail I was taught.

I took a taxi through a wet London to the Imperial Hotel on Russell Square, found a telephone booth in the lobby and dialled a West Berlin number. I studied the lobby as it rang and the tone of an answer machine came on.

'The meeting went well,' I said in German, the code to let Abu Leila know that I had arrived without incident. I told him I'd speak to him soon. I'd just had a *tref* with Abu Leila in Berlin, where he'd given me the money and some documents. He called our meetings *tref*s because that's what East German intelligence officers called meetings with their agents, and I suppose I counted as Abu Leila's agent, although he had never used that word. I hung up but kept the receiver to my ear, using the time to scan the lobby for familiar faces from the airport. I called the speaking clock so no one could find out what number I'd dialled.

I changed out of my suit into jeans, T-shirt and tennis shoes in the hotel toilets, putting the suit in the holdall. I didn't like to look out of place; it was important to blend in. Be grey, not colourful, my trainers in Moscow had said. I always matched my shoes to my clothes. I'd heard that immigration officers checked for illegal immigrants by looking at their shoes. I ripped my plane ticket up and threw it into the toilet bowl, urinating on the scraps before flushing them away. It is easier to flush soaked paper than dry – this is detail I've picked up with experience.

From the hotel I walked to King's Cross Station and jumped onto a bus going to Kentish Town. I loved these open London buses; you could get on and off when you liked, which made it a little harder for anybody in pursuit. You should always sit at the back of the bus when you get on, because surveillance like to sit at the back to get a good view of you embarking without having to turn around. Your job is to make their job more difficult without it being plain that you know what you are doing. All this I have been taught.

I ran through my meeting with Abu Leila.

'Keep an extra eye out for the competition,' he'd said. 'The competition' was our name for Mossad; it was our little joke: the idea of PLO security competing with such an organisation was laughable. Apparently 'the competition' were trying to reassert themselves in England after recent setbacks – Mossad's station in London had been closed by Margaret Thatcher two years earlier, for having an agent in a PLO cell implicated in the shooting of a Palestinian cartoonist on a South Kensington street. But Abu Leila had another reason for his warning – he wanted to host a secret meeting in England, a meeting between Israelis and Palestinians. His warning was unnecessary; I'd been trained to be constantly alert. It was always better to be safe than sorry, even if being safe meant not being able to relax.

By the time I got to Kentish Town I had reassured myself that I was travelling alone. I walked the dark and quiet residential backstreets up to Tufnell Park, avoiding the main road. The recent rain had freshened the air and cleansed the streets. I stopped occasionally, once to do my shoelaces, twice to shift my bag to the other shoulder, always giving a quick scout behind as I crossed the road. But it was late on a Sunday and nobody else was about.

It was with some relief that I reached my road in Tufnell Park where I rented a small room – just a bed, cooker and sink in a three-storey terraced house – what the English call a bedsit. Six rooms in all – occupied, as far as I could tell, by mature students or itinerant workers. It had been home for a year, and I paid the rent every month in cash. Since each of the rooms was self-contained (apart from shared bathrooms on each floor) I exchanged only greetings with the other inhabitants when passing them on the stairs, which suited me fine.

I hung up my suit and took the money from inside the newspaper. I'd spent the first fifteen years of my life in a refugee camp, so I appreciated how much money I was carrying, although Abu Leila handed it out indifferently, not even expecting me to account for it. I took no advantage though; I just lived the life of a student, as instructed. My modest monthly expenses were paid through to a UK bank account, transferred from a trust fund in Qatar ostensibly set up by my parents' executors, although I don't think my parents had ever even opened a bank account. My fees at the School of Oriental and African Studies, where I was registered as a student, had been paid upfront, from the same account. The last thing Abu Leila wanted was for me to look out of place. He gave me strict instructions to stay out of exiled Arab circles, and particularly to avoid the Palestinian student community and their organisations, like the General Union of Palestinian Students. Abu Leila said that Western intelligence agencies saw anyone involved in such activities as a potential threat, and that such groups were infiltrated by the competition. I wrapped the money and the Swiss passport in a towel, thinking of several ways it could be put to good use in the camp, although I didn't know what it was for, just what I had to do with it.

I saw light coming from under the bathroom door on the landing. As I turned to go back into my room, the door opened and my housemate emerged trailing steam, wrapped in a towel that reached mid-thigh, another wrapped turban-like around her head. I'd only seen her once or twice before as we passed each other on the stairs. She'd been there a month, replacing a middle-aged man who I'd never seen use the bathroom.

4

We shuffled awkwardly on the small landing, and she gave an embarrassed smile as she walked past me with her freshly bathed smell. The shabby but clean bathroom was still steamy. I caught the herbal aroma of her bathwater as it swirled down the plughole. She'd left a candle on the side of the bath – a thin snake of smoke emerged from the blown-out wick. I wet my forefinger and thumb and squeezed the smoking wick dead with a hiss.

The house was quiet as I checked the alignment of the screws that held the plastic side panel of the bath in place. They were as I'd last left them. Using a tiny penknife attached to my key ring, I removed the panel. Lying on my back parallel to the bath, I reached under and unhooked an A4-sized plastic package attached to a water pipe running along the wall under the tub. It was still warm from the bath. I pulled the package out. Undoing the zip-lock, I took out a Lebanese passport and replaced it with the Swiss passport and the dollars. Even in thousand-dollar bills the money was a tight fit. The zip-lock had a Greek passport and £2,600 in it, from which I removed £1,000. I closed it and replaced it on the pipe, which took some effort since I had to do it blind. Not an ideal hiding place, but you had to make use of what was around you. I never kept anything incriminating in my room – that, according to my trainers, you should never do. I screwed the bath panel back on, making sure the screw heads were aligned as before.

Back in my room I lay in bed with the lights out and the curtains open, the room lit up by the street lamps. Again I went through what little Abu Leila had told me yesterday. My job was to make sure his secret meeting went ahead smoothly, my first task being to research a venue and find somewhere for the Palestinian contingent to stay. As ever, Abu Leila had been light on detail, but then Abu Leila had his own piecemeal way of revealing information, and it wasn't my place to ask questions, not after all he'd done for me. He did say that the meeting would change the course of history and that everything – my training, my cover, the necessary lies, my exile – had been leading to this moment. I reached into the drawer in my bedside cabinet and took out a packet of codeine. I swallowed three tablets with water and lay back down on my bed. I could hear muffled voices from the adjoining room, then the sound of a creaking bed and a man groaning.

I closed my eyes and tried to relax. It was with relief that the codeine started to work and the warmth suffused my body. It was like being tucked in by Mama. It was like Esma stroking my head. I listened to the noises coming through the wall until I fell asleep.

TWO

The Lebanese passport was real, according to Abu Leila, who had given it to me when I left Beirut for Cyprus five years ago. It even had my real surname on it, Khoury, rather than Anton, the surname in the Swiss passport. Khoury is a common Arab Christian surname (meaning priest); Anton could be French or German or Swiss. I have been told that, on looks alone, I could be mistaken for either Swiss or Lebanese, and have also been mistaken for French, Italian, Greek and even an Israeli; all of which is handy when you are travelling on passports from these countries. I was born in the Sabra refugee camp in Beirut – just one of the many hundreds of thousands of Palestinians born outside Palestine who has never actually set foot there.

I'd never tested the Lebanese passport in Lebanon, because Abu Leila had forbidden me to go back. He'd clutched it tightly for a moment before letting it go, looking at me intently and saying, 'From now on you are Lebanese. You were born in east Beirut, and a stray bomb killed your parents during the war.'

East Beirut was mainly Maronite Christian, and we were from west Beirut, although my family was Christian – Greek Orthodox, to be precise – rather than Maronite, who are of the Catholic doctrine. The Phalangists – a neo-Nazi Lebanese group intent on Lebanon being 'pure' – are Maronite Christians. It was the Phalangists who had killed my family on that black day. Abu Leila, once he had made his point, let go of the passport and relieved me of my United Nations card identifying me as a Palestinian refugee. He'd then gone through the details of my reconstructed past. Much of it was true. Abu Leila's genius was in connecting lies to the truth as much as possible. This was later reinforced during my training – if you can believe just a bit of your cover story then you can convince your listener (and even yourself) that it is *all* true.

Because I'd been born and raised in the Sabra refugee camp in south-west Beirut, speaking in a Lebanese vernacular came easily, as many of the camp residents were Lebanese, united with the Palestinians in their poverty. My father had looked down on these Lebanese, because, he said, they had no excuse being there, not being subject to the same disadvantages we Palestinians were with our refugee status. Mama would tell him to shut up, saying they were just refugees within their own country, and that we were in no position to look down on anyone. Mama used to clean and cook for wealthy Lebanese families. During the summer, when the camp-based United Nations refugee school I attended was closed, I sometimes accompanied her to the more affluent areas of west Beirut and sat in large kitchens while she kept house for the owners. If they weren't present Mama allowed me to look around ('Don't touch anything!') and I was amazed that people could have so many rooms, as well as enough things to fill them all. Sometimes the woman of the house would be around and I would be restricted to studying at the kitchen table while Mama made coffee for the gossiping, freshly coiffed women who sat in the formal living room. I would take my school books with me, and it always struck me that, despite the wealth of Mama's employers, few of them had books on their ornament-filled shelves.

After the killings I wound up (via the Zionist army, the Red Cross and the Red Crescent) living with such a family. Except that they were Palestinian and Christian, and it was an eye-opener to meet Palestinians who lived outside the camp, never mind ones who had a live-in maid and ate meat every day. But before that, in the immediate aftermath, this elderly childless couple had taken me in and fed me and clothed me and sent me (at great expense) to the International School of Beirut. It was only much later, when I was no longer able to thank them, that I appreciated their generosity. Kind as they were, I didn't take to them, and my memories of them are vague. They were reserved to the point of being formal, and again it was later that I understood that my stay was only ever going to be temporary, that they never intended to let me into their hearts. No one had thought to tell me this at the time. It hadn't occurred to me, once I was settled in to my new and comfortable home, to go back to the refugee camp, nor was it ever suggested by anyone. What was the point? After all, I had no one to go back to – a result not just of the efficiency of the killers who had murdered my small family – all five of them – in one fell swoop, but also because I was an only child and came from a Christian family. These things made us a minority in the camp and meant we had few real friends. Or at least my parents (mainly my father) had chosen to have few friends: he hadn't just looked down on our impoverished Lebanese neighbours, but also on our Muslim neighbours, muttering with annoyance at the daily calls to prayer and the pre-dawn pot-banging in the streets during Ramadan. So I had no extended family, no friends to take me in, and little supporting infrastructure since the Israelis had forced the PLO out of Beirut just before the killings. I was told by the Red Crescent worker who handled my case that I should feel lucky to have found such a good foster family so quickly, that other children had ended up back in the camp with other families. She told me this as if it was a bad thing.

I kept to myself in my new alien environment, avoiding my new classmates after school, who called me 'the refugee' in that offhand cruel manner that children have of picking up on any difference. I steeled myself against this rejection, determined to do well at my lessons, to show that I was as good as any of the other kids despite my schooling thus far, which in itself was cause for mockery. So I filled this family-free and friendless void with studying, principally languages, for which my teachers said I had an aptitude. And although I busied myself with school and books and study, it was at night – after I had finished reading – that I found my circumstances most difficult; that was when I had no way of deflecting my thoughts from Mama's receding screams or the dying weight of my father pressing down on me. At the time these memories were still fresh and overwhelmed me, rekindling the panic I'd felt at the time.

I know that it was shameful and weak, but in those first weeks after arriving in my new home I cried every night, muffling the sound with my pillow so no one would hear me. I cried until I exhausted myself to sleep.

I worried that my new foster family would hear the nightly crying and be embarrassed that they'd adopted a fifteen-year-old cry-baby, but I learned that by rocking my head back and forth on the pillow I could displace the bad memories until sleep caught up with me. This action created a rushing sound in my head, a soothing white noise. After a few days of acquiring this new skill, Esma, the Kurdish maid who lived in the box room next to mine during the week, came into my room late one night.

'What are you doing?' she asked in a harsh whisper. 'You're keeping me awake with your banging.' I looked at her framed in the doorway, dressed only in her slip, and couldn't answer. She studied me, and something overcame her well-earned need for sleep, for she came in and sat on my bed and stroked my head to stop my rocking. The next night, though, imagining her sleeping on the other side of the wall, I vacillated between rocking my head in the hope that she would come in and keeping still so as not to disturb her. Sometimes I rocked my head with abandon and she would come, but on the whole she didn't, banging on the wall instead.

'I'm not your mother,' she said one night, after coming into my room. She was right, she wasn't Mama. I was ashamed, and she could see that. 'I work all day,' she added, more softly. 'I need to sleep.' So I no longer tried to attract her attention, but learned that if I put my ear to the wall I could hear the steady breathing which told me she was asleep, and that became my cue to rock my head. At the weekends, when she went home to her village outside Beirut, I could start rocking as soon as I tired of reading.

THREE

When I first arrived in London a year ago, I was travelling on my Lebanese passport stamped with a twelve-month visa and papers indicating that I was registered at the School of Oriental and African Studies. I was enrolled to do a ten-month-long foundation course – essentially an advanced English language course for foreigners intending to do further study. I had graduated in English and German from the Freie Universität in West Berlin a few months before arriving in London; I didn't need the postgraduate language course, but being at SOAS was good cover and gave me time to do my real job without being burdened with too much work.

The morning after getting back from West Berlin I called in at SOAS to pick up some coursework. I received a lecture from my tutor on my lax attendance: I had been going to the minimum number of lectures required to qualify for credits. Her heart wasn't in it though, because my coursework results were excellent and I never missed an assignment. I gave her my most penitent face and she smiled and shook her head, pointing at her door. A couple of the students invited me to an end-of-course party. I told them I'd think about it – I don't think they expected me to attend and I didn't plan to.

Afterwards I stopped at a private postbox bureau in Westminster. One of the first things I had done on arriving in London was to register at three of these services using different identities. All I needed was a fake driving licence and a matching utility bill. I kept a variety of these documents in a bank deposit box registered under yet another name, along with other documentation and money. Six large envelopes were in the postbox, five of which contained sales leaflets and technical documents that related to military radio equipment that I was collating for Abu Leila. The sixth envelope was one I had had couriered from West Berlin the day before yesterday, given to me by Abu Leila. I hadn't wanted to carry it, especially since I was carrying the money and didn't want the two things connected. I could perhaps explain the money, but not the money and whatever was in that envelope. I also found a letter posted from Rome. I opened it before leaving the bureau. Inside was a single sheet with a list of twelve names and addresses typed in Arabic, but no explanation of what they were. The addresses were all in towns on the West Bank; they could have been informers or potential recruits, it was not my concern. I bundled the brochures into one large envelope and posted them to a PO box in West Berlin that Abu Leila checked on a regular basis.

Thirty minutes later I entered Westminster Reference Library off Leicester Square, where there were few people at that time of day. Removing a *Shorter Oxford Dictionary* from a shelf, I sat at a desk and ciphered the names in the letter using a code that Abu Leila had come up with.

I had to rewrite the names in English, using an agreed transliteration of the Arabic. Western intelligence agencies had great problems processing and cross-referencing Arabic names because of the variety of ways one could spell them in English, but Abu Leila had standardised the process, adding a layer of consistency. The system involved using the *Shorter Oxford* to generate a reference number for a word, a combination of the line and page number. The downside was that I had to have access to the same dictionary as Abu Leila, but it couldn't be one that I kept at home, hence my use of the library. It was laborious and there were surely better and more secure ways of communicating, but we had stuck with it because we were the only ones who used it, and I liked it because I came across new words every time. When completed, I destroyed the original letter, flushing the torn and soaked remains down the public toilet in the library. I posted the coded letter to Berlin as soon as I was outside.

Back in Tufnell Park I had a bath. I thought of the girl who had lain in it the night before. I thought of the towel high on her long legs. I thought of the noises I'd heard in her room. I didn't have much to go on from last night so I thought of Kurdish Esma. I missed her for her head-stroking, but I missed her for other things too.

The last time I had been with a woman was several weeks ago, someone I'd picked up in a Berlin bar and taken to my hotel room. I couldn't remember her name or what she looked like, except that she had large breasts, thick ankles and stubbly legs. All of my sexual encounters were of this nature, as little was expected by either party beyond a certain release. I found it easier to say nothing than to lie, as getting to know someone unfortunately meant telling them about myself, letting them see beyond the façade. I'd been taught to be wary of women, especially those who initiated contact: I heard many stories (from Abu Leila and my Soviet trainers) of people falling foul of this most ancient of honey traps. An Israeli nuclear scientist had been lured from London to Rome by a Mossad agent who had picked him up in Trafalgar Square, of all places. I knew that one's ego could blur the reality of a situation: it is easier to believe that a woman finds you irresistible than that she is trying to ensnare you. So on the whole I ignored the women who started things and always made the approach myself, although I was aware of the signals that could be given out to make you initiate contact: a smile, a lingering look, someone asking for directions or a light. It was hard work, having to be alert all the time, and once or twice I had considered using a prostitute. I imagined that with a prostitute you could relax completely; a transaction was entered into. Logically it made sense, given my circumstances, and yet something, a sense of shame or pride, stopped me from going through with it.

I often wondered what it would be like to be completely honest with someone about myself, even considering asking Abu Leila whether I could be coupled with a woman in the same position. I had a recurring fantasy involving a pair of agents travelling Europe, staying in hotels and going to restaurants together (I hated eating in restaurants alone) once our business was done. It made sense from an operational point of view, as a couple attracts less attention than a person on their own. As I drained the bath I promised myself that I would bring it up with Abu Leila when I saw him next.

FOUR

On the whole, my foster 'auntie' and 'uncle' (I could never properly think of them as surrogate parents) left me to my own devices, although they obliged me to be sociable when they had visitors. A lot of people came to the apartment in the first weeks, and it became clear that they had come to see me. Not to talk to me but to look at me, as if my tragedy might have some physical manifestation. I felt uncomfortable in their presence, sensing their curiosity and pity.

'Poor thing,' the coiffed women would say to each other, as if I couldn't hear them. 'Imagine, his whole family in one go!'

I would say nothing, withdrawing to my room, where I conjugated French verbs and practised writing joined-up English in ruled notebooks. Sometimes Esma the maid would come in brandishing a duster and pretend to clean. I could not determine Esma's age beyond that she didn't seem much older than me, and I sensed that she would rather be doing anything but cleaning for this kindly but reserved couple. I would jokingly admonish her in my beginner's French, telling her not to disturb me or that she had missed dusting a shelf, and she would laugh because she couldn't understand me, covering her mouth to hide her gold-filled teeth. But by then

I had caught the spark in her pitch-black eyes and would try to provoke her further.

'Please would you tell me the way to the Louvre?' I would ask her in French. When she was doubled up I would continue in a deadpan voice, 'Do you have a double room free for the night?' until she was in hysterics and biting into the duster so her employers wouldn't hear. On one occasion I had hidden in my room to escape some gawping guests, and lay on my bed reading an abridged *Huckleberry Finn*, wrestling with the language with the aid of a heavy dictionary. Esma came in and pretended to wipe the dust-free surfaces. As always, she had her maid's floral housecoat on; I'd never seen her in anything else apart from her slip that first night she had come into my room.

'What are you reading?' she'd asked, obviously bored. The voices of the visitors in the sitting room travelled down the hall, although their words couldn't be made out. I started to read aloud to Esma. She giggled and started to flick at my legs with the duster. I put on a mock angry French voice, telling her to behave or to go to her room. She flicked at me some more and with careful timing I caught the duster and pulled, underestimating how light she was and so jerking her onto me. We wrestled briefly, grunting and huffing quietly, and she got astride my chest, trying to pin my arms to the bed with her knees. I let her do it. I could see her white thighs and feel her hot breath, and for a second we were still and panting at each other, her unravelled black hair tickling my face. Then my dictionary slid off the bed and thudded to the floor and she was off me and gone, leaving the duster on my chest and red knee prints in the soft inside of my biceps.

A chain-smoking Abu Leila visited my foster aunt and uncle's home six months after the killings. It was the first time a man had visited the apartment on his own. He filled an armchair and would not allow his hosts to take his raincoat, preferring to drape it over his knees. He dismissed the selection of different cigarette brands on offer, fishing in his raincoat for his own, a flat-boxed brand that I had never seen before, with oval-shaped cigarettes inside. He lit up and peered at me through glasses so heavy-rimmed he had to repeatedly push them back up his hooked nose. The smoke from his cigarettes was sweet and rich, like the incense I used to smell in the Greek Orthodox church Mama took me to at Easter. I had never spoken to anyone in a suit before and I was nervous, associating him with officialdom. The feeling was reinforced when I entered the room and saw him handing over an envelope to my foster aunt and uncle, who expressed their gratitude with an effusiveness I'd not seen before.

'Michel,' Abu Leila had said, 'let me speak with these good people alone, then we will talk.' He spoke in a Palestinian accent, with a voice damaged by years of smoking. I had never been asked to go to my room before and I didn't move, not knowing what to do. 'Go,' Abu Leila commanded softly, waving at me with his cigarette and winking through a grubby lens.

Forty minutes or so after re-reading the same page of algebra at my desk I heard a knock at my door and Abu Leila came in, closing it softly behind him. He sat on the bed and lit one of his cigarettes, filling the small room with pungent blue smoke. I turned to face him and watched him run nicotine-yellowed fingers through his thick hair. He had his raincoat with him. I opened the small window above the desk and watched the smoke escape. No stranger had come into my room like this before.

'Tell me what happened in Sabra – tell me everything,' Abu Leila said, pushing his heavy glasses up his nose and peering at me. The request was made in a tone that could have been used to ask how I was finding school, or whether I liked my new bedroom, but it was this lack of emotion in Abu Leila's voice, the fact that he did not affect concern, that allowed me to consider telling him about the killings. It was also the first time that anyone had asked me what had happened, apart from the enemy soldier who had found me wandering around outside the camp in my bloodstained clothes. Not my own blood, it turned out, but the blood of my father. I recalled that the Israeli soldier, an Arab-looking Israeli (another revelation to me, as I had never seen one before), had hidden his M16 rifle – hidden it because I'd started to shake when I saw it – before crouching down to question me in a funny-sounding Arabic. The soldier had listened as an Israeli medic checked me for injuries, looking at the ground and holding his face in his hands as if it had happened to him. And so I told Abu Leila the story, starting with my family and me sitting down to dinner and ending with me escaping from the camp into the arms of the Israeli who handed me over to the Red Cross.

It had felt good to tell it, like when you've been keeping something from your parents and come out with it at last. It feels good even if the consequences of telling it may not be good. And when Abu Leila heard it, he lit another cigarette and after a silence said, 'Do you want to see justice done, Michel?' I looked up and blushed and nodded, because it was as if he had looked into my head and seen my secret wish: that I should somehow avenge what happened and make up for not doing anything to help Mama. He carried on, saying, 'Then you need to know why this was done to you.' Did he not mean *who* had done this to me? 'Do you play chess, Michel?' Yes, I told him, my father had taught me, and we'd played until I'd started to beat him. He smiled and dragged on his cigarette. 'The pawn is often sacrificed, Michel, so the bishops and the knights can live on to achieve greater victory.' He looked at me intently. 'Do you understand me?' I said yes, although I didn't fully at the time. What I did intuit was that he was offering me a way out of my situation, a way to rebuild my shattered life – he was giving my experience a reason and purpose. He smiled and shook my hand, as if we had just signed a contract satisfactory to both parties.

Now, according to an older Abu Leila in Berlin, my purpose was becoming clearer, but I always clung to that first conversation, even though we never talked of my family or of revenge again.

FIVE

'It's Roberto, can I speak to your father?' I said to the boy who answered the phone. I was calling from a phone box outside Finsbury Park underground station. It went quiet at the other end and I could hear raised voices in the background, women and children shouting in Turkish. Then a man's voice shouted and it went quiet.

'Roberto! My favourite customer,' a male Turkish voice boomed into my ear. 'When are you coming to visit?'

'Lemi, I'll be there in an hour,' I told him. I sat in a café diagonally across from Lemi's house, just three streets from the station. I watched the traffic, looking for people sitting in parked cars or standing around, the same person coming and going, anything that indicated Lemi was being watched. I wasn't that thorough, relying on the fact that Lemi would only be of interest to the police rather than the intelligence services, and any surveillance they carried out would be obvious. A lot of my time was spent watching and waiting.

During my training the Soviets had told me that waiting for contact with agents was a third of the job, avoiding surveillance a third, and reassuring agents that they were doing the right thing another third. But Lemi the Turk was no agent of mine. He was just one of the people, a technician, that I used for specific jobs. He was a genius at adapting everyday luggage and objects so that things could be smuggled or hidden in them. He'd once shown me a whole chess set that he'd hollowed out in his attic workshop, ready to be filled before the bottoms were faultlessly glued on. When I'd asked what was worth smuggling in such small quantities Lemi told me that he was adapting twenty such chess sets for a bulk shipment of cocaine. Although I found such things interesting, I lacked confidence in the Turk's discretion, a requirement in such an occupation. Intelligence agencies would have a whole department to do just what Lemi did, but I had no access to such facilities, except through Abu Leila and the Stasi and KGB, and although Abu Leila had been happy to use them for training, he trusted them not one bit with anything operational.

'We are useful to them and they support our struggle to an extent, but we are not fighting for the same thing,' he'd once told me. Abu Leila was particularly wary of the East Germans. 'The Stasi are obsessed with spying on their own people and the West Germans,' he said. 'And for some reason they are also obsessed with the English,' he'd added on reflection. 'All they want to do is recruit British academics. Just be glad that they don't know you are in England.'

Ten minutes before Lemi was expecting me, I knocked on his door and was let into the house by the small dark boy who'd answered the phone. Lemi's security was non-existent; he thought it was enough of a cover to be a family man and sculptor. He greeted me from the top of the stairs, a broad smile under his thick moustache. He looked like he ate well. He owned a whole house in a neighbourhood where most people lived in houses sectioned into smaller units, much like where I lived.

'I won't offer you any coffee, my friend, I know you are always in a hurry.' He pretended to look hurt and I followed the big man upstairs. I could hear children on the lower floor and smell Middle Eastern cooking. A woman was shouting at the children in Turkish. I always felt at home in Lemi's house. The atmosphere and the smells were so familiar, even if the language was not. The Turk had a workshop (he called it a studio) in the attic, where he did his modifications. You could only get up there using a pull-down ladder, which didn't look like it would take Lemi's weight. I had been referred to the Turk by a Parisian woman who sometimes forged documents for me. She was another artist, not just in what she did, but because she painted larger-than-life canvases of male nudes lying on crumpled sheets. I had once seen her work on sale in a gallery in London. With her the forgery was to support her artwork, whereas with Lemi the carving was just a front for his real passion. She was in her fifties, twice as old as any of her models; they were all young and looked into the viewer's eyes with a sensuality that made me uncomfortable. What struck me was that they all looked equally vulnerable.

'On the outside you look like a man,' she told me when I'd first gone to pick up a fake driving licence from her studio. 'But you have something of a boy about you on the inside.' She'd looked me up and down and asked me if I'd pose for her. I'd fidgeted and declined, worried not so much by being naked in front of her but by ending up looking like the others in the paintings, although in retrospect it would have been an excellent excuse for my visits. 'Perhaps next time,' she'd smiled, openly appraising me. I'd been relieved to get out of her studio.

Lemi handed me a hard suitcase, the sort you could take on to an aircraft. It had little wheels and a retractable handle. I'd sent it to him two weeks ago by minicab.

'Go on, have a look,' he said. He was like a kid showing someone a puzzle. I opened the case and felt along the inside, looking for clues. I pressed the inside but could detect no telltale give of a false bottom. The lining was flush. Lemi laughed. 'Good, eh? You'll never open it, my friend.' He then bent down next to me and unscrewed one of the feet. By pushing in the resulting hole with his finger the bottom lining came away slightly at one point inside the case, a big enough gap that he could get his finger inside. He ran it between the lining and the edge and the whole thing came away in one rigid piece. Lemi chuckled as it revealed a gap two centimetres deep. 'When you put whatever you want in there, make sure you fasten the lining back on around here,' he said, indicating the lip of the removed lining. 'It will stick to the case.' He demonstrated. 'But this is not for drugs, is it?' he asked as he closed it. It was obvious that the hidden compartment was not big enough for drugs but I let the Turk think what he wanted. I thought maybe I should use someone else: an Algerian I knew in Paris, for instance, although he was too politically active for my liking. The Turk had no political connections, which meant that he was unlikely to be on any intelligence service radar. I said nothing as I handed over £500, plus £20 for one of his teenage sons to take the case to a locker at Victoria Station and post the key to the PO box address I gave him. I inhaled the cooking smells before I stepped out onto the street.

My next job was to change the $75,000 into shekels. This meant I had to pick up the money from Tufnell Park and take it to a money changer in Notting Hill. It was run like any other bureau de change, except it was owned by an Armenian who laundered money. You gave him large amounts of cash and he split it up into small transactions, redistributing it through the banks, all for a hefty percentage, of course. I had to leave the money with him in a plastic bag and go and wait in a café for a couple of hours while he sorted it out. When I picked the bag up it was a lot heavier than when I had left it, a testament to the poor value of the shekel compared to the dollar. I disliked hanging around there; I suspected that, like Lemi, he was involved in the drugs business and would possibly be of interest to the police.

SIX

Esma avoided me for several days after the incident on my bed, and had stopped coming into my room to flick her duster. This had made bedtime even more of an ordeal for me, and I reverted to rocking my head again. But one night I heard my door open and, fearing it was my foster aunt or uncle coming to tell me off, I turned my face to the mattress, pressed my pillow hard over my head and pretended to be asleep. But I could smell Esma, a soapy medicinal smell. Her hair was on my back before her hands and lips, and she muttered something in Kurdish that included my name. I turned over and she wiped my wet cheeks, sliding under the cover with me. We explored each other in the dark until we were breathing fast and shallow. Then we lay face to face, our noses touching, and used our hands on each other until hers were sticky and mine were wet. We lay together for a bit, catching our breath. In a fit of whispered giggling we searched for her underwear in the tangle of sheets – then she was gone. The next morning she'd stripped my bed and washed my sheets, and had to do it again for three days running. On the fourth day, a Friday, I trudged back from school in the afternoon to find she had gone to her village, as she did every weekend. I spent an interminable three nights and two days waiting for the moment when I could race back from school on Monday, but she wasn't at home, and when I enquired about her I was told she wasn't returning. I hadn't dared ask why in case they'd become aware of our nightly trysts. The next day Esma was replaced by an old woman who smelled of homemade yoghurt rather than soap and I went back to rocking my head.

Abu Leila continued to visit me intermittently in Beirut, always talking with my aunt and uncle before spending time alone with me. We would sometimes walk on the American University campus opposite the International School, and Abu Leila would explain the Palestinian struggle for self-determination, how it needed to be fought on many fronts and on different levels. Sometimes Abu Leila would talk as if I wasn't there, speaking of internal politics and machinations that I didn't understand, mentioning people that I didn't know. He always talked of the Palestinians in the third person, as if they were a people he didn't belong to. Then he would catch himself and tell me to focus on my studies, tell me that my language skills were second to none, that I was destined for important things.

So I studied a lot of books given to me by Abu Leila, right up until I left for Cyprus. Sometimes Abu Leila had to explain them to me, as many of the books were in French and English (they weren't available in Arabic) and at that time I was still struggling a bit with them.

'You need to know your enemy,' he'd told me, giving me history books and pamphlets. I read how Zionists believed in the inalienable right of Jews to Palestine, and how it emerged from the belief that creating a Jewish state was the answer to anti-semitism. So I read about anti-semitism, and began to understand the relentless nature of it through the ages, from Tsarist Russia onwards. Then I came to the Holocaust, the seemingly natural culmination of all this centuries-old hatred expressed in a whole industry of death. My only knowledge of the Holocaust until then was my father's mention of Hitler, when, aged nine, I had asked him why he and Mama had left Palestine.

'Hitler is to blame,' was all my father had said, in that infuriating way he had of trying to explain things in one sentence. I knew all about the Jews coming to Palestine, every Palestinian did; they'd been coming for years before the diaspora. But nobody had properly explained to me the reason *why* the Jews had come, apart from that their religion told them to. I'd never contemplated the reasons – it didn't seem to matter – until Abu Leila explained it to me.

Some years later, during the 1982 siege of Beirut by Israel, and several weeks before the day of the killings, we'd been sheltering in a hospital bunker as Israeli F16s dropped bombs when my father decided to angrily expand on his original comment.

'If Hitler had finished what he'd started we wouldn't be cowering here being shelled by these people.' I hadn't understood what he'd meant at the time, and two months later my father was dead so I couldn't ask him. It was only after listening to Abu Leila and reading the books he'd given me that I understood, and was ashamed of the sentiments my father had expressed. When I'd related my father's comments to Abu Leila, he said my father was an ignorant and uneducated man trying to make sense of a helpless situation in which he couldn't protect his family from the phosphorous and cluster bombs.

'What is true is that Palestinians are paying the price for the Holocaust,' he said, 'a uniquely European crime that they are taking a beating for. But it is the Europeans and Russians who are responsible for the persecution that preceded it – it goes back a long way.' So I learned that those bombs were dropped by the direct descendants of people who'd been forced to live in camps such as the one I was living in at the time, although they were then called ghettos. I learned that the same people who called Palestinians 'two-legged animals' were the descendants of people who had suffered endless jibes and dehumanisation. I found it difficult to reconcile these two things. In my reading about the Holocaust I discovered that the Nazis, having invaded Poland, used sympathetic Ukrainians, who hated the Poles, to 'cleanse' the villages and ghettos of Jews for them and to work in the concentration camps. These were tasks they took on with relish and imaginative cruelty. I thought of the fascist Phalangists in Beirut, let into Sabra camp by the Israelis, who sealed it to stop anyone escaping. When I pointed this out to Abu Leila he told me that I had described what was called an 'irony' in English, and that people inevitably repeated history, changing its presentation to suit the present.

'It's like a child who is beaten by his parents. If he grows up to be a parent himself he will probably also beat his children,' he said.

'How does it stop then?' I asked, thinking of us, sooner or later, with our own country oppressing someone less fortunate – maybe Kurds like Esma, maybe the Bedouin; no state liked a roaming people after all.

'Self-awareness,' was Abu Leila's response. 'You have to be constantly vigilant of your own behaviour and make sure the price you pay for self-preservation does not come at someone else's expense.'

Abu Leila also gave me the poetry of the Palestinian, Mahmoud Darwish, the writings of the Lebanese mystic, Kahlil Gibran, the love poetry of the Syrian poet, Nizar Qabbani, the plays of the Egyptian, Naguib Mahfouz, and the novels of Abdul-Rahman Munif, whose books are banned in his native Saudi Arabia. But he saved his real admiration for Moroccan writers like Tahar Ben Jelloun, who wrote in French.

'This is to build an appreciation of your own literary culture,' he'd said. But I had to leave all the poetry and books behind when I went to Cyprus, apart from Gibran, because he was consistent with my cover of being a Lebanese student. That was when I handed over my refugee card, as Abu Leila had refused to let me take anything that gave a clue to my heritage or past in Beirut. Given what Abu Leila had told me about the importance of remaining connected to the past, I understood that this also was an 'irony', but said nothing.

SEVEN

A couple of days later, after a morning of attending lectures at SOAS, I picked up Lemi the Turk's modified case from Victoria Station and took it back to Tufnell Park. I had filled a shelf in my bedsit with some of the books I hadn't been allowed to take to Cyprus from Beirut, and widened my interest along the way. As a concession to Abu Leila, the poetry books were bilingual, and some of the novels were translations to 'help' with my English. I laboriously removed the panel from the bath and took the shekels and the sealed envelope from the bulging zip-lock case. Back in my room, I removed the lining from the case as instructed by the Turk. I layered the money and the envelope into the false bottom of the case and had to pad it with newspaper to prevent the money from sliding around and to make it as uniform as possible. With the money inside and the bottom back in place, I checked it to make sure it looked and felt OK. I put the case in my wardrobe and heated up a can of minestrone soup on my single gas ring.

I'd finished my soup and was washing the bowl in the tiny sink when I heard shouting in the hall: a woman's voice. Then a door slammed hard enough for my own door to rattle in its frame. I carried on washing up; these were just the noises of communal living.

I opened my door to go to the bathroom and was surprised to see the young woman from next door sitting on the bottom step of the stairs, smoking a cigarette. She looked just as startled to see me.

'I'm sorry, I didn't realise you were in,' she said. 'I wouldn't have slammed the door.'

I shrugged to indicate that it was nothing. She was dark-haired but very English – if I was asked to point out a typically English girl to someone she would be that girl, even though she wasn't particularly fair-skinned. Her hair was wavy and just reached her shoulders, and I'd studied enough women to be able to tell that it had been expensively cut. She pushed it behind her ears to keep it from her face.

'Are you all right?' I asked. I could hear a man sobbing in her room, and wondered what sort of woman could make a man cry. She rolled her dark eyes and pointed her cigarette towards the door.

'I'm fine, just having a little man trouble,' she said. She was not a real smoker; she held the cigarette awkwardly, like she didn't know what to do with it in between puffs. And when she did put it in her mouth it was held gently between her lips as if she was afraid to damage it by clamping too hard. She was probably smoking because it was what people do in times of stress, a physical indication of it. I have never smoked, and avoided going with women who did because of the smell and taste. I stood awkwardly, not wanting to go to the bathroom knowing that she was sitting just outside and not wanting to go back into my room because it looked like

I'd come out to see what the noise was. She, on the other hand, looked completely at ease on the stairs, leaning back, her elbows on the steps behind her, lifting one arm to puff on her cigarette. She was barefoot, dressed in jeans and a white T-shirt. When she leaned back on the stairs I could see that she had no breasts to speak of. She wore a chunky man's watch with a stainless-steel strap that slid up and down her arm when she lifted her hand.

'You could wait in my room,' I said, and as soon as the words left my mouth I wanted to take them back. She looked at me briefly then stood up, pushing her rucked jeans down her long legs. She was tall, even in her bare feet, though not as tall as me.

'OK, just for a minute,' she said. Back in my room I went to clear the only chair but she sat on my narrow bed before I'd finished, her back against the wall, crossing her long legs. She flexed a narrow bare foot and I wanted to reach out and touch it, to run a finger along the arch. She scrunched up her face at the cigarette and offered it to me. I took it, running it under the tap and putting it in the bin before filling the kettle, having offered to make tea. I'd left the door ajar as a gesture of my honourable intentions, but wasn't sure she noticed or even cared – she was looking around my room with interest.

'I've never been in any of the other rooms in this house,' she said.

'Is he your boyfriend?' I asked, pointing to the wall that adjoined her room. She was studying the books on the shelf over my bed.

'Not really. I think he likes to pretend he is.' She reached for a book. 'I see you like Kahlil Gibran.'

'Yes, I do.' How stupid I sounded. I poured boiling water onto tea leaves in my small teapot.

'He's married though. He sometimes forgets that when he drinks,' she said. She looked at me to gauge my reaction. It took me a second to realise she wasn't talking about Gibran. I gave no response, because I wasn't sure whether she was looking for approval or trying to shock me. I poured the tea and sat on the chair at the bottom of the bed, wondering what kind of a man drank at lunchtime and cried over a woman. I passed her a mug and watched her fold her legs underneath her so she was sitting on her bare feet. She looked comfortable and relaxed, considering that a man was snivelling in her room while she was sitting on another man's bed. I liked that she wasn't embarrassed. I didn't know what to say, so I drank my tea.

'Do you think men are weaker than women?' she asked, pushing her hair from her face and tucking it behind her ears – a wasted effort as it fell back immediately.

'That's not a fair question when you have a man crying in your room.'

She laughed, and it was an artless, instinctive, surprisingly masculine sound that I wanted to hear again. I began to feel more relaxed about her being in my room.

'I suppose I should go and see whether he's OK.' She unfolded her legs and got off the bed.

I stood up. 'I'm Michel, by the way.'

She stood at the door and pushed her hair back again. She was only half a head shorter than me.

'As in "Michel, *ma belle*", like in the song?' She smiled and offered me her hand to shake. I saw a playfulness in her eyes, an arching of her eyebrows. I shook my head, not knowing what song she meant, just that *ma belle* was wrong for the masculine. Her hand was cool and soft, and, unusually for a woman, her grip was firm. 'I'm Helen, Michel. Thanks for the tea and the use of your room as a refuge.' I smiled and started to close the door behind her but she pushed it back open, sticking her head close to my ear. I was drawn to a small mole or piercing on her left earlobe and I could smell the shampoo on her shiny hair. 'I'll try to keep the noise down,' she said in a low voice. Then she was gone.

I washed her cup. She was the first person to have been in my room other than the landlord, who emptied the electricity meter of coins when he picked up the rent.

EIGHT

The next morning I sat in a coffee shop in the outpatients department of University College Hospital near Euston Square station. It looked out over the entrance and I could see everyone who came and went. Before coming to the hospital I'd taken the case by taxi to Euston Station and deposited it in left luggage. A jaundiced man in pyjamas and a hospital gown sat at the next table. He had a needle in his forearm which was connected to a drip hanging from a wheeled stand. I didn't understand why they let sick people wander around like that. I drank what passed for coffee in England and watched the elderly and the infirm walk the corridor past the coffee shop. I couldn't wait to get my business done so I could leave. My eyes tracked an olive-skinned man in glasses and a white coat as he came out of the lift and passed me by. He left through the main exit. I'd rung him last night, pretending to be his cousin. During our conversation I had mentioned another imaginary cousin working in the Gulf, which was the signal to meet in this location. We had several 'relatives', each designating a different place to meet. I finished my watery coffee and watched people come and go before getting up to follow him.

On a side street around the corner from the entrance to the outpatients department was a service area with unmarked double doors that led into the bowels of the hospital. Inside and down some steps was a long corridor with hissing pipes running the length of the ceiling. The walls and floor were unpainted concrete. Ramzi, the doctor I had followed in, was waiting just inside the door. We shook hands and I looked around. Cleaners, delivery people and the lower strata of hospital staff were walking by. They were mostly black or Asian and took no interest in us. I noted that Ramzi had grown sideburns since we'd last met; it was fashionable among certain men at the time. Ramzi was a fellow Palestinian, although he was born to a Christian family near Jerusalem on the West Bank, not in a Lebanese refugee camp. He was going to visit the Occupied Territories in a couple of days, travelling via Jordan.

'So, are you all set?' I asked in English.

'How many more of these trips do I need to do?' Ramzi asked in careful English, accentuating the 'e' at the end of 'these'. I switched to Arabic for the benefit of passers-by.

'I'm not sure what you mean,' I said. Ramzi had couriered stuff back and forth to the Occupied Territories for a couple of years without much complaint. He used to stop over in Germany before I came to the UK, and his trips were financed by money I gave him.

'I mean I have a wife and she wants to start a family.' Ramzi had told me about his new wife the last time we'd met. She was a Palestinian from Nablus who worked as a lab technician in this very hospital, where Ramzi was a senior house officer. From what I could gather, Abu Leila had paid indirectly for Ramzi's medical training, although you wouldn't think it the way he was talking now. On his last but one trip to the West Bank six months ago Ramzi had taken this woman with him, along with another adapted suitcase. They'd come back married. Abu Leila had been angry at this development, mainly because he'd not been forewarned. He worried that Ramzi would develop new priorities and told me we would have to cultivate another courier. It looked like he might be right.

'I'll talk to the man,' I said to Ramzi, who was polishing his designer glasses, 'but I'm not sure that having a family means the struggle is over.'

Ramzi snorted and raised his thick eyebrows. 'The struggle takes many forms, my friend. There are many paths to the same destination. Some are more effective than others, like being more engaged with the real struggle instead of sneaking around like thieves.'

It sounded like something Ramzi had read or heard someone else say. I wasn't sure how to deal with this. Ramzi hadn't expressed such reservations before. I concentrated on practicalities; I had a job to do, and so did he.

'The case will be picked up when you make the crossing on Sunday. It's the usual procedure: you'll leave the case in the taxi to Ramallah and pick it up on the way back.'

Ramzi sighed and shook his head. 'You guys don't know what is happening on the West Bank, or in Gaza. That is where the real resistance is taking place. Perhaps you should pay a visit to Gaza and see for yourself.'

I said nothing, but I doubted whether a nice middle-class Christian boy like him had ever been to the Gaza Strip.

'They've been throwing stones for two years, but it hasn't changed anything,' I said.

Ramzi looked at the floor briefly then took a deep breath. 'I'd like to speak to the man myself,' he said.

I shook my head. 'That's not possible.' I wasn't even sure if Ramzi knew Abu Leila personally; 'the man' was just an expression we used to indicate whoever I reported to.

'Then tell the man that I'm eternally grateful for all his help and everything, but this may be the last time I deliver for him.' He didn't raise his eyes to look at me until he had finished. I was sure he wouldn't be talking like this to Abu Leila's face. I gave him the ticket to the luggage deposit office at Euston Station. He glanced at it then looked at me.

'Not man enough to bring it yourself?'

It was my turn to take a long breath. I counted to five in my head and told myself he was emboldened because he'd worked up the courage to say what he wanted to say and didn't know when to hold back.

'It's the way things are done, Ramzi,' I said.

'What's in it anyway?'

'Just papers,' I told him.

He shook his head again. 'You people outside the Territories won't make a Palestinian state by playing these games. You don't play games with the Israelis.'

'There'll be something to bring back. Just make sure you use the same taxi driver on your return,' I said.

We shook hands, and Ramzi kept hold of my hand. His palm was clammy, which it hadn't been when we'd met. His other hand gripped my wrist and he leaned forward, holding my gaze with a pleading look. 'Please tell the man what I've told you … My wife is having a baby.'

'Congratulations,' I said. 'The money to pay for your trip is in the case.' I had to shake off his grip to escape. I suspected, despite my clothes and mastery of language, that Ramzi could tell that I was a refugee camp boy, born and bred, and that he looked down on me.

NINE

I had boarded at The English School in Nicosia in Cyprus for two years after leaving Beirut in 1984. It was in the middle of Nicosia, but set in a wood so you wouldn't know it was there. I had to sit some English exams to get in, to show that I could cope with the lessons because they followed the English curriculum. We had to learn Modern Greek too, along with our other lessons, and once again I threw myself into this task as if my life depended on it, because I wanted to catch up with the other students and not to stand out. I shared a room with Jack, a podgy boy whose English father and Greek mother travelled constantly on business. He told me how he had been in boarding schools since he was seven, and was vague when it came to what his parents did. We developed an unspoken agreement whereby I asked him no questions about them (and deflected other people's) and he asked none about mine, beyond knowing that they were dead. He mocked my constant reading, and often sat jabbering away at his desk in our room as I tried to absorb information from books. He filled his mouth with the biscuits and cakes his parents sent instead of the postcards and letters that other children received. I picked up a lot of English expressions rooming with him, which served me well once in England. He would come out with things like, 'This island has gone to seed since the Turks invaded,' or 'Has the cat got your tongue, Michel?' or, when showing me one of the pornographic magazines he hid under his mattress, 'Look at the jugs on that! I'm putting her in my wank bank.' Or, rather optimistically, and when homework got in the way of sneaking into town, 'That's scuppered our plans to get laid.' All of which I asked him to explain to me. Sometimes, when waiting for him to fall asleep so I could rock my head, I'd hear him sobbing into his pillow and I'd lie still until he'd finished: I myself was done with crying.

'Are you a *shlomo*, Michel?' he once asked me while I was reading. I had shaken my head, not sure what he meant. 'A kike, a yid, a Jew?' I shook my head again. 'Then why are you always reading about the bloody Holocaust? Let's go out and rustle up some skirt.'

He was right, I was becoming obsessed. Reading Primo Levi's account of his time in Auschwitz, I was struck by his understated and matter-of-fact description of his terrible ordeal. I'd read a few other accounts, as Jack had obviously noticed, but most of them screamed at you hysterically and you had to close your ears to it – one account I'd read even turned out to be invented, and it wasn't the first. Primo Levi whispered these things to you, and if you'd survived a tragedy such as I had you knew that it rang true. It whispered to you afterwards, usually at night, because that was when there was nothing else to drown it out. Except maybe Esma, or rocking your head, or, as I discovered later, the magic of codeine.

The idea that Fat Jack (as he was known) and I could get anywhere with girls was laughable, but the fact was that girls found him quite charming. By my first summer in Nicosia my Greek was good enough to communicate with the locals. So, in the afternoons (we were finished by 2 p.m.) and at weekends, we went to the beach, although with women we were bumbling and (as Jack would have said, had we been self-aware) cack-handed. Then we discovered that holidaying English girls were a better bet than the locals, less prudish, and keen to escape from their parents getting drunk by the pools of the many hotels and villas along the coast. They were looking for fun: they knew they'd be gone in a couple of weeks and wanted to pick up experiences not available at home. So we chatted up these pale, gawky, bony teenagers, but then they'd get drunk and ride off on the back of scooters in their bikinis, holding onto bronzed shirtless locals who took over from our fumblings. By the end of the holidays these girls sometimes looked different, sometimes scared, like they hadn't been ready for what they'd done, but mostly smug, like they knew something you didn't. When they left their white skin was burned a painful-looking red, helped by the constant application of palm oil. I never managed to go with any of these girls (I found them simultaneously silly and scary) but enjoyed being on the periphery of the beach parties and disco evenings.

Abu Leila would visit once a month, posing as my uncle. At that time he passed for a smoking, spectacle-wearing semitic version of the popular TV detective Columbo. After he had received a progress report from the principal we would go into Nicosia and he would buy me whatever I needed, be it Levis or books or Adidas trainers. Then we'd drink coffee and chat and he would tell me how well I was doing, although I already knew it. He was proud that my English was now better than his, and I was keen to impress him.

During one such visit he said, 'I would like you to study German.' And I enrolled for it without even asking him why.

My time in Cyprus was happy enough in the sense that I had nothing to worry about and I had grown used to my memories, although I still couldn't get to sleep without the head-rocking. What had happened in Sabra, to my family, had become a part of me. They say that a personal tragedy fades over time, but that is just a lie to make you feel better. What happens is that it becomes suffused into your system, more integrated into the everyday fabric of your life. It is like homogenising the cream into the milk, rather than it sitting at the top of the bottle: the cream is still there, you just can't see it.

Occasionally, however, I was violently reminded of it. One night, after sitting our final exams before graduation, I was in bed reading a book Abu Leila had given me, an account of a Jewish boy's experience in Poland (Falenica, I think), and for a minute I thought I was reading my own story. He too had been sitting down to dinner when the Germans had come for him and his family and taken them outside. He too had survived by using the same means I had. I got up, dizzy and sweating, and had to open the window to keep from hyperventilating. Jack, sitting in his bed drinking cocoa, shouted at me to close it.

'I knew all that fucking reading would make you ill,' he said. I had to wait three weeks until Abu Leila's next visit so I could show him the pages about Falenica from the book, and he had just nodded without reading it.

'I know,' he said. 'That's why I gave it to you.' He sighed. 'No suffering is unique, Michel,' he said. I needed to know what he meant and how these things could happen again and what had happened to the boy and whether you could be normal after such a thing, but Abu Leila had just lit a cigarette and taken the book from me. If I am to be honest, a part of me also hated that Jewish boy. I hated him for the very reason that Abu Leila had pointed out – because he had taken away the uniqueness of my experience.

That was when he chose to tell me that I would be going to West Germany after I graduated from The English School. It was all part of the longer-term plan, he explained, although the plan itself was only revealed to me bit by bit, as it unfolded, like watching a TV soap opera in which you are the star. He must have seen the confusion in my face for he said, 'Things will become clearer in Berlin.'

TEN

I flew back to West Berlin a week after giving Ramzi the case. I'd received a postcard from Abu Leila – the scene on the front told me where it would be (East rather than West) and the numbers in the message told me when.

The plane flew low along a narrow flight path over the German Democratic Republic. It had to execute a steep turn over West Berlin to get into position to land at Tegel, as they had limited space in which to manoeuvre to avoid flying over the east of the city. This was great if you were on the right side of the plane and liked a good view of Berlin, but for me it was just a reminder of the fact that we were in a large and heavy machine twisting and turning in the sky, taking the mechanical structure to its limits. I closed my eyes and clutched the armrests.

I preferred certain aspects of West Berlin to London. Although not literally under siege – you could take a flight or train out any time – it was certainly surrounded by the GDR and this gave it the feel of an island. An island of capitalism in a sea of communism. The highest building in West Berlin, the Europa Centre, had a revolving Mercedes star on it, to remind people in the East what was important. The East had the television tower, to remind the West what was important; you could see it from nearly everywhere. It wasn't difficult for people to go to the East; they did it all the time as tourists, although they had to be back by midnight. Of course very few people could come from the East. The main thing I liked about West Berlin was the Kreuzberg suburb, where I would sometimes go for a faint taste of the hustle and bustle of the camp – you couldn't get the same atmosphere in London as the Arabs were wealthier there.

After clearing passport control at Tegel I took the bus to Zoologischer Garten Station, which drug dealers and prostitutes used as their office, then walked to where I had booked a cheap room, in keeping with my student status. I washed and went out again, walking to the centre and mingling with the other tourists to bore any possible watchers.

My first time in Berlin was a shock to me after Mediterranean Cyprus. Too many people contained by a wall that kept the West out of the East, or the other way around, depending on who you listened to. Initially I had found it cold and lacklustre, the buildings too big and overwhelming. I was enrolled at the Freie Universität to study English language and literature, and of course German. This choice was made by Abu Leila, based, he said, on the recommendations of my teachers at The English School in Nicosia, who spoke highly of my linguistic abilities. At one point I had asked him whether I shouldn't learn Hebrew, thinking it would be useful. But he had just shaken his head and I hadn't pushed it.

I stopped at a falafel stand run by some Egyptians. I ordered a large sandwich and stood at a table on the pavement, washing it down with Coca-Cola. I watched people go by. West Berlin attracted refugees, exiles and the dispossessed from all over the world. They congregated in this besieged city, smoking, drinking and agitating in the Berlin bars. Berlin was famous for its large number of bars and I made a point of never visiting the same one twice, particularly if I had picked up a woman there.

I did once have a relationship, with a student in my first year at university. I remember her with affection, a short Romanian girl with dimples and black curly hair. Her parents had managed to escape Romania the year before. She made me laugh, and I lost my virginity to her (Esma and I never had a chance to go all the way). But a month into our relationship, Antanasia or Atanasia (I can't remember her exact name) wanted to know more, asking the kind of questions you would expect someone to ask after dating them for four weeks. I would sneak her into my room at night, as no visitors were allowed to stay over, and we would share my single bed. At the time I was living in a large anonymous boarding house in Wilmersdorf, as Abu Leila didn't want me staying with the other students in university-appointed accommodation. I shared my floor with Polish migrants, exclusively men, who spent every night drinking and talking into the small hours. Antanasia would light a candle to make love by and would always end up sitting astride me; that's how she liked to do it. After she'd caught her breath she would start asking me questions – who were my parents and where did I go to school and what were my plans after university, and she would trap me underneath her, sitting on my chest and pinning my arms down like

Esma had done that time. At first she would try cajoling and tickling answers out of me, and I would pretend to plead for mercy to avoid telling the lies I'd rehearsed with Abu Leila. On one of these occasions, after a couple of weeks of this, she got off quickly and, with her back to me, started to get dressed, not even bothering to wash herself in the sink.

'I feel sorry for you,' she said in German, blowing out the candle and putting on the harsh main light. 'It would be nice if you could be open with me, if you could be honest.'

I could see that she was angry. 'I didn't mean to hurt your feelings,' I said.

'I'm not hurt. I'm sad. I'm sad for you because you cannot be close to anyone.'

'There are other ways of being close,' I said. I'm not sure what I meant but she probably thought I was talking about sex because she just glared at me, with her heavy brows creased together. I never saw her again after that, except in passing on campus or during the odd class that we shared. She did slip me a note a few weeks later that read: 'I hope you find what is in your heart.' She had drawn a small broken heart at the bottom of the page, like oversized punctuation. That was the last time I'd had a relationship that lasted more than a week.

The next morning I took the S-Bahn east to Friedrichstrasse – the only crossing into East Berlin that foreigners and diplomats could use. Diplomats had their own channel, and I'd used it occasionally when I needed to cross for long periods. The East Germans would let you through without stamping your passport if they were expecting you, provided you gave them the correct password. That's how I went to Potsdam and Beeskow to do some training, or once for three months to Moscow via Schönefeld Airport in East Berlin. This time I was just going across to meet Abu Leila, so I went across as a tourist.

The station on the GDR side at Friedrichstrasse was a maze of corridors. A couple of hundred people were queuing, most of them tourists going across for the experience of being in a communist country for a few hours. Abu Leila didn't want the East German Intelligence Service seeing us meet – although he fretted equally about other PLO people – so I did the tourist thing for an hour, then walked east from the television tower, crossing Karl-Marx-Allee into a residential area. Fewer people were around and I wandered dilapidated shop-free streets until I reached a faceless residential block. I went through a courtyard and up to the first floor, where I rapped on a door. An elderly North-African-looking woman opened it and let me in silently. She pointed into the living room and disappeared into the kitchen from where the smell of cooking was wafting. I went through to see Abu Leila sitting at the coffee table playing Patience under a blue haze of smoke. The main light was on and the shutters were closed.

ELEVEN

Abu Leila and I embraced and kissed cheeks. He held me at arm's length and appraised me.

'You are looking well,' he said.

I had often wondered whether he had a daughter called Leila or whether 'Abu Leila' was simply a *nom de guerre.* It was not the kind of thing I could ask him though. I'd once asked him which town he came from in Palestine and he'd thrown me an irritated glance, even though it was a usual question for any compatriots meeting abroad to ask, particularly Palestinians.

We sat on drab, hard-edged furniture with thin cushions. Abu Leila didn't look well. He had rings under his eyes that matched his grey stubble. His suit was more creased than usual and he looked shrunken, like an old man. I felt a fleeting swell of fear, fear of what would happen if he were to die.

'I've been doing a lot of travelling,' he said, polishing his glasses. 'There are many changes going on in the world and few of them are for the better.' He put his glasses on and peered at me through the clean lenses, then smiled, showing me his nicotine-stained teeth. 'Did you know that in some places it is no longer acceptable to smoke in public?' he said.

He lit up a cigarette and showed it to me as if to demonstrate its innocence. 'Every year it gets harder to find these. The KaDeWe in West Berlin is the only place in Germany that stocks them. Harrods in London also do them. So what's happening with you?'

I told him about my conversation with Ramzi.

'It was only a matter of time,' he said. 'This is what women do. They fall in love with what they find, then want to change it.' He should have been more angry at Ramzi instead of empathising with him. Instead he told me to keep a look-out for someone who might be able to help with the couriering. He smiled. 'Perhaps you know of a woman who wants to travel to the Middle East?' he said. Helen came to mind but I shook my head; I was hoping he would suggest someone. The old woman brought tea in small glasses. Abu Leila closed the door after her and sat down.

'I'm not sure how much longer I can stay in the East,' he said. He examined the playing cards on the table. 'The East Germans are living in denial for the moment, they do not think what is happening in Moscow has any relevance to them.' I assumed this was a reference to Gorbachev and what was called Glasnost; the Soviet Union had just held elections for the first time and Gorbachev had publicly stated that the Berlin Wall should come down. I hoped Abu Leila wasn't going to start one of his political diatribes. 'What is it they say in English about the writing on the wall?' he asked.

'They can't see the writing on the wall,' I told him.

'Exactly so,' he chuckled, and we drank our tea. I was trying to absorb the ramifications of him moving from the

East when he said, 'Let us talk of other things. How are you getting on with finding a venue for my meeting?'

I told him that I thought it best if it was outside London and that Cambridge or Oxford looked good. I explained that they had good access and plenty of tourists and visiting academics. A group of foreigners wouldn't look out of place. 'Also, Cambridge has a small airport and you can fly to it from Amsterdam or Paris easily,' I said. So did Oxford, but Cambridge was easier for me to get to from London.

'OK, I like the sound of Cambridge. I'd like you to rent a house for the summer. Big enough for eight people. Tell them ...' He waved his hand.

'Don't worry, I'll come up with a story,' I said.

'Of course you will.' He gathered the cards.

I looked around the room and took a breath. 'What's the purpose of the meeting?'

He looked at me, still shuffling the cards.

'OK, you should know, since you are organising it.' He put the cards back in the pack and sat back. 'Palestinians do a lot of lamenting about their plight. Sometimes I think they are too attached to playing the victim. It is true that they are victims, but it is a limited role: you are victimised and pitied and nothing else.' He lit a match and pointed it at me. 'The man who thinks he is unlucky will always trip up,' he said. He ignited another cigarette, stood up, walked to the shuttered window, realised he probably shouldn't open it and turned around. 'What this means is that they lack imagination when it comes to dealing with the situation. By "they" I mean the leadership, of course – the people on the ground who live and breathe the occupation know what is needed – the leadership just don't have the imagination to deliver it for them. Children have taken things into their own hands, literally, using stones and burning tyres.' He stubbed out his cigarette and said, almost to himself, 'We must think the unthinkable.'

Emboldened by his unusual candour, I asked, 'What is the unthinkable?'

He sat down and pushed up his glasses.

'You believe in an independent Palestinian state and,' waving his arms around, 'the right to self-determination, blah blah blah?' he said. I nodded, slightly taken aback by his sarcastic tone. 'Alongside Israel's right to exist, blah blah blah?'

'Yes …' I wasn't sure where he was headed.

'What if I told you that I, and a few others like me, don't believe in two states?' He smiled, he was enjoying himself.

'What do you mean?'

'I mean what if there was just one state?'

'You mean getting rid of Israel altogether?' As far as I knew, only a couple of PLO groups still took that approach, and the PLO executive had already accepted that Israel existed and would continue to do so.

Abu Leila shook his head, still smiling. 'No, I mean a secular, democratic state for Jews, Christians and Muslims. A country where everyone would have equal rights, regardless of their religion.'

One country, I thought. It was such a simple and appealing idea that I wondered why it hadn't occurred to someone before – although later I learned that it was mooted as early as 1948, then swept aside by post-Holocaust guilt. Yet it seemed impossible to achieve – I could see obstacles wherever I looked. I said as much.

'Yes, I know, many Israelis would not like it because it does away with the Jewishness of the state. But things are changing in Israel, there are people who are thinking the same, since they realise that the alternative is both inevitable and tragic. Zionism is on a road to nowhere except a cliff edge.' He fiddled with his box of matches. 'Also, many Palestinians wouldn't like the idea, especially those living in the past, before 1948 or 1967. Some exiles still carry their house key with them as if they are going back home. Incidentally, these people would not be going home under any two-state solution deal, let me tell you that for nothing.' I had heard my own father and uncles complaining about how their right to return had been written off by the PLO. 'Don't forget, Michel, that one and a half million Arabs live within Israel. A two-state solution does not even begin to address them.' I hadn't thought about those still living within 1967 borders. Mama's village of Lubya was within 1948 Israel, but had been demolished when they fled the Haganah. Abu Leila stood up and removed his glasses. They were smaller than the ones he'd worn when I first met him in Beirut. He started to walk up and down, addressing some invisible crowd in his oddly self-conscious manner, like he sometimes had when visiting me when I was still at school in Beirut.

'Already secret meetings are taking place to discuss having initial talks regarding status negotiations. But the Old Man has certain ideas about how these should work, which limits the capacity for negotiating. He wants to constantly rotate the negotiators and will not choose the right people. One of them can't even speak English properly!' He shook his head. 'I've seen the names on the Israeli side and they would easily out-negotiate the Palestinians. They'll come out feeling pleased that they have been allowed to shit in their own toilets every other Wednesday.'

I had not seen Abu Leila talk so intensely about the internal politics of the struggle before, or known that he was close to the Old Man, the nickname given to Arafat. My head was reeling as I tried to think of a sensible question. He sat down again.

'That is why we must arrange this other session, and draw up a joint proposal before anything comes of these talks they want to have in Norway. We'll call it the Cambridge Declaration!' We laughed, but I was fired up.

'Are you with me, Michel?' He smiled, knowing my answer already: how could I not be with him? I'd been with him this far without question because he had given me something to live for. I had done everything he'd said because I believed that it was in the interest of the struggle. That the struggle was headed in a slightly different direction made no difference to me. We shook hands across the table. My intention to broach the subject of working with other people was gone. How could I bring up such a self-centred thing as my own loneliness after this?

He picked up the cards. 'Let's play while we wait for lunch. It's my favourite: lamb tagine with honeyed prunes.'

TWELVE

At Tegel Airport later that afternoon I bought a copy of *Le Monde* because I'd noticed a reference on the front page to a piece inside about Sabra and Shatila. I had no time to read it before the flight, so I opened the newspaper on the plane to distract me from the terror of take-off. The article profiled the Phalangist leaders who had led the militia into Sabra and Shatila and what had become of them. Most of them were now respectable politicians in the new Lebanese government. The rest were running large businesses, one had even gone to South America. The whole thing made me sick. I tore the article out and put it in my jacket pocket, to add to my collection.

It occurred to me, as we dropped through the sky to Heathrow, that the meeting Abu Leila was arranging ran counter to the official line. Wouldn't he get into trouble with the Old Man? I never questioned my lack of contact with other members of PLO security, although I knew they must exist: the letters, the forged documents, the tiny cameras, the telephone scramblers; all things I'd delivered or bought or arranged delivery for. Yet I'd never met anyone who worked for Abu Leila – I knew of nobody that even knew him, except perhaps Ramzi, although he had never met him. I assumed it was just the way things were, a matter of sensible containment. But what if I was known only to Abu Leila and no one else? All my training had been on my own; I'd spent a whole summer in Moscow living in a small apartment with no company except the guy assigned to look after me, the various trainers and the woman who'd come to cook and clean. I didn't know what was normal, all I knew was Abu Leila and what he told me. It was clear that other points of view existed that I was not aware of, other people with other ideas of how to do things. My reflections were cut short to concentrate on the stress of landing in one piece.

It was close to ten by the time I got back to Tufnell Park, and I was looking forward to some codeine and bed.

Helen was sitting on the stairs again, but this time wrapped in a bath towel.

'Oh God, how embarrassing,' she said. She put her face in her hands and pushed the towel between her thighs.

'Man trouble again?' I asked.

'You could say that. I'm locked out.' She gave a weak smile. She looked as tired as I felt: her eyes were dark and puffy.

I stuck the key in my door. 'I don't hear him crying. Is it the same man as before?' I asked.

She gave me a look and her mouth tensed and I wished I hadn't said it. 'The bastard left while I was in the bath,' she said gesturing at her towel, 'and I'm not exactly dressed for travel.'

I opened my door. 'You mean he's not in your room?' I asked.

She shook her head and her hair fell forward. She pushed it back from her face. 'There's no answer. He must have left while I was in the bath.' She combed her hair out with her fingers. 'We had a row and I thought a bath would help. I find a bath usually helps.' She sounded better but looked awkward, repeatedly checking that the towel was still wedged between her thighs. I avoided looking at her legs. I didn't know what to do – then it occurred to me that I *could* do something.

'I can open your door,' I said. 'Wait there.' I took out a set of small electrical screwdrivers from the cupboard under the sink in my room. I picked up a paper clip from the chest of drawers that doubled as a desk and went back into the hall. Her lock was the same as mine, a basic Yale, and in training I'd managed to open them within thirty seconds. Not a record, according to the Russian who'd taught me, but good enough for the field. Every day he would send me a new lock and I would practise on it in my Moscow apartment, to kill the long evenings alone. Although I did have a lock-picking set, I didn't keep it in my room, for obvious reasons; it was hidden in the garden.

'Are you going to pick the lock?' Helen asked. I put my finger to my lips and pointed upstairs. She forgot that she was naked under a towel as she stood beside me at the door. I knelt down and examined the lock more closely. It was well used and the plug (the round bit that turns with the key) was loose in the hull. I decided I would scrub the lock rather than trying to pick each pin. You want to be quick in this field, although I doubted whether opening doors for women dressed only in towels was what my trainers had in mind. I knew it was mad to be doing this, even as I bent the paper clip open and created a small kink in the end. I put it in the keyway and inserted the screwdriver to act as a torque. I was vaguely aware of Helen kneeling beside me on the threadbare carpet, of her newly bathed smell. Soon the pins began to set and I pulled the paper clip in and out more rapidly, increasing the torque with the screwdriver as I did so. The lock gave abruptly and the door was open. Thirty seconds tops. Helen laughed and I stood up. She clapped her hands, jumped up and put her arms around my neck. I didn't reciprocate.

'That's fantastic, I'm so impressed!' She stood back and considered me with tilted head. 'Where did you learn to do that?' she whispered, then punched me on the shoulder. I grinned idiotically, pleased to have found a happy use for this skill, and she opened the door.

Her room was bigger than mine and better furnished. She had Indian-type throws on an armchair and a screen to cover the cooker and sink area. She also had a naked man lying on his back on the single bed, half a bottle of gin in the crook of his arm. Helen put her face in her hands again. I checked his breathing. He was older, maybe in his late thirties or early forties, and flabby. He wasn't Caucasian – it was difficult to tell in this light but he could have been Mediterranean. He wasn't going to die so I pulled him onto his side to stop him choking, in case he vomited. His belly sagged onto the mattress. Helen covered his lower half with a sheet. I took the gin bottle and put it on the table.

'I'll leave you to …' I struggled to think of what I was leaving her to do.

'OK, yeah. Listen, thanks again for your help,' she said, her tone cooler than her earlier exuberance. I went into the hall and she stuck her head out after me, keeping the door half-closed, as if to hide what was inside. 'Goodnight,' she said. I wanted to tell her she didn't have to stay in there.

'Goodnight,' I said.

I took three codeine before getting into bed and felt the effect within minutes. I'd forgotten to eat anything, what with the problems next door. But with codeine it no longer mattered. I remembered the article from *Le Monde* in my jacket pocket. Perhaps I could do something about the people in it, although I wasn't sure what. Then I thought of Helen and her lover. What was she doing with such an older man? How did they both sleep in that bed? I fell onto the mattress. It was a nice sensation: my whole body was warm and safe and swaying, very slowly, from side to side. I smiled because I was on a warm, soft cloud.

THIRTEEN

Before I'd left for Moscow from Schönefeld Airport in the GDR, Abu Leila had told me that on arrival at Sheremetyevo Airport I should look for a man carrying an English edition of *Crime and Punishment*. When I disembarked I was pleasantly surprised to see someone not much older than me, casually holding the book up to his chest under a folded arm as if he'd just been reading it. Close up, though, the spine looked unbroken. He was round-faced and smiled as if I was arriving for summer camp. His fair hair was cropped short and he wore a wedding ring.

'*Ahlan wa sahlan*,' he said, surprising me with his Arabic. 'Follow me.' He turned and I followed him through an unmarked door, on the other side of which he showed someone ID. I wasn't searched and my passport wasn't taken from me, although he filled out my details on a form which he signed and gave to the official. We went through a network of corridors until we emerged in the foyer of the airport. Outside we found his unmemorable car and inside it he gripped my hand tightly.

'My name is Vasily,' he said. 'Welcome to the Union of Soviet Socialist Republics.' He drove carefully down the Leningradskoe highway towards a darkening Moscow. I looked for familiar landmarks but all I recognised were large pictures of Gorbachev. He noticed my gaze. 'We are on the brink of a new era,' he said. 'As long as the West does not push us too hard. To them we are just a virgin market waiting to be deflowered.' We drove around the outskirts of Moscow and parked in a residential area. Vasily took my bag and led me to an ancient block of flats where we took a creaking lift to the top floor. Vasily had the key to the only door on this floor. He opened it onto a little hall, from which double doors led into the living room in which a coffee table was covered with a variety of dishes, some Russian beer and an iced bottle of vodka. A woman, in her fifties, I think, came through from the kitchen. She wore an apron, which she removed.

'This is Marina,' Vasily said. 'She will come each morning and cook and clean. She speaks Georgian and a little Russian.'

'*Spaseeba*,' I said, speaking the only Russian I knew and bowing my head to her because I didn't know what else to do. Vasily told me that Marina would use a special knock on the door when she came in the morning. She demonstrated the knock on a sideboard, then put on a headscarf and left. I would be on my own in the evenings and at weekends, he told me. We sat down to eat but I had no appetite. Vasily looked disappointed that I didn't drink.

'I was told you're not a Muslim?' he said, sounding concerned that he may have insulted me by offering alcohol.

'I'm not,' I said. 'I just don't drink alcohol.'

'That is good.' He poured himself a chilled shot of

Stolichnaya. 'Many people in our business rely on it too much.' He didn't say for what, but showed me around the flat, which took no more than sixty seconds. The living room looked north over the city and no other buildings were in the proximity because of a large tram and bus depot below. The bedroom at the back was overlooked, and Vasily suggested I keep the shutters closed. A small kitchen and bathroom completed the tour. Vasily shook my hand and said he had to leave.

'When you have finished your training the world will not look the same again,' he said.

Left alone, I tried the television in the living room but it was dead. I picked up the Dostoyevsky that Vasily had left and started to read.

Different people came to the Moscow apartment over the summer. One man came with a shoe box and a rolled-up plastic play mat. We moved the coffee table out of the way and he unfurled the mat, which had streets and buildings drawn on it. They were not like European streets though, they were more like American streets, straight and parallel and in blocks. He took a selection of toy cars from the box. He didn't speak English, so Vasily had to translate.

'He says you are the red car.'

'But I want to be the blue car,' I said, and although Vasily laughed he did not translate my joke. The red car was the target and the other cars were following it. I moved the red car on the mat and the man moved the other cars, to show that wherever I went they would follow, although 'follow' isn't an accurate description. Despite what you see in films, some of the cars will be in front of the target car and some will be on other streets parallel to it.

Evenings were spent alone reading. I read Dostoyevsky until I was sick of him, so Vasily took me to a bookshop where they had a small selection of English books. We bought some Dashiell Hammett, which they stocked because he was a communist. Driving back to my apartment, Vasily said he had read John le Carré, although you couldn't buy him in the USSR. He said that all KGB trainees read him for the tradecraft.

'He has been in the business,' he said. 'You can tell.'

I contemplated all this as I lay in bed the morning after finding Helen's unconscious lover. I contemplated it because I experienced the same disorientation upon waking that I had my first morning in Moscow. The bewilderment you might get, I imagined, from too much alcohol, or, in my case, too much opiate, or when you don't know how you got to the place you have woken up in, or even who you are. Something about those first few minutes of the day can either make or break the rest of it. I usually overcame it by doing my push-ups and sit-ups until my arms and stomach ached.

I hid the *Le Monde* article under the bath and went to lessons at SOAS for a couple of hours. Then I checked my PO box in Westminster, taking surveillance counter-measures along the way, using the underground. Going underground forces any surveillance behind you (rather than parallel and in front) and they hate that. Carrying out that manoeuvre often exposed them, particularly when few passengers were about.

All this and more I learned in my summer in Moscow, practising on Moscow streets against the KGB. The idea, said Vasily, was to do it without making it obvious that you were doing it, otherwise you were advertising your guilt. He would come with me, and we began by me trying to spot any surveillance in the first place, without trying to avoid it. He said that they were using KGB trainees for the exercise.

'They have to learn too,' he said. I found the trainees too easy to spot. Their clumsy efforts at trying to change their appearance by taking off jackets and coats and putting on hats did not help them. I could spot their individual gait and mannerisms, the way they muttered self-consciously into microphones hidden under their sleeves. I could spot their obvious mirroring of my actions: if I stopped, they stopped too; if I moved, they moved. They had no subtlety. Afterwards I would have to recount to Vasily how many people I had seen and where. He gave me no feedback on these efforts, but, smiling one morning, he said that an experienced team had replaced the trainees. 'I do not even know if they will be there or not,' he said, 'sometimes they will be busy following real spies.' I enjoyed these games and learned to be constantly alert, memorising faces and looking for places that would force a team behind me or up close. Sometimes, though, you decide to do things that don't require you to be constantly, if metaphorically, looking over your shoulder. So you take a few days off, go to the cinema, sit in the park, stay at home and read a book. In fact, it's a good thing to do if you have any suspicion that you're being followed.

'Make them bored,' said Vasily. 'A bored surveillance team is a careless one,' he said. 'After a few days they might even call it off. Do anything odd or different though, give them just one idea that you know what you are doing and they will stick to you like dog shit on the bottom of a shoe.'

So you have to be on continual alert: every public place is a potential meeting place; every alley or public toilet could be a dead-letter drop; every street, store and restaurant needs to be assessed for its counter-surveillance potential. You need to be constantly on the look-out for places to cache money and documents. Everyday objects must be considered potential concealers of microphones or cameras. Every person you meet could either be an agent wanting to get close or a possible recruit to the cause. Every woman that talks to you wants to trap you with the promise of sex. Every postcard has a hidden meaning. Everybody behind you could be following you, and it is your job to shake them off.

FOURTEEN

When I got back to Tufnell Park I lay down. I must have fallen asleep as I was woken by knocking, and the light in the room had changed. Helen was at the door.

'Hello.' She waved at me by holding up her hand and wiggling her fingers. 'I want to repay you for what you did yesterday.' In my dopey state I thought she wanted to give me money; perhaps some English etiquette I was unsure of. I stood in my bare feet and ran my hand through my tangled hair. She looked different, like she had a little make-up on. Not much, but enough to make a difference. 'I'd like to take you out to dinner,' she said. I'd never been asked out to dinner before.

'You don't have to pay me back,' I said.

She shrugged and pushed back her hair.

'OK then. Let's just go to dinner. We can go Dutch, if you like.'

I was trying to remember what going Dutch meant, and for some reason I looked behind me into my room, as if something there could rescue me from making a decision.

'Do you have a girl in there?' she asked, trying to look past me.

I smiled and shook my head.

'Then maybe you have better plans for tonight?'

My plans consisted of heating up a ready-made meal of meat and vegetables and gravy. I was going to eat it from the plastic container it came in so I'd only have a fork to wash up.

'I have no plans,' I said. 'Give me fifteen minutes to get dressed.'

We went around the corner to a Chinese restaurant on the high street. She was telling me how good it was and asking if I had been before. She looked great, in simple linen trousers and a shirt. They were understated but looked expensive. Her hair was pinned back for a change, and she had little dangly earrings on, like silver peas. She still had the enormous stainless-steel man's watch on, and for some reason I found it reassuring. I chose a table in the corner and sat down with my back to the wall, where I could see the door. I worried about being on a date initiated by a woman.

'So tell me how you learned to open doors like that,' she said.

I'd forgotten to concoct a story to explain the lock-picking, so I smiled stupidly in order to buy time to think. 'It's just something I picked up,' I said.

'Picked up where? Prison?'

I told myself that these were innocent questions.

'Relax,' she said. 'You look like a deer caught in headlights.'

I sat back in my chair and tried to smile. My knee was springing up and down under the table in a rapid displacement of nervous energy. A waiter approached.

'Perhaps we need a drink,' she said.

'I don't drink alcohol,' I told her, wishing I did.

'Then we'll drink green tea,' she said. 'It has the same effect.' We ordered, and while we waited for our food we sipped our pale tea.

'I've sent him back to his wife,' she said. I kept a blank face, even though I knew who she was referring to. 'You know, my pretend boyfriend?'

'It's none of my business,' I said, glad at least that the subject had been changed.

'Well, you have become involved in a way, and I feel I owe you an explanation.'

She didn't owe me an explanation but I understand that sometimes women have to talk through their problems – they don't want a solution necessarily, just someone to listen. She told me that she was a postgraduate anthropology student and that he was her supervisor and that they naturally spent a lot of time together because of her work on her PhD.

'We attended the same field trip and things got out of hand.' I didn't want to hear this but I let her carry on. 'He told me I made him feel complete,' she said, as if this explained everything. Our food arrived and we were quiet as they laid the dishes out.

'And how did he make you feel?' I asked, when the waiters were gone.

'Do you ever feel that you are only living half your life, like something is beyond you, just out of reach?' I nodded, although truthfully I didn't know what she was talking about. She put rice on her plate. 'I feel like that all the time, like there must be more to life, something more real than ...'

She waved her chopsticks around. 'Anyway, I have something missing, a gap. A gap ... I let other people fill.'

I supposed she meant men. We ate our food. She asked me what I was studying and I told her about the language course.

'It doesn't sound like you need it,' she said.

'It's a requirement,' I lied.

'And then what? What do you want to do?'

I was flummoxed by the question, it wasn't something anyone had asked me before. I didn't know what Abu Leila had in mind. Maybe he didn't know, or maybe he hadn't told me yet.

'English literature,' I said. It just popped into my head.

We ate: she used her chopsticks and savoured her food, making noises of satisfaction when she liked something. Her big watch slid down her forearm when she raised her hand.

I used a fork and ate quickly without much noticing the food; I'd forgotten how hungry I was. Occasionally I looked around the room at the other diners, or at people coming through the door, checking for anyone who looked like they were in the business. We didn't talk for a while but I didn't feel uncomfortable, like you do sometimes when you struggle to make conversation. We looked at each other with our mouths full of food and she smiled at me with her eyes.

'You don't say much, do you?' she said.

I shrugged. 'Does that bother you?'

She shook her head. 'No, I like it.' She removed sauce from her chin with her napkin. 'I find that men can't wait to talk about themselves. But not you.' I wondered how many men she'd based that generalisation on. 'I hate the fact that I talk too much,' she said.

'Then try shutting up.'

She laughed her natural, muscular laugh and made a zipping motion across her lips. They brought us more tea and we sat drinking it. She looked at me over her cup and I looked back. I winked at her to make her say something. She stuck her tongue out at me. I rolled my eyes. She batted her eyelashes. We kept up this silliness until the waiter came and put the bill on our table.

We walked back to the house more slowly than we had left it. I asked her to explain anthropology. She said it was a big subject but that in a nutshell it was the comparative study of humankind. I told her I was no wiser.

'Well,' she said, becoming animated, 'different societies deal with the same universal events in different ways. My area of interest is death. More specifically, I'm interested in how different cultures cope with death. That's what my thesis is on: I'm comparing the burial rites of ancient Turks with those of a Celtic tribe of the same period, looking at what they have in common and what they do differently.'

We walked a bit more, and when we were near our house she asked me where I was from. I told her I was from Lebanon – avoiding saying I was Lebanese.

'Is that why you don't drink, for religious reasons?'

'As a matter of fact, I'm not a Muslim,' I said.

'No, of course you're not.'

'Why wouldn't I be?'

'I don't know. I'm sorry, I haven't quite got my anthropological stripes yet. As you can see, I have yet to hone my cultural awareness skills before I'm awarded them. Am I babbling again?'

'A little,' I said, smiling.

She zipped her mouth. Could she be as nervous as I felt? She seemed so self-assured. We both took our keys out to open the door but I got to the lock first. Upstairs we stood on our shared landing. We kissed each other on the cheek, my right hand resting gently on her hip with hers on my arm. I hoped that she wouldn't ask me into her room; I certainly wouldn't ask her into mine. Maybe because I could still see her naked tutor on her bed, or maybe I didn't want yet another brief encounter. I was certainly still wary of her. Besides, we hadn't had the usual pre-one-night-stand dance of easy compliments and accelerated physical contact.

'Shall we do that again?' she asked. I thought she meant the kiss, but when she turned to her door I understood she meant dinner.

'I would like that,' I said.

I lay on my bed in the dark and listened to her running a bath. I wondered if she was using her herbal bath oil. Later, I had to make myself get out of bed to take some codeine because I'd forgotten to take any and had nearly fallen asleep.

FIFTEEN

Teaching me the art of picking locks was the responsibility of a short, bald Russian whose face had the vodka-induced ruddiness of many Muscovites I had come across. He arrived with Vasily one morning, carrying a bag that clattered when he put it on the floor. Like my surveillance trainer, he only spoke Russian, so Vasily was on hand, although by then I was practising my own attempts at Russian on anyone I came in contact with. He had a basic lock which he had dismantled, and he showed me the brass bits laid on the table like a dismembered clock. He matched the pieces to a cross-sectional drawing of a lock with Russian labels. He explained that picking was an art – because you cannot see what you are doing – and the resistance in your fingers becomes your guide. It is such a tactile thing, yet at the same time abstract – in that you have to mentally visualise what you cannot see – that it becomes addictive.

Later, when I arrived in London, I bought myself a picking set from a company that supplied locksmiths and hid it in the unused garden at Tufnell Park. I hadn't used them on Helen's lock because their possession would need even more explaining than the skill itself. The only time I'd used them was when the man I usually bought codeine from disappeared for three weeks. I had allowed myself to run out completely. I thought I could cope without it for a few days but I was wrong. I picked my way into a nursing home (where the English keep their old people) two streets from my bedsit. I got through a back door, an office door and a drugs cabinet all in a matter of minutes.

The day after dinner with Helen I was standing in a phone box near SOAS calling Ramzi. He was due back two days ago and should have sent a postcard to let me know he was in London and wanted to meet. I needed to get the case from him; it would have papers in it for Abu Leila from the Territories. I watched students walking past as I dialled, talking about their plans for the coming summer. I was filled with vague despondency. The receiver felt heavy as I took it from the hook. It rang for a while and a part of me was relieved that I'd have to hang up, but then a woman's greeting replaced the ringing. I was taken aback; it was usually Ramzi at the other end. I took her to be Ramzi's wife. She didn't sound happy.

'It's Muneer, is Ramzi there?' I asked in Arabic.

'Muneer?' she asked, as if I had insulted her.

'His cousin from Qatar,' I said, sticking to the cover Ramzi and I used.

'He has no cousin from Qatar,' she said.

This didn't sound good.

'Is Ramzi there?'

'You're the guy who gave Ramzi the case, aren't you?'

I should have put the phone down at that point but I

needed to know what was going on. I wondered how much Ramzi had told her.

'Is he there?'

'No, he isn't here, you shit, I've had to leave him in an Israeli prison!' She was shouting and I pulled the receiver from my ear, glad I was in an enclosed phone box. 'He took your fucking case in for you but they stopped him on the bridge when we were coming out.' The earpiece buzzed with the force of her voice.

'What about the case? Was he bringing the case back?' I asked, thinking of the papers that were supposed to come back for Abu Leila.

'The case, the case? Did you hear what I said, you cowardly shit? They've got Ramzi. Do you understand? Do you know what they do to people in prison?'

I knew exactly what they did to people in prison, I'd heard the reports; it had even been in the English newspapers. I needed to know what had happened to the case though.

'Have you got the case?' I asked.

'I want to know what's so interesting about this case?' she shouted. Before I could answer she called me two Arabic words I had never heard a woman use before and I jumped as I heard a loud crash in the earpiece. There were two other loud crashes and the line went dead. I hung up. She must have been hitting the receiver very hard on something.

Vasily once told me that if you had planned for a crisis then you couldn't have one. It seemed an optimistic pronouncement that I challenged with the observation that the definition of a crisis was that it was by nature unforeseen.

'OK,' he'd said, 'Let me explain it like this. It is inevitable that things will sometimes go bad. You just need to contain it when it happens.'

I needed to get a message to Abu Leila. I gave myself some time before ringing his emergency answerphone in West Berlin; I wanted to think. So I went to a large Waterstone's bookshop nearby and browsed for a bit. I picked up Primo Levi's *If This Is a Man*, which I had read in Cyprus all those years ago. I bought the book and went outside to make the call.

I chose a different phone box to the one I'd used before and dialled the memorised number. It rang twice and I heard the messageless tone. I spoke slowly and clearly in German.

'Hello, it's Roberto. I just wanted to let you know that Giorgio has been approached by the competition while travelling back from his trip to the factory. It seems that they are still having talks with him and he has probably been with them for two days. He may have had some of our samples on him, so they probably know about the new products he was bringing from the factory.' I also told him that I would be away for three days. That was to let him know that I would wait by a certain phone box tonight, the three days indicating which one. If he couldn't ring me that night he would try again in the morning. We always stuck to a 6.30 p.m. or 9.30 a.m. call, and he had numbers for adjacent phones if the first one was busy or out of order. After leaving the message I dialled the speaking clock, just in case.

With a few hours to fill before Abu Leila rang, I went up to my local library in Kentish Town and did some SOAS coursework. I had a week before the summer break and needed to hand in my final piece of work. Then, with the help of a librarian, I got the names and numbers of some letting agencies in Cambridge, as I needed to arrange a time to go up and view properties suitable for Abu Leila's negotiation team. I usually used the Kentish Town Library exclusively for studying, but I wanted to have some progress to report when I spoke to him later. I had no doubt that things had to carry on despite Ramzi's predicament – if anything, it probably added some urgency, although I knew of no connection between the Cambridge meeting and Ramzi's activities.

SIXTEEN

Abu Leila didn't ring that night so I had to go to the backup phone box the next morning. It was on a quiet residential square near Highbury & Islington underground station, where the people who occupied the big houses would never need to use a public phone. I got there just before 9.30, having checked my watch earlier against the BBC World Service time signal. I didn't want to be hanging around in a residential area such as this, because the inhabitants tended to be vigilant against any potential threat to their property, and a foreign-looking gentleman (as Jack called me) loitering on their street could result in a call to the police. I picked the phone up on the first ring.

'I know about Giorgio,' Abu Leila said, after some mechanical greetings. 'You need to find out if he has the samples with him or whether his secretary brought them back. He was certainly given them when he left the factory.' I told him that I had tried to speak to his 'secretary' but that she was upset at what had happened. 'I am working on the assumption that he has them with him and is showing them to the competition, but I need confirmation as soon as possible,' he said. His tone was urgent, more urgent than I'd heard before.

'I can let you know tomorrow,' I said, thinking I'd have to speak to Ramzi's wife again or get into their house before morning.

'Leave me a message before ten tomorrow morning,' said Abu Leila. 'You should work on the assumption that the competition know about the samples, so if Giorgio doesn't have them they will be looking for them. If his secretary has them you need to get them before they do.'

I called Ramzi's wife and let the phone ring for some time before remembering that she had smashed the receiver during my last call. I wanted to avoid going to their house, a small mid-terraced place in the East End of London, in case it was being watched. It was a possibility that they had let her come back to England for a reason. I recalled that she worked as a pathology technician at University College Hospital, but I didn't know her name or whether she still worked there. But if she did, and since they were married and had probably taken his name, then the hospital would be a good place to start.

Hospitals have no security to speak of. You can wander almost anywhere unchallenged, particularly if you don a white coat – best acquired from the doctors' lounge in the A&E department. Or go dressed in a suit carrying a briefcase and pretend you are a drugs salesman. I didn't need either, as it happens. I went up to the pathology department and watched a noisy group of white-coated females coming out for lunch – none of them looked like they could be the woman I was looking for. I held the automatic door open with my foot while I asked one of the women if she knew

Ramzi's wife. The door had a keypad lock on it, one not capable of being picked.

'You mean Fadia,' she said. 'She works in cytology.' She rushed off to catch up with her colleagues before I could ask her where cytology was. Inside the department, I walked up the central corridor studying the signs on the doors until I hit the jackpot. Through a glass panel on one of the doors I could see four people sitting at benches working. There were tubes and microscopes and machines that looked like dishwashers everywhere. One woman, sitting at the back, looked promising. She had frizzy black hair and fine features, like the bust of Nefertiti I had seen in the Egyptian Museum in West Berlin. If that was her, I could see why Ramzi had married her and why his dedication to the cause was waning. She was sitting on her own with her back to the window, squinting into a very big microscope.

No one took much notice of me when I went in – a big bearded man writing in a notebook glanced at me as I passed but then quickly returned to whatever it was he was concentrating on. The frizzy-haired woman looked up as I walked towards her and we held each other's gaze. At first she looked at me with absent-minded curiosity, but then her dark eyes grew blacker and her face clouded and she stood up as I approached her from the other side of the laboratory bench.

She was heavily pregnant and looked like she was going to give birth at any moment, but I was no real judge of these things. It rattled me though.

'You're Muneer,' she said in Arabic, not disguising her

loathing. 'I've been expecting you.' She stood with small fists clenched at her sides.

'I just want to know about the case,' I said. 'Did you bring it back?'

'Get away from me!' she said loudly in English. I could hear a chair being scraped back on the floor behind me.

'Is everything all right, Fadia?' a man's voice said from the same direction. Presumably it was the man with the beard.

'I just need the case and I will disappear,' I said to her, not looking around.

'You have ruined our lives and all you can think of is your stupid case?' she said, switching back to Arabic. 'Is it going to liberate Palestine, this stupid case of yours?' She held her swollen belly and started breathing through her mouth.

'Is this man bothering you, Fadia?' The big man with a beard came into my peripheral vision; I didn't look at him – I didn't want to engage with him unless I had to, as it would divert me from my goal.

'I just need to know whether the enemy has the case,' I said to her in Arabic, keeping my voice low and my eyes on her.

'If you tell me who you really are, I will tell you where the case is,' she sneered. I had to fight to maintain eye contact; her dark eyes affected my concentration. She turned to the man with the beard. 'Yes, he is bothering me. He is making indecent suggestions while my husband is away.' Then she started crying – quietly though, dissipating the rage. I could feel the man's hand on my shoulder, but it was a tentative grip. It took a lot of effort to pretend it wasn't there.

'More people could be imprisoned, or worse, if the Jews have the case,' I said to her in Arabic. 'It is a real possibility. Do you want that on your conscience?'

She jerked her head up. 'You are all the same, you sons of whores, playing at revolution, ruining people's lives. You are no better than the enemy. Why don't you go the West Bank and throw some stones, join the Intifada? It might do more good.' I blinked at her and waited until her shoulders relaxed. She waved her colleague away. 'I didn't let him bring it over the bridge,' she said. 'I carried it across myself. I have it here.'

SEVENTEEN

Dead-letter drops, explained Vasily, are just a way of exchanging things with another person without having to meet them face to face. You don't even have to know who the other person is. You leave something for them and they pick it up soon after. It means that you are not in the same place at the same time and therefore less likely to be connected. My last week in Moscow was spent wandering the streets with Vasily, looking for suitable places to hide things. It was not as easy as I'd thought after my success with the counter-surveillance training.

'This is how our trainees collect their pay cheques,' he'd said, and I wasn't sure if he was joking or not. I was stuffing a 35mm film canister into a wall cavity in an alley, hoping that I wasn't being watched by the team on our tail. 'Some agents can do these drops while under overt surveillance and not be spotted,' he said. He told me of an agent at the Russian London embassy who used to make a drop next to Marx's grave in Highgate Cemetery. 'He would take a walk there every day, right under the nose of MI5, and they saw nothing. What could be more natural than a Soviet citizen visiting the grave of Karl Marx?' He laughed out loud as I tried to replace the brick over the canister. It wouldn't stay in. He declared my efforts a failure: I had taken too long. I told Vasily that I thought that this would all be redundant with the developments in personal computing.

'I don't think so,' he said. 'People will still need to take photographs of documents, and those negatives will still need to be transferred somehow.'

I preferred the use of public buildings rather than holes in walls. Toilets are good. You can stick something in a bag in a cistern or on top of a condom machine without much risk of being seen doing it. Not all public toilets are suitable though. Department store toilets are good, or museums or hospitals, or even your doctor's surgery. The latter is good because it is somewhere you can legitimately go, even if you are being followed. Somewhere like that, where you have a good reason to be, or regularly go, is best. Don't use a park toilet unless you usually walk in the park. Don't walk in the woods unless you always walk in the woods. A drug-dealing pub is no good either as the toilets are often used to do business in and sometimes undercover policemen lurk there. These are things you learn over time.

I was standing in such a drug-dealing pub toilet, having come straight from Westminster Reference Library, where I'd filed a blow-by-blow account of my previous day's encounter at the hospital. Last night I'd left a message for Abu Leila telling him I had the 'samples' and asking him what he wanted me to do with them. I had recovered the case, which Fadia had in her locker at work, and in the false bottom sat a single, letter-sized white envelope, sealed with tape. It was fat with papers and I'd hidden it under the bath in Tufnell Park.

In the toilets I handed over £300 to my dealer in exchange for a multi-pack of codeine phosphate tablets, each packet containing twenty-eight tablets of 30mg strength. It was still cellophane-wrapped and in its barcoded delivery pack. I put it in a plastic bag. I'd rung the dealer from near the pub, telling him to get there within the hour, which I'd spent watching the place before he arrived, then for half an hour after he went in – the last thing I needed was to be picked up by the police while buying prescription-only drugs.

'If it's not the real thing I will come back and find you,' I said, only half-joking.

He pretended to look offended. Like so many English men he was badly dressed, in his case a shabby, ill-fitting suit. With his battered briefcase, he looked like an unsuccessful accountant. He scrunched up his pale and pimpled face. 'Roberto, my friend, have I ever sold you anything that wasn't pharmaceutically kosher?'

No, he hadn't, he was reliable in that respect. Some dealers had tried to sell me codeine combined with other drugs, which meant that to make it worthwhile you had to extract the codeine by dissolving and filtering the tablets. Outside the pub I was in Knightsbridge and bright sunshine. People sat at benches drinking beer. Some men had taken their tops off to reveal white chests, and the women were in sleeveless T-shirts and sunglasses, pulling their skirts up to brown their egg-white legs.

I put half of the codeine in my safety deposit box in the basement of Harrods department store and took the remaining packets back to Tufnell Park. I was considering taking a couple of tablets for an afternoon nap when I heard someone (definitely not Helen) on the stairs, then a key was tried in her lock. Someone knocked on her door. It was a gentle knocking but persistent, with some urgency to it. Then the sound of a man's voice, a low, pleading tone. I put an ear to my own door to hear better.

'Please, my love, let me in,' the voice was whispering. '*S'agapo*, Elena. Let me in, *agapi mou*,' he was saying. So he was Greek, her tutor, her lover or ex-lover. He didn't want to go back to his wife, that was certain, or more likely he still wanted Helen as well as his wife. I wondered how he'd got in the front door.

I opened my door quickly to surprise him. He was talking into where the door meets the frame and his right hand was tapping continuously against her door in a rhythmic accompaniment to his pathetic whispering. He stopped when he saw me and pushed himself away from the door, standing up straight with some difficulty. He pulled at his jacket and smoothed back his thick hair, which was shiny with oil or gel. It curled up slightly before it met his shoulders, but was greying at the temples. He couldn't do anything about the two-day growth of stubble and the drinker's eyes: watery and unfocused.

'I don't think she's in,' I said, folding my arms and leaning sideways onto my own door frame. He looked more respectable than when I'd last seen him, mainly because he was clothed, but I could smell the alcohol from where I was standing, just an arm's length away. He didn't speak but knocked more firmly on her door, like he'd just arrived. I waited with him for an answer. 'I'm sure she's not there,'

I said. I was tempted to say something in Greek. Instead I said, 'Shall I give her a message?' He started to go down the stairs. 'Who shall I say called?' I said to his back. He turned to give me a long look, as if to remember my face, but I met his stare until he looked down at the carpet. I knew then that he was no real threat. When he turned back around he stumbled on a bit of frayed carpet, nearly tripping headlong into the front door before finding his feet. 'Be careful!' I shouted after him.

Back in my room I lay down again and two minutes later heard a tapping on my own door. Helen was outside in her white T-shirt, jeans and big watch. She had just come out of her room and was barefoot. She tilted her head.

'Do you like jazz?' she asked.

'I don't know,' I said. 'I've never heard any.'

EIGHTEEN

It turned out that no, I didn't like jazz, at least not the style she took me to hear; she assured me jazz was a broad church. We'd walked down to Camden Town and the club was so crowded and smoky and loud that I was glad to be out walking by the canal afterwards. I found the music chaotic and startling. Helen said that was the whole point, that it could go anywhere. It was a bit like those Impressionist paintings Abu Leila told me to see in Paris, swirly and unfocused. She'd enjoyed it though. She'd drunk four glasses of wine and it showed in her languorous stride. Since it had been too loud in the club for us to talk much, I'd spent the evening watching her, or, more particularly, watching other men watching her. She appeared oblivious, though, to their attention. Some women are self-conscious about that sort of thing and you can tell they are pretending it isn't happening. Others, although they may not consciously encourage it, would be troubled if it didn't happen, as if defined by their attractiveness. With Helen it was as if she was immune to the attention. I didn't believe that she wasn't aware of it, she'd have to be obtuse not to be, and I'm sure she'd been told how attractive she was, but she just carried on regardless. I know that women have to be careful that their signals are not misread, because on the whole men like to interpret things to their own advantage, but Helen didn't care; after all, it was our own fault if we saw something we wanted to see. It came to me later that the men weren't ogling her exactly, more hoping that she would notice them, in the way that a dog desperately craves the attention of its master. But she gave them nothing, not even a glance. I wondered how she chose the men she wanted to be involved with, whether, as she'd intimated, not much thought went into it. I didn't know her enough yet to distinguish what she told me from what she actually did.

'Perhaps we should have started with something more accessible,' she said. She took my arm, and it felt good, walking along like that. We passed a drunk propped up against the wall, wrapped in a coat and scarf despite the warm night. He held up a bottle to us as we passed. Helen had a silk scarf tied around her neck and was wearing big dangly earrings, then just a man's white shirt over her jeans and flat shoes. I got a hint of expensive scent; I could smell it when she drew close, as she did now. She still had that watch on.

'So what are you going to do about your PhD?' I asked.

'What do you mean?'

'I thought he was your supervisor. Won't you need a new supervisor?'

She let go of my arm. 'I can't exactly change supervisors at this stage, not without getting him into trouble.'

I wasn't sure why she cared if he got into trouble. 'But how can you still work with him? He obviously hasn't accepted the situation.' She didn't speak. 'I'm sorry,' I said. 'It's none of my business.'

'He just needs time to understand that I'm serious,' she said.

'And *are* you serious?' I asked.

She laughed and put her arm through mine again. 'Michel! I think you're jealous.' Her remark caught me off guard and I was glad that she couldn't see my face in the dark.

'I just worry that he'll turn up drunk and uninvited, like this afternoon,' I said. It was the first time we'd mentioned the incident.

'You'll protect me from the nasty man, won't you, Michel?' she said in a mock girlish voice, huddling against my arm. I supposed she was making fun of me, perhaps it was the wine. But I knew that if it came to it I would protect her, and she probably knew that too.

Back in Tufnell Park we sat in her room, me in her armchair and her cross-legged on the bed. I drank proper coffee from a fragile china cup with an elephant on it and worried that I might break it. She had insisted on putting on some 'gentler' jazz, and it sounded more bearable than what we had listened to earlier, soothing even. A bedside lamp covered by a silk scarf gave the room a reddish glow. I thought about whether we would sleep together, whether the time was right. I thought about it only because I cared what would happen the following day, and the day after that. Helen closed her eyes and sat with her back against the wall. I watched her neck and the line of her jaw. I thought of Fadia alone, and of Ramzi in prison, but tried to distract myself by concentrating on Helen's face – her long lashes curling up from her closed eyes. She was behaving as if I wasn't there, not in a bad way, just as if she was comfortable in my presence.

'My bed is on the other side of that wall,' I said.

She opened her eyes, but only slightly. 'I know,' she said, her voice soft. 'I've imagined you lying there, just six inches away.'

We looked at each other and she patted the bed. I went to sit on it and she ran her fingers up and down my forearm.

'I love your arms,' she said. 'It's like you have cables running under the skin.' I undid her buttons with my free hand and opened the shirt. As I suspected, she wore no brassiere, but then she hardly needed it. 'Do you think I'm too small, Michel?'

'I think you are just right,' I said, moving my fingers gently over her chest. She smiled and started to remove her shirt.

'You too,' she ordered. So I took off my shirt.

Afterwards, we lay side by side on her bed, and I wondered how she slept on it with her Greek lover Zorba, or whatever his name was, who was twice my size. She was asleep, breathing easily. I felt good, peaceful. I had been with maybe fifteen women before Helen. With the exception of Esma (who didn't count), and perhaps Antanasia in Berlin, sleeping with women had always been an insular experience, one where we were both doing our own thing, stuck in our own individual bubbles of gratification. With Helen I understood what had been missing: there'd been no overlap, no intersection. With Helen there was overlap, my experience was tied to hers, I wanted her to feel good. I told her how good it felt while we were doing it and she told me how good it felt and it fired us up even more. I looked down at her, a sheen of sweat still showing between her breasts. Like strawberries, her nipples were. Her neck had gone red, the redness spreading like a rash from her throat down her chest. I wondered whether she knew it happened, whether someone else had told her. I slipped gently off the bed, picked up the key to my room and tiptoed to the door. I put her door on the latch and checked that she was still asleep. I went onto the landing, still naked, half-expecting to see Zorba, even at this late hour. In my room I took an open packet of codeine from the dresser next to the bed and popped three tablets, putting one back. I downed the tablets with water and went back into her room. She stirred as I got into bed.

'Where were you, *ma belle*?'

I smiled at the endearment, but it wasn't the time to correct her grammar. 'Bathroom,' I said.

'I was afraid you'd gone.' She put her head on my chest and was soon asleep again. I lay awake for a while, matching my breathing with hers.

NINETEEN

I woke in Helen's bed but Helen was gone. The only trace of her was several dark hairs on her pillow. There was a note propped up on the bedside table.

'Gone to UCL,' it said. 'Last night great, let's do it again! See you tonight?'

I had a look around her room. I wasn't looking for anything in particular, just curious. Of course it crossed my mind that Helen might be more than she presented – after all, she had arrived in the house after I had. Although, if she was suspect, looking around her room would provide no clues; if she had anything to hide she wouldn't leave a trace of it here, just as I left no trace of my real activities in my room. She had the luxury of a small desk, which I examined without disturbing anything. I didn't want to open any drawers, in case the contents had been carefully arranged to make it obvious if they'd been gone through. I did discover from papers on her desk that she was at University College London (which explained the acronym on the note) and that her faculty was within a mile of SOAS and five minutes from where Ramzi worked at UCH. I flicked through an anthropological journal on the desk, stopping at a smarmy-looking headshot of her tutor. It was over an article that Helen and he had jointly published, although her name was under his and in smaller letters. It said that he was an authority on Near Eastern burial sites. I memorised his name just because I didn't like the look he'd given me the other day. A jealous Greek was not someone I needed on my tail.

As I got dressed I considered various scenarios of how Helen and I had got together and whether the whole thing had been engineered. I tried to forget our lovemaking and be objective, but it was too difficult, so after a while I gave up.

I went out to make some phone calls. I rang three letting agencies in Cambridge, told them what I wanted, then rang them back an hour later to see what they'd come up with, all from three different phone boxes. I settled on an efficient-sounding woman who was eager to do business; she'd lined up four places, the others had managed three between them. She wanted me to come up and have a look at the properties as soon as possible. I told her I'd be up on the Friday, two days away.

Later I sat in the SOAS canteen drinking tea, thinking about my last day in Moscow. Vasily had arrived early, to take me to the airport. I remember giving him my battery-operated electric razor, because he had admired it when I'd first arrived.

'It's a symbol of Western decadence,' I said.

He laughed but I could see he was touched. 'You will understand that I cannot give you anything in return?'

'You've given me a whole new world,' I said.

Vasily had insisted we sit together on the sofa for a minute because it was a Russian tradition to rest briefly just before embarking on a journey.

It was late at night and Helen and I were both in the bath, facing each other, me with my back to the taps. We couldn't stretch our legs out fully.

'What's the most dangerous thing you have ever done?' Helen asked.

I panicked at the question, thinking that she was testing me, that she knew who I was. Perhaps she had been planted in the house after all – it was all horribly possible despite my earlier rationalisations. I was a fool to get involved with someone living in the same house. I was a fool to get involved with anyone at all.

'What do you mean?' I asked. I sank into the water to my chin, but that just made my knees stick out even more. They looked like hard and hairy islands.

'Well, I once went hang gliding, which is quite dangerous.'

I smiled and contemplated the line of water across her chest, her breasts forming little peninsulas in the water.

'Well?' she said. 'Has the cat got your tongue?'

I had to remember what that meant: the cat getting your tongue.

'I think the most dangerous thing I've done is to get into this bath with you,' I said.

'You think I'm dangerous, do you?' She flicked water at me. 'What do you think I'm going to do to you?' She ran her hands up my legs to my knees. I put a foot on her stomach. I was hypnotised by the light of the candles, the herbal smell of the bath, the low timbre of her voice, her soapy touch. I let my eyes relax and my vision blur. She became a ghostly apparition, shifting in the water before me. 'What are you doing this summer?' she asked.

I was alert again. I was making sure a secret meeting was going to take place between arch enemies with a view to creating a single, secular state for them to live in together – and by the way, we were bathing on top of a lot of cash and forged passports and an envelope that Mossad were desperate to get their hands on.

'I don't know yet,' was what I actually said.

'You're not going home to Lebanon, to see your family?'

I shifted in the water. 'I don't have any family,' I said. 'Well, only a distant relative in Berlin.' It was always useful to have a distant relative up your sleeve.

She sat forward and took my hands, looking me in the face. 'What happened to them?'

'They were murdered,' I said, although I had meant to say killed. I always say killed because that was what I had agreed with Abu Leila: killed by a bomb. Murdered had slipped out.

'I'm sorry. Was it in the war?' I nodded. 'Poor baby.' She started to kiss my hands. I heard the front door open and close downstairs and the candles flickered from the draught that travelled upstairs and under the door, as it had done several times that evening. The flames nearly went out but then recovered. We heard footsteps on the stairs, but they stopped on our landing. Someone knocked at one of the doors. It wouldn't be the landlord at this time of night, and it wouldn't be for me.

'Elena, *agapi mou*?' It was her tutor's whiny voice. Helen leaned forward to snuff out the candles behind me so he wouldn't see the light under the bathroom door. She put her fingers to my lips. Her face was close to mine.

'I can't bear to be without you, my sweet,' he said, his voice slurred. My eyes grew accustomed to the light from the window. Helen sat back slowly with her face in her hands. I decided that this needed to stop and put my hands on the side of the bath to get out, but Helen put her hands on mine to restrain me. She shook her head violently and mouthed a silent 'Please!' Her expression was desperate, so I sat back slowly so as not to slosh the water. I thought that if he came to the bathroom door, I would have to confront him. He started whimpering into her door. He was a sorry specimen, that was for sure. I couldn't understand why he had a key to the front door but not her room. Helen sank her head into the water until only her face was exposed and she was looking at the ceiling. It meant that her behind was pushed down against me. She had to lift her legs and put them on either side of my head. Perhaps she couldn't hear him with her ears underwater. In the dark the steaming water looked like hot oil. We waited for two minutes like this, then I heard him go downstairs and the front door opening and closing. The candles flickered.

I leaned over her, taking my weight with my forearms on the sides of the bath. 'I think he's definitely over you,' I said.

She raised her head out of the water. 'Stop it, it's not funny.'

'Why does he have a key to the house?'

She put her arms around my neck. I dropped my pelvis between her legs.

'Because I gave it to him.'

She wrapped her long legs around my waist and pulled me down. I was pushing at her, ready.

'No, not in the bath,' she said. We got out of the water and I thought she wanted to go into her room but she stood dripping before the full-length mirror, putting her hands either side of it and spreading her feet, sticking her behind out. This was a different Helen to last night. Last night was looking each other in the eye and whispering and kissing; this was something else. I stood behind her and ran one hand over her stomach, using the other to guide myself into her. Despite her length, she still had to lift her heels off the floor to get the angle right. When I was inside her I held still and we looked at each other in the mirror.

'Why doesn't he have a key to your room then, if he has a key to the house?' I asked.

'I changed the lock to my room because he wouldn't give me the keys back,' she gasped. That explained him trying to open her door when I'd caught him outside her room before. She pushed against me and said, 'Are you going to interrogate me or fuck me?'

TWENTY

One of my first tasks after finishing training in Moscow was to go to Geneva, buy six tiny Minox cameras and bring them back to Berlin for Abu Leila to take through to the East. Abu Leila said they were for the Russians, a 'thank you' for my training. Each camera was no bigger than a Swiss army knife and you could fit two of them inside an empty cigarette packet. They were used primarily to photograph documents, and produced a tiny negative that was easy to smuggle or put in a dead-letter drop. The Soviets had tried to make their own version of the camera but it had proved unreliable. I told the supplier that they were for a pharmaceutical company that was having an exercise to test their own security against rival companies. I 'thanked' the Russians on a number of occasions for a couple of years after I said goodbye to Vasily, although it was never anything heavy, just making the odd pick-up of documents or microfilm and taking them to West Berlin, where Abu Leila would take it across through diplomatic channels. Then it all just stopped, although sometimes it was difficult to know whether I was doing things for Abu Leila or for someone else, as nothing I did was explained to me.

In fact, the Cambridge meeting was the first time I'd

understood the purpose behind my actions. I'd delivered packages without knowing their contents, passed on telephone messages that I didn't understand, made large payments of money to people at airports, checked names against public records and carried out counter-surveillance for Abu Leila when he held meetings in West Berlin. I didn't know what these meetings were about, but since I was a student and looked like one, no one paid me any heed when I wandered around with my books. The meetings were always in public places (steakhouses were a favourite of his) and usually involved only one other person. I even heard Abu Leila talking Hebrew at the start of some of these trysts, before I'd moved out of earshot. I would scout the venue beforehand, looking for the telltale surveillance box, and would also watch the target go into the venue (always first) before giving Abu Leila the all-clear.

Only once did we have a situation where the meeting had to be aborted. I had arrived at the restaurant where the *tref* was to happen an hour beforehand, to make sure that whoever Abu Leila was meeting didn't have backup. I had checked the inside of the restaurant, then gone to sit in a café across the road with my newspaper to watch for the target, with the intention of scouting the neighbourhood afterwards for any company he may have attracted. He arrived with two other men, and the three of them stood outside the restaurant chatting before he went in alone. The two men then came over and sat at a table next to mine. They were wide men in suits, speaking Arabic with a Syrian accent, discussing their flight plans to Romania the following day. I assumed they worked for one of the many

Syrian intelligence agencies. I left the café and walked the two blocks to where Abu Leila was waiting in a taxi. I put my newspaper in a bin as I passed him, the signal to abort the meeting.

Afterwards, when we met up in East Berlin, Abu Leila said they were probably Syrian Air Force intelligence operatives, since most of the Syrian security services (there were many) were preoccupied with spying on their own population, as well as Palestinians living in Syria. Most Arab countries thought of the Palestinians they hosted as an undesirable revolutionary force that needed to be contained and tolerated rather than welcomed, despite the supportive rhetoric you might hear spouted. The last thing they wanted were subversive ideas of democracy or free speech trickling into their own populations.

Ask any Palestinian who they'd rather be interrogated by, an Arab or an Israeli, and they'd be hard pressed to choose between them.

Ramzi would be suffering, that's for certain, and I thought of him as I passed UCH, where both he and Fadia worked. I had just sat my 'viva' at SOAS (it was, as Jack would have said, 'a piece of piss') and was on my way to meet Helen for lunch. I thought of the beautiful, angry Fadia, alone and pregnant. Maybe I should have felt guilty. I felt bad for her, but not responsible. They have an expression, the English, about making an omelette: you cannot do it without breaking eggs.

I met Helen in a café off the Euston Road. It was run by Italians who did an all-day English breakfast. When we'd ordered, she said, 'Niki wants me to go on a field trip this summer, to visit some ancient burial grounds in Turkey. It's related to my thesis.'

Niki would be short for her supervisor's name, Nikolos, as I had seen on the article in her room. I asked a question I didn't want to ask. 'And will Professor Niki be going on this trip as well?'

She shook her head but did not look up from her plate.

'No, I don't think so.'

My chest and throat became constricted by her lie. 'Will you be gone the whole summer?'

'No, it's only for a week or two. Anyway, I don't know that I'll be going yet.' This was another lie, I thought. 'I'll probably go up to Scotland as well, my mother has a house there.' We ate for a while without looking at each other, mopping our plates with toast. My face must have betrayed my feelings, for she said, 'You mustn't get too attached to me, Michel. I'm not worth it.'

I looked at her for a few seconds and I got a glimpse of a different, more mature person. 'You seem so sure of yourself but you are like a leaf, going whichever direction the wind blows. You don't know what you want so you just do whatever's easiest, whatever someone suggests to you,' I said.

She crossed her arms and looked out of the window. Maybe I had gone too far. She turned back to me and said in a low voice, 'And what about you, *ma belle*, do you know what you want or where you're heading? Are you so different to me?'

'It's *mon beau*, not *ma belle*. *Belle* is for a woman.'

She stood up, scraping her chair back in the process. I paid the bill and caught up with her outside. Then, as if nothing had taken place between us, she asked, 'Have you ever been to Scotland?' I shook my head. It was true, I had never been. 'Perhaps you'd like to come up for a few days. It's on the beach.'

I had no love of the beach, but to spend some time with Helen without Professor Zorba knocking on her door would be good. The only fly in the ointment (as Jack would have said) was the liberation of my people from occupation. I had no idea how long the Cambridge meeting would take.

'I would love to go,' I said, but I was still thinking about her trip to Turkey. We parted with a hasty kiss and she strode off to college. The cursory nature of our parting hurt me, as did the knowledge that she was on her way to be near that man. I told myself not to be an idiot and to concentrate on what was important. I went to Knightsbridge to pick up some money and ID from my safety deposit box in Harrods, as I was going to Cambridge the next day.

TWENTY-ONE

The first thing I registered about Cambridge Railway Station was that it had only one exit, whatever platform you arrived at. There was also just one exit from the station building onto the street. I phoned Rachel, the estate agent, and she offered to come and get me. I waited outside, noticing that a single road led to and from the station; this meant that it would be easy for one person to watch for arrivals. I wondered why only one person was working the security for such an important meeting; a team of six to ten would be needed to do it properly. I was trying to work out Abu Leila's thinking when Rachel's black BMW came up the road, just as she'd described it.

I'd dressed to give an impression of money: in an expensive but casual suit and shirt, no tie, and good shoes. She stopped at the kerb and I got into an air-conditioned interior that reeked of cloying perfume. She looked too small for the BMW. She wore a pinstripe suit with a skirt that was very short when sitting down. Her uniformly blonde hair was tied up hard at the back of her head. Her make-up was copious but meticulously applied, and she had a gold Star of David around her neck. The star didn't bother me, except that, according to Abu Leila, it was not unknown for pro-Israeli Jews outside Israel to be asked for help by the Israeli 'competition'. Someone who could provide empty properties would no doubt fall into that category. On the other hand, I had given my name as Roberto Levi, so she could just be wearing it for my benefit; sales people will stop at nothing to clinch a deal. She may have fished it out of a drawer, perhaps forgotten since she'd been given it by her grandmother.

But I was being unfair to Rachel; I was tired and irritable from waiting up for Helen last night, not wanting to take any codeine and fall asleep in case she knocked on my door. But she hadn't come home and wasn't there when I knocked early in the morning. I'd thought about picking the new lock but decided it wouldn't be a good idea, just in case she was inside. I sat back in the leather seat of the BMW while Rachel explained the housing market in Cambridge. I listened to very little of what she said, but her voice was pleasant enough and it was a nice car with comfortable seats. Every once in a while, when it was safe to do so, I treated myself to an eyeful of her legs.

The first house we went to was unsuitable. I knew it before we even got out, but I didn't say anything. It was a semi-detached house on a narrow street of terraced houses; exactly what I had said I didn't want. It would be a nightmare to secure. We went in anyway. Rachel had to put her heels on before getting out of the car, but even with them on she only came up to my shoulders. She looked worried.

'You don't like it, do you, Mr Levi?'

I shook my head.

'I knew it wasn't right, but my boss made me include

it – he's been trying to shift it for months.' She seemed genuinely upset.

'Don't worry, Rachel. Let's look at the ones that you chose for me.' We drove for ten minutes to another property, and I could see a finger-width of stocking top. I wondered what it would be like to be with her, and whether she wanted me to wonder. She was intent on the road though, having to peer over the top of the steering wheel because she was so short. She was not the type of woman I ordinarily found attractive, she had made too much of an effort with her appearance so that you noticed that more than the person underneath. Though I was vaguely interested in knowing what she was like under all that make-up, pinstripe and perfume. Helen possibly went to the same effort but always looked like she hadn't bothered. Again I wondered if she'd spent the night with Zorba somewhere, to avoid bringing him back to Tufnell Park. I didn't understand Helen and her insistence on maintaining contact with that buffoon. I hated myself for being drawn to her, knowing it to be a weakness and a distraction from what was important.

'I think this is more what you're looking for,' Rachel said, as we turned off a main road onto a quiet street with large detached houses. Each house had its own big frontage so it was set back from the road. She turned in to one of them. A gate led onto a drive, but it looked like it had never been closed and you didn't want to attract attention by changing the status quo. Rachel was telling me that the owners were in Australia and needed tenants for the summer. I'd told her on the phone that I needed the house for a group of businessmen of various nationalities who were looking to buy into some of the innovative technology companies starting up in Cambridge: I had done my research. They didn't want to stay in a hotel, I told her, because of the expense, but needed somewhere comfortable.

'I like this one already,' I said, as we drew up on the gravel drive. She unlocked the front door for me and ushered me inside. It was expensively furnished and had several rooms downstairs, six bedrooms, two bathrooms, a TV. Rachel kept up a running commentary as we went around. I walked outside and looked around the garden. None of the house was overlooked, although the bottom of the garden could be seen from the adjacent houses. I couldn't imagine that whoever was staying would have time for the garden but there would have to be some rules, some areas would be off limits. I'd said to Abu Leila that if I was going to arrange this then I needed to be fully in charge of security and be able to lay down the law. No wandering into town on their own, no telephone calls telling family or mistresses where they were, no visitors. People were stupid when it came to security, even those who should know better.

Rachel followed me around like a happy puppy, pleased that I was pleased. I made her show me where the house was on the map, which she had to clack off in her heels to get from the car. Looking at the map, I liked what I saw and told her that we didn't need to look at any other places.

'I'm happy with this one, Rachel.' I looked at my watch, it was only mid-morning.

'Do you want to go and do the paperwork then?' I looked at her round, powdered face. Her mascara-thickened eyelashes moved up and down rapidly. We were standing alone in the large open-plan kitchen, alone in the 'good-sized, well-appointed house'. Maybe Helen was right, maybe I shouldn't get too attached to her; perhaps she wasn't the right person for me after all.

'When does your boss expect you back?'

'We were due to see four places, well, five, with the one he threw in, so I'm not expected back until later this afternoon.' She splayed her stubby fingers on the worktop, her immaculate red fingernails contrasting against the shiny black granite. She raised her shaped eyebrows and smiled. 'Why, Mr Levi, what are you thinking?'

I smiled. I didn't know what I was thinking. I was thinking Rachel and I could go upstairs and try the 'well-proportioned bedroom with queen-sized bed' and I could forget about Helen. 'What I am thinking is that I have never seen Cambridge. Maybe you could show it to me and we could have lunch. What do you think?'

'I think I would like that.'

'I'll tell your boss that you showed me all the houses,' I said.

'You're a nice man, Mr Levi, not everyone would do that.'

'Call me Roberto.'

She locked up the house as I waited in the car. I watched her walk around and get in. She turned to look at me, taking in my face and said, 'Where shall we go first?'

'I understand there's an airport here?'

'You want to see the airport? It's tiny.'

'Indulge me, Rachel.'

The Star of David sparkled at her neck as she refreshed

her lipstick in the rear-view mirror. The lipstick matched the colour of her nails. It was such an intimate thing to do, I thought, as she reversed – to put on lipstick in front of a stranger.

TWENTY-TWO

Back at King's Cross Station I left a message on the Berlin answer machine to the effect that I'd sorted out the accommodation and identified several opportunities for an actual meeting place. I got on the bus up to Tufnell Park. I'd left Rachel three months' rent and filled out some paperwork back at her office. I didn't pursue my curiosity about her, although I sensed that she would have been willing, particularly after her two glasses of white wine at lunch. She'd shown me around town and the colleges and I'd pretended to be interested in all that history. On the other hand, I didn't give her, as Jack might say, the cold shoulder. I told her I would be back in Cambridge over the summer and would look her up: it would be useful to have a local contact there. I had her business card in my wallet, her home number written on the back in fountain pen. I even got a kiss on the cheek in the car, when she dropped me off. I was glad when I was on the train, it was hard work playing Roberto Levi all morning, even though I did get a bit of a kick out of the whole thing.

It was early evening when I knocked on Helen's door.

'Michel, at last, you're here.' Wearing a strappy summer dress and sticking an earring into her earlobe, she looked like she was ready to go out. She took in my clothes. 'You're looking expensively stylish – been on a date, have we?' I shook my head but she wasn't interested in my answer. She grabbed something from her room then came out into the hall.

'Looks like you're going on a date yourself.' She twirled on some shoes with a slight heel, a third of the size of Rachel's.

'You approve?' She pulled a wrap around her shoulders. The whole effect was offset by her masculine watch.

'I take great pleasure in your appearance,' I said.

'You're such a smoothie, but I'm so glad you're here.' She pulled on my sleeve. 'Come with me, Michel.'

'Where are we going?'

'My departmental end-of-year party. I need you there.' She stood holding a small handbag covered in little shiny sequins. How could I have even thought about sleeping with Rachel? Everything about her now seemed so contrived and overdone as I stood next to Helen. The truth was that spending time with Rachel had made me ache for Helen.

'Can't we go into your room so I can take more pleasure in your appearance?'

She smacked me on the arm with her handbag. 'Later, when we come back. I want you to, I really do.' She kissed me and pulled me by the hand down the stairs I had just come up.

Twenty minutes on the upper deck at the back of the bus and it hit me, where we were going. I stopped caressing her neck. 'Won't Professor Zorba be at this party?' I asked.

'Yes, he will, and his name isn't Zorba.' She pulled her

shawl over her shoulders where I had tugged it to expose her lovely skin. She said, 'He'll be there with his wife.'

I thought about it for a minute, him being there with his wife. 'So are we going as a couple?'

'Yes, we are. I want them to see us together.' She put her head on my shoulder and squeezed my thigh. 'Aren't you pleased?'

I had to consider whether I was pleased. 'It depends,' I said reluctantly.

She sat up and frowned at me. 'On what exactly?'

'On whether the idea is for him to see us together or for his wife to.'

She gave me a look. 'That's a shitty thing to say.' Maybe she did want me to be there for her sake, or to show him that she'd moved on. But maybe she'd thought this up with him last night, perhaps after they'd had sex. They'd possibly had a laugh about it when she explained how easy it would be to get me to come along and play boyfriend for the evening. Perhaps she even teased him with the idea that she might have to sleep with me afterwards. I tried to rein in my thoughts but instead I just saw him on top of her. 'Why don't you go home then, Michel, if it's going to be a problem for you?' The bus had turned onto Euston Road.

'I'm sorry,' I said, although I wasn't sure what for. 'I didn't get much sleep last night.'

'Neither did I, as it happens.'

'I don't want to know what you were doing.'

She snapped her head round. 'What's that supposed to fucking mean? You really are behaving like an arsehole, Michel.' She took out a tissue from her bag and blew into it.

I put my arm around her but she shook it off. She shredded the wet tissue. 'I was with Maria, an old schoolfriend. We were talking most of the night.' I gave her a cotton handkerchief which she blew into noisily. 'We were talking about how I always manage to fuck things up.' She looked at me. 'I was telling her about you, about how you might be different.' This said as if to suggest that maybe she'd got it completely wrong.

'I'm sorry, Helen. I imagined all kinds of stupid things – I don't know what to say …' Her mascara had smudged onto her cheeks. I told her that I didn't think we should go to the party.

'I thought it would be a good idea, but maybe you're right.' She blew her nose again and gave me my wet handkerchief back. 'They all hate me anyway.'

'I don't believe that,' I said.

'Then you're a fool – I've been sleeping with the head of the department, remember.' Her voice was full of bitter self-loathing.

'You can't tell who you're going to fall in love with,' I said, although I found the idea of her being in love with him nauseating.

She snorted. 'Love has nothing to do with it, Michel. You really don't know me at all.' She pulled away again and looked out onto Euston Station.

'Then we need to get to know each other better,' I said, pulling her back to me.

She relaxed into my shoulder. 'Is that so? And how do you propose we do that?'

I had rehearsed the answer to this. 'Eating, talking and making love,' I said.

'You're such a charmer,' she said, sniggering in my ear and prodding my ribs. 'Seriously though, I like those suggestions – I'm just not sure I like the order they're in.'

We did eat first though, at a vegetarian Indian restaurant behind Euston Station. I resisted the urge to ask her if she'd taken Zorba there or whether she was still going to Turkey with him, and I was pleased that I didn't spoil the mood. We ate, then took the bus back to Tufnell Park.

After we had made love she told me she was going to visit her mother in the morning. I asked her whether her father was still alive, as she never mentioned him. We were lying naked on her bed, her throat and chest still flushed. The window was open and a cool breeze dried the sweat on us. She'd chosen a different scarf to cover her bedside lamp; one that blocked out most of the light. She had a drawer full of silk scarves, and one was still tied to her right wrist, although I'd undone the other end from the bedstead. I had to repeat the question about her father.

'Do you have to think about whether he's alive?' I joked.

She sighed. 'I want to believe he's alive, but I haven't seen or heard from him since he disappeared three years ago, so I'm not sure.'

I looked at her. She had that look I'd seen on her face once before, like she was older than her years. 'Disappeared?'

'Yes. Mum and I came home one evening after a girls' night out to find that he had cleared out all his things.

Clothes, papers, letters, books, toothbrush, even his umbrella. Everything that was his. It was as if he was trying to expunge himself from our lives. There was no note, nothing. He was just gone.'

I had to think about what she had told me. After a minute I asked, 'Did you try to find him?'

'What do you think? The police said it was not unknown for men to disappear like that, although usually they just leave everything behind. Apparently it was unusual that he took all his things. My mother thinks that he may have had another woman somewhere. He travelled a lot, he was – maybe still is – a successful businessman.'

'What about his business? Surely—'

'Michel, we followed up every lead. He'd sold the business some weeks before leaving. We were well provided for. It was all very carefully planned.'

'So what do you think happened to him?' I asked.

'I don't know; maybe he had another family somewhere. Or maybe he committed suicide.'

'What do you think?' I asked.

She turned away from me but I held her close. 'I don't know. It was more important than us, whatever it was.' I started to mutter platitudes but I could see she'd set her face hard so I shut up. 'He did leave one thing,' she said. She reached out to the bedside table and put something cold and metallic in my hand. I could tell without holding it up to the light that it was her big stainless-steel watch.

TWENTY-THREE

Before Helen left the house to visit her mother the next morning she kissed me and said, 'I've not told anyone about my father, Michel, except for Maria.' Maria, I recalled, was the friend she'd been with two nights ago, someone she'd known since school, someone she confided in. I was pleased to be a fellow confidant; it answered an unspoken question, although I wondered whether Zorba had used the scarves in the same way I had. I tried to put that from my mind. Did it even matter? Yes, somehow it did. The more I thought about it, the more it mattered. What did she see in that fool? I did extra sit-ups until I could do no more and had to lie on the floor till the fiery ache in my belly subsided. It was a first for me, that business with the scarves. I'd found the whole thing disturbing and exciting, but I didn't want to reflect on why it was disturbing, just as I didn't want to reflect on why I hadn't gone back into the house after Mama's screams had ended and the men had left.

I ran a bath and while it filled did an inventory of what was underneath it. I saw the article I'd torn out of *Le Monde*. I had a lot of other material on the massacre, culled from hours spent in libraries reading newspapers on a microfiche machine. I'd printed out anything of interest – interviews, stories and pictures. I'd requested official reports by various agencies. I'd read books by journalists, tearing out pages relevant to that day. It was all collated in a large folder in my safety deposit box underneath Harrods.

I wasn't sure what I was going to do with all this information. I had an idea that I wanted to punish the people responsible. But who I would punish and how wasn't yet clear to me.

After Moscow I'd had five weekends of training in East Berlin before leaving for London. It took place mostly in Potsdam, but sometimes in Beeskow, south-east of Berlin, where I was driven from East Berlin by an elderly man who spoke not once in the ten times we were together. The training involved the use of weapons, self-defence, interrogation techniques and technical surveillance. I would go over on a Friday night and come back on Sunday afternoon, staying in a cell-like room. I shot various handguns at paper targets in sound-proofed basements. I stripped the same weapons and reassembled them with a stopwatch going, all weapons you could carry about your person. The training was all given in a deadpan manner that lacked the humour of Vasily and his comrades. To kill someone you need to shoot them at least four or five times in the head, just to make sure. And it needs to be up close with a hand-held weapon. You have to put it right up against the head or very close to it, otherwise you could miss; some weapons give a massive kick, and any shot following the first could go wild. If you can't get close enough to kill the target with your first shot, then you will need to incapacitate them with a body shot first and finish the deed close up, a *coup de grâce*. All this I learned so as to understand what I might be up against, not so that I might put these things into practice – this was made clear to me when I asked Abu Leila about it. In the back of my mind though, I pictured the men on that black day. I had seen those that took part, at least in the beginning, when they'd come into our house and interrupted our dinner, although some had worn ski masks to cover their faces. I couldn't even be sure of the numbers involved: at least five and possibly as many as eight. People had come and gone. I could still hear their voices, but only one name was used, and it wasn't in the article I was holding. I made a big effort to learn everything I was being taught by the Stasi. They told Abu Leila I practised with uncommon zeal.

I counted the money in the zip-lock bag and put it back with the Greek and Swiss passports. I removed the fat envelope I had retrieved from Fadia, weighing it and holding it to the light before putting it back in the bag with everything else; I was still awaiting instruction from Abu Leila.

Lying in the bath, I wondered whether it was possible for me to have a real relationship with Helen. The obstacles were big, not least of all Abu Leila, to whom it would be a betrayal. I visualised myself telling him, but cringed at the thought. I would have to tell her the truth about myself, and no amount of insistence on my part that I would stick to the cover story would convince him otherwise. And why would it? The reality was that the attraction of having a relationship was in part telling her about my life, sharing its burdens. I'd given up much for a greater cause: I couldn't mix with certain people, had to deny my origins, couldn't travel to my place of birth. I lied to everyone I met and had no real friends. I envied Ramzi his wife. To have someone like Fadia who worried about your well-being so much she would take such a risk for you – that would be something.

I got out of the bath. I was beginning to feel sorry for myself. I reminded myself again of the people who hadn't survived the massacre at Sabra, and what had happened to those that had some years later. It was these events that had led me to use codeine for the first time.

I'd been at university in West Berlin for a year when news reports came through of another attack on the Sabra and Shatila refugee camps. This time it was by Syrian-backed Amal (Shia Muslims) rather than Israeli-backed Phalangists (Maronite Christians) – incongruously united in their desire to rid Lebanon of all Palestinians. Within two weeks my end of the camp, the Sabra end, had been defeated and the inhabitants had either fled to the adjoining Shatila camp or been killed. After a year-long ceasefire Amal attacked the Shatila end, but the inhabitants were better prepared and put up a stiff resistance against a force ten times mightier. They were besieged for six months, with no help apart from some occasional shelling of the besiegers by friendly leftist factions situated in the mountains overlooking Beirut. Women and children were shot down by snipers as they tried to sneak out to find water, food and greatly needed medical supplies. Others were shot trying to retrieve the fallen. A year later and near starvation – this was just as I was graduating from my second year – the camp residents had asked Islamic leaders for dispensation to eat the dead. I had found the whole situation very difficult, and was desperate to do something, although I didn't know what. Abu Leila convinced me I was already doing the right thing.

'Your time will come, Michel,' he'd said, as we drank coffee on the upper floor of the Kranzler Café on the Ku'Damm on one of Abu Leila's rare forays into West Berlin. 'You need to stay focused on the bigger picture, look to the longer term.' He waved a cigarette as he spoke, drawing a hazy vision in Turkish smoke. At the time I didn't think to ask him to be more specific, but I was angry. Angry because I was having to relive something that should not have happened the first time, never mind a second. Angry because nobody did anything about it – nobody. Angry because I didn't know how to express my anger and because Abu Leila appeared insensitive to my feelings.

I'd left him at the Kranzler and gone to a party with some people from university. This was unusual for me, as I never attended parties. If I'd been a drinker I would have got drunk, but I wasn't; it had made me sick when I'd tried it in Cyprus. A woman at the party, on learning I was teetotal, offered me a cannabis cigarette. I declined, telling her I didn't smoke. She made it her mission to find something for me.

'You don't look right, you need something to make you right,' she'd said. She returned later with a pack of codeine from the bathroom.

'They're my mother's. They'll give you happy thoughts,' she said, passing me a glass of water.

She wasn't lying. It did make me feel right, righter than I'd ever felt, and I told her so. I also told her, as we lay on her bed – the party raging below – that I loved her. We didn't have sex because it didn't cross our minds; it's not that type of drug. That night was the first night that I slept without rocking my head, or even feeling the need to.

After my bath I went into Westminster to check my PO box. The only thing in it was a postcard postmarked the previous day. It was a picture of Big Ben and on the back all it said was, 'I miss you a lot.'

It meant Ramzi was back and wanted to meet.

TWENTY-FOUR

I absently scanned faces at the other tables while sitting waiting for Ramzi in the outpatients café at UCH: an elderly couple drinking tea, two doctors eating wilting sandwiches that the English like to make, a couple with a pasty child in a wheelchair and a tube in her nose, a man in a jacket and tie reading yesterday's *Sunday Times*. I could read the headline from where I was sitting: 'Israel in Hostage Swap Bid with Iran.' I was so absorbed in straining to read the subheading that I didn't notice Ramzi until he was standing right in front of me. We were meant to meet in the service area like we had last time, so I felt wrong-footed when he sat down. He put a can of Fanta and a Mars bar on the table.

I don't know what I was expecting but he didn't look too bad to my eyes. He was bouncing his leg up and down under the table and glancing around nervously. It was contagious, and I started to look around the place myself, more worried about his wife Fadia turning up than anything else. I was sure, now that I'd met her, that she had primed him to cut ties with me. In fact, I was surprised that he had contacted me at all, but maybe he still felt some responsibility to what we were doing. I concentrated on getting some facts.

'Was it bad?' I asked. He broke the metal seal on the can

of Fanta and unwrapped the Mars bar. I drank from a bottle of water. The place was busy with patients and their relatives, clinics being in full swing this time of the morning.

'I was held in the Russian Compound,' he said, as if this answered my question. The Russian Compound was a prison in Jerusalem built by the Turks and still used by the Israelis. It was notorious among Palestinians. 'Do you know what *al-shabah* is?' I knew what it was, it meant ghost, but he was going to tell me anyway. 'They make you sit on a stool, so low that you have to squat on it. Then they tie your hands to the wall so your arms are stretched. Then they put a cloth sack over your head,' he said. 'A sack that stinks of piss. You panic because you think that you will suffocate.' He took a mouthful of Mars bar and spoke while chewing. 'They leave you there for hours until your arms and legs go numb. It gives you a terrible pain in the shoulders after a while.' He showed me his wrists; they were still marked from the plastic ties used to bind them.

'What reason did they give for stopping you?' I asked.

'They don't need a reason,' he said, 'but they were interested in my luggage.'

'But you didn't have the case,' I said. 'You gave it to Fadia.'

'Fadia insisted that she take the case once she realised what was going on, that I was planning to take it back across. She knew about it because I'd given it to the taxi driver on the way in and it turned up on the way back. It was her that insisted we go across separately.' He looked at me to see whether I had anything to say. 'She was insistent,' he repeated. I nodded sympathetically; I imagined she would be. She could easily have told him to dump the case though, rather than bring it through herself, so I had to admire her for that. I asked Ramzi why she hadn't just left it.

'She did want to leave it at first, she was going to leave it with the driver, but he said that it was very important it left the country and that he would get into trouble if he took it back. He was a different driver, not the one who picked us up.'

'A different driver?'

He nodded and took a bite of chocolate and a swig of drink. I asked him to describe the new driver. A thin balding man with designer stubble, except for where a small scar on his chin meant no hair could grow.

'And Fadia wasn't stopped?'

He shook his head. 'Fadia said that since she was pregnant it made sense for her to carry it. She moved her clothes into the case in the taxi. The driver agreed that this was a good idea.'

A new driver, and one with opinions. We talked some more. I asked for names and dates and asked the same questions in different ways, just to check his story.

Essentially he'd been stopped at the bridge once Fadia had gone through, accused of being a member of a terrorist organisation, then taken straight back to Jerusalem to the Russian Compound and left to stew with the sack on his head for a couple of days. Once Fadia realised he wasn't coming across she had sorted out a lawyer for him when she got to Amman, although Ramzi said he might as well have been a postman for all the good he did.

'Of course this whole business has made her stressed,' Ramzi said.

I needed to get to the heart of things before I let him go. 'What questions did they ask you?' I asked. 'I'm sure it was hard going, you'll have had to have told them something.'

He finished his chocolate and scrunched up the wrapper. 'If I'd had the case on me I would have said something, because the evidence would have been there. But I didn't tell them about the case because they weren't concerned with it. The truth is they didn't ask me anything.' He drank some more, swilled it around his mouth and said, 'I didn't tell them about you, if that's what's worrying you.'

I ignored that and continued, 'And the driver, did they ask about him?' The taxi driver was the only link Ramzi had to Abu Leila's network on the West Bank.

He shook his head. 'They asked me no questions, that was the thing, they just ripped my cases apart. In the end they had to let me go. They took me before a judge to apply for an extra seven days' detention, but surprisingly she said they had to let me go.' I studied him for evidence of lying but I could see nothing beyond nervous energy.

'OK, I'll let you get back to work,' I said.

'Did you speak to the man,' he asked, 'like we discussed last time?'

'I think you should concentrate on your family from now on,' I said. He had become a liability, obviously burned and on the enemy's radar. Even if he wasn't, his wife made things too difficult, although based on her performance at the crossing she would have been of more use than he was.

'You mean I'm no longer any use to you,' he said, a sneer

on his lips, although he was probably just masking his relief. I could have reminded him that he was the one that wanted out, but I was already compiling my report in my head and wanted to get it down on paper before it faded. Then he sat up in his seat and cleared his throat. 'Fadia, well, Fadia and I, we are starting a medical charity. We want to organise for doctors and medical technicians here to go to Gaza and train people there, a sort of exchange programme, if you will. Obviously this does not sit well with what I've been doing to help you and the man.' He looked different when he said this, betraying an enthusiasm and confidence I hadn't seen before. It made me aware that my dealings with people were very limited and that they had whole other lives that I didn't know about.

'Good luck with that,' I said, shaking his hand.

'You need it more than I do, my friend,' he said, clapping me on the back in a familiar manner that betrayed his relief at not having to see me again.

I stepped into the street, glad to be out of the hospital and away from Ramzi.

After leaving Ramzi I went over to Euston Station. I needed to speak to Abu Leila, or at least leave him a message to let him know that Ramzi had been released. Was it good news or not? I wasn't sure. Certainly Abu Leila's network in the Territories was compromised in some way, but the Israelis didn't seem to care if Ramzi knew – or perhaps they wanted it known. I stood in a phone booth and looked out onto the station hall, half-empty after the morning rush. I was formulating what I would say on the phone. I watched as parents tried to herd children and luggage to the right platform; the summer holidays were starting. A man standing by the escalators and looking up at the departures board caught my attention. He looked familiar, but I wasn't sure where I'd seen him before. I turned around and made the call to the answerphone, just saying that Ramzi was out and that the competition were possibly aware that he was a member of the sales team. I told him that I would follow up with a more detailed report. I hung up and dialled the speaking clock. It came to me, as the voice on the other end told me it was 11.36, where I'd seen the man in the hall before. It was in the café at the hospital, reading yesterday's *Sunday Times*. He'd changed his appearance somehow, but had the same rounded shoulders. I turned around to see if he was still there, but he'd disappeared.

TWENTY-FIVE

I stepped onto a bus going towards Leicester Square as soon as I exited Euston Station. I was keen to get my report written and sent off as soon as I could; seeing the same man twice made me anxious. It could have been coincidence, of course; Euston was the nearest train station to the hospital so it wasn't impossible. But still, training had taught me that I couldn't dismiss these things lightly.

Inside Westminster Reference Library I grabbed my big dictionary from the shelf and went to my desk. Only two other library users were seated, one of whom was the tramp sleeping at his desk, wrapped in his coat despite the heat. As I passed him I held my breath, knowing from experience that he would smell. An elderly woman sat at one of the microfiche viewers which whined as it sped back through years of newspaper headlines. I had used the same machine myself many times in my research. I sat in my usual place, with my back to the wall and overlooking most of the desks. No one could pass me without my seeing them approach, which gave me time to cover what I was writing. I started to jot down the account of my conversation with Ramzi, leaving out nothing because I'd been taught never to judge what was or wasn't important.

I'd got to the bit about Ramzi's wife Fadia calling a lawyer from Amman, and looked up to give my eyes a rest from the small print of the dictionary. Someone else had come into the library and was poring over a book some three rows away. He looked up at the window and I recognised him as the man at Euston Station, the same one I'd seen when meeting with Ramzi. Twice was a coincidence, three times was not. He had taken off his tie, of course, and was now jacketless. He'd even combed his fair hair differently. But it was him. He had the same pale face and rounded shoulders, which he couldn't disguise. I was aware of someone else moving among the book stacks to my right, but looked down at the desk again so as not to appear concerned. I was annoyed with myself because I'd not noticed them come in to the library. I slipped my incomplete report into my pocket and scrunched it up, my first thought being that I should get rid of it immediately. I felt trapped and had to work hard to slow my beating heart – an exercise I'd learned in Moscow. I resisted the urge to get up and run. I imagined Vasily beside me, telling me what I should be looking for.

I wondered what size of team was waiting outside, it could be anything from five to ten on foot, maybe more in backup vehicles. If they were the 'competition' then there wouldn't be so many, as they would have had to come from Israel or use the few people they had here. I looked at my watch. I was due to meet Helen in an hour and wanted to confirm their presence before then, or at the very least lose them. I didn't want her connected to me.

Without looking at anyone, I got up and replaced the dictionary on the shelf. It would have to be the last time I used it. I walked slowly outside and stood in the doorway, as if deciding which way to go, which I was, but it also gave me time to look around. I didn't remain there long enough to confirm who was watching the entrance, but it was enough time to take in all the people that potentially fitted the bill. I looked for people putting a hand to their ear, fiddling with radios under their clothes, loitering with no purpose. I memorised faces so that I could spot them later. The operator inside would have signalled my leaving by using a couple of clicks on a radio. They would have someone covering every direction I could go in, and possibly a car somewhere nearby, if they were using radios, to act as a command-and-relay point. My plan of action, therefore, was to get underground, where radios would be useless.

I walked up St Martin's Street and across Leicester Square and tried to figure out where I had been picked up. The obvious place was the hospital, when I'd met Ramzi. This, perhaps, was why he had been released, so they could trace the source of whatever was coming into the Territories. Did they ask him to set up the meeting? I replayed our conversation, looking for clues, but found none to suggest Ramzi had set me up, apart from the fact that he didn't meet me in the specified place but came up to me in public. This was idle speculation though, and besides, they knew he would make contact on his own; all they needed to do was to keep him in sight. Perhaps they'd held him in Jerusalem to give themselves enough time to set things in place, get people over here. If this was the case then they wouldn't know how Ramzi made contact, or about my PO box. And if they had just picked me up this morning then they didn't know where I lived. They had no reason to even suspect that I was anything but Ramzi's cousin, as I'd made out on the phone when arranging the meeting. Perhaps all I needed to do was convince my surveillance team of my innocence. But all this reassurance was undone by the knowledge that they had picked me to follow rather than any of Ramzi's wide circle of friends; they certainly wouldn't have had enough people to cover everyone.

I turned onto Charing Cross Road and changed my mind about going into Leicester Square tube as that was the nearest station and they might have someone in there ahead of me. Instead I walked up the road, not even trying to detect them, and went into Foyles Bookshop. As soon as I was inside I made my way as quickly as I could, without running, to the second floor, where I went to the front of the shop overlooking Charing Cross Road.

I looked out of a dirty window onto the street, trying to spot the pale man from the library. Since they knew I had seen him up close they wouldn't deploy him in the shop and risk what they thought would be a second sighting by me – unbeknown to them, I had already seen him three times. They would send someone else in though. I saw a couple on the other side of the road, both wearing jackets despite the heat, standing facing the bookshop. He was dark, more semitic-looking than me. He was talking but not looking at her, leaning his head slightly into his collar. Then the man from the library walked past them and went into a café up the road. The woman crossed the road towards the bookshop and out of sight. I walked back through the store, then turned right until I got to the windows overlooking a side street. I knew there was a second entrance to the bookshop here, and it made sense for them to cover it. Bingo. There was my jacketed woman, looking into a guitar shop window on the other side of the road. I had three of the team now. There could be at least one other with me in the bookshop. I checked my watch. I had half an hour before I was to meet Helen.

TWENTY-SIX

Inside the bookshop I pretended to peruse a book on what was called the 'Arab–Israeli Conflict'. It wasn't a conflict, it was an occupation. Indeed Abu Leila always referred to it as a colonisation by the West.

'The idea that there's a war on is a myth, Michel,' he'd once said. 'It implies two equal powers fighting on equal terms.' He puffed on a Turkish cigarette. 'This David and Goliath idea is part of the mythology, a mythology that only involves white Jews, by the way.' I don't know why this should have come into my head at that particular moment, when I had what I believed to be the competition on my tail, except that I was in a bit of a David and Goliath situation myself. I put the book back on the shelf and went up the escalator to the next floor. Near to where I got off I pulled out a heavy book of photographs on the Vietnam War. I stood facing the top of the escalator, where I could see the people coming off over pictures of the remains of napalm-burnt villages. I would only be visible when they appeared near the top of the escalator and would be so close that they would have to be very careful to avoid looking startled. Surveillance operatives try to avoid eye contact, but sometimes it is difficult to do without being obvious and giving themselves away. If they do make eye contact with the target then they have to be pulled from the team, as they might be recognised next time.

A couple of people came off the escalator and paid me no heed beyond a glance. Then a familiar head of shiny dark hair appeared, then Helen's pretty face. Just behind her was the slack unshaven face of her tutor Zorba, or Niki, or whatever the fuck he was called. Helen went bright red when she saw me and he went pale. Stepping off the escalator, Helen spoke with exaggerated gaiety.

'Michel! What are you doing here?'

As if I had been banned from bookshops. Her neck became flushed as in lovemaking. I ignored the Greek, who moved over to a section of books. He was out of earshot but still in my peripheral vision, so able to see us. I was conflicted: I didn't want to be seen with Helen by my pursuers, but just as equally I didn't want to see her out with Zorba.

'We're just getting a couple of books on Turkey,' she said. He pretended to study the back of a book but smoothed his hair back self-consciously. I looked at my watch.

'I thought we were meeting for lunch,' I said. Her embarrassment, which had been fading, was renewed with a fresh reddening. Her face told me she'd forgotten, but all I could think was that someone could come up the escalator at any second and see us talking. 'Will I see you later?' I asked, then, unable to stop myself, 'or will you be reading to each other all afternoon?' Helen's eyes brightened with anger, but before she could reply I saw the top of a head behind her on the escalator so I turned my back on her and walked away fast.

I was so angry when I left through the side entrance of Foyles that I crossed the narrow road too fast and bumped into a woman as she turned from a shop window. Instinctively I apologised, holding onto her arm to steady her before realising it was one of the female operatives. In my rage I'd completely forgotten about her. She had a form-fitting flesh-coloured earpiece in her left ear, much as a deaf person might have, and a similarly coloured wire ran down her neck and disappeared behind her hair. At ten paces you wouldn't see it. This close I could see the alarm in her eyes. But she was a professional and suppressed it. I smiled, feeling reckless, just to see what would happen. She smiled back.

'Are you all right?' I asked her.

'Yes, I'm OK.' Her accent gave her away; they must have flown her over from Israel. I decided to push my luck.

'That's an unusual accent. Where are you from?' I asked.

She shook her head and smiled, like she'd heard that line before. 'I'm OK. Don't worry, it was nothing.' Her hand worked beneath her jacket. No doubt summoning help on the radio. I glanced to my right and saw the Arab-looking operative walking fast towards us from Charing Cross Road. He was muttering into his collar, restraining himself from sprinting. I thought I heard a buzzing from the woman's ear, but I might have imagined it. I was in a mood to take this all the way, I didn't care what the consequences were.

Besides, what could they do in broad daylight? They were obviously just a surveillance team, nothing more.

'Maybe I could buy you a coffee – to apologise?' I said. 'There's a place just around the corner.' She shook her head and her companion reached us. Up close he definitely looked as semitic as I did, but she didn't, she was definitely Caucasian, probably Israeli, with that accent. He reminded me of the Arab-looking soldier who had picked me up outside Sabra on the day of the killings. Abu Leila had once told me about research that showed that Sephardic Jews and Palestinians were no different genetically. He said the research had been withdrawn after publication in an academic journal because of the outcry it had caused. According to one of his many monologues, the Palestinians and Arab Jews, the Mizrahis, were probably the original Jews, and the European Jews, the Ashkenazis, were later converts with no genetic link to the region. Could this man, standing not two metres away from me, and I be from the same genetic pool? I reminded myself that he was still an enemy. Even a neighbour can be your enemy, even a father or brother.

'My boyfriend,' the woman said, gesturing at him, putting on an apologetic smile. She moved over to him and put her arm through his. He had removed his earpiece and had tried to tuck it under his collar, without much success.

I raised my hands in apology and bowed my head in defeat. 'I'm sorry,' I said. 'Of course you would have a boyfriend.'

The man forced himself to smile, then they turned away and walked back towards Charing Cross Road. I followed behind quite happily, knowing there was probably one person behind me as well as the pale-faced man in the café. I followed them as they turned left onto Charing Cross Road and passed them as they crossed it to go into the café, just as the pale-faced man came out. It was straight out of the manual: one operator following behind and one on the other side of the road. This was the time to go underground and channel them behind me. I quickly turned into the entrance of Tottenham Court Road tube and, as soon as I was out of view, took the stairs three steps at a time.

TWENTY-SEVEN

After much prevarication, I got back to Tufnell Park. I'd travelled by taxi, bus, tube and on foot, and it was getting dark when I made it to my room. I didn't knock on Helen's door as I passed it, figuring that she would still be out. Let her come to me, I thought, too tired to even think about what had happened between us in the bookshop. I warmed up a ready-made meal and ate it from its plastic container. It tasted like the plastic had leached into the food. I took three codeine and lay on the bed in the dark.

The codeine had long since converted to morphine in my brain when I heard a knock at the door. I couldn't answer it, not without it being obvious that I was doped up. I heard Helen's door close and a few moments later some music seeped through the wall. I wished I could make the wall disappear and for our rooms to become one. I considered knocking on the wall, but then I would have to get up to answer the door, which was physically impossible. I was content where I was, comfortably floating on my cloud. I would have liked Helen to be on my cloud. She would like the codeine, I thought. It could help her like it helped me. I thought of Mama and wondered why I had no siblings. Helen had no siblings, as far as I knew. Mama used to do everything for me – cook, clean, fetch me water when I was thirsty, make me a sandwich if I was hungry. She would wash and dry a particular shirt for me if I wanted to wear it that same day. Mothers here weren't like that. I felt a bit embarrassed for Mama now. She'd seemed happy enough looking after all us men, but I now understood that she wouldn't have complained even if she hadn't been happy. Helen's music took on a melancholy tone, it sounded like more of her jazz. It washed over me like a slow wave, making me sad yet not quite depressed; you couldn't get depressed on codeine. Instead I was filled with an indistinct longing.

I had a dreamless sleep and was awoken by more knocking. I staggered from the bed, still in my now wrinkled clothes. I opened the door, and Helen was there in a towel revealing her long legs.

'Good morning, neighbour,' she said. She clutched the towel to her chest. 'I'm having a bath and need someone to wash my back. Would you oblige?'

I didn't smile, believing she was just trying to distract me from yesterday. 'I haven't had breakfast,' I said.

'Well, Mr Grumpy, we'll get breakfast afterwards. I'll buy you some to make up for forgetting lunch yesterday. You can wash my back to make up for turning yours on me in the bookshop. What was that about?'

Before I could answer, the front door opened and closed downstairs and she gestured desperately for me to let her into my room. I closed the door behind her as someone's feet hit the stairs. She stood inside the door and let the towel drop. I studied her body and listened to the footsteps arrive on the landing and go up the next flight. A door closed somewhere upstairs.

'Do you want to punish me, Michel? Is that it?' She moved past me into the middle of the room and turned her back to me. She looked over her shoulder, sticking out her behind. 'Do you want to smack me?' She was smiling but I didn't know if she was making fun of me or was angry or what. I was also getting aroused. Then her voice got softer and deeper and she lost the smile. 'If you want to punish me, you can,' she said. She knelt on the chair, resting her elbows on the back of it so her behind was pushed out. I put my hand on her buttocks, then between her legs. She was wet and gave off a musky smell. She said something but I couldn't be sure what because her face was turned to the wall and the words came from deep in her throat. I started to unbutton my trousers, overwhelmed with a need I didn't even think of controlling.

'No, not there. Get on the bed,' I said. She got off the chair and lay on her back, her legs apart. I got on top of her in my clothes, undoing my trousers just enough to free myself. She lay with her arms either side of her head, as if she was being held at gunpoint. I was crazy with lust and anger. I took my weight with arms outstretched, like I was doing push-ups, my knees between her thighs, my hands pushing down on hers, our fingers intertwined. She grunted with her eyes half-closed, until I was done, which wasn't long afterwards, and I flopped down onto her. I was panting and could hear my heart, or maybe it was hers, thumping rapidly. Her arms came around me and her hands stroked the back of my head. She whispered gently in my ear, 'Do you feel better, Michel?' I nodded, my face in her hair. I'd attained a certain serenity that I couldn't explain. I wanted to apologise, but I wasn't sure what for. 'Good. So do I – now let's have that bath.'

I washed Helen's back while I considered my next move. I hadn't finished my report for Abu Leila, detailing my meeting with Ramzi, but I had more urgent news to report. Although I'd left him a message last night from somewhere on my circuitous route home, it was restricted to telling him that the 'competition' were here but that I was not, as far as I could tell, known to them, apart from by sight. Of course I wasn't sure of this. Ramzi could have told them what he knew about me, which, although little, was enough for determined professionals to trace me, given time. I needed a *tref* with Abu Leila, that was certain, a written report wouldn't be enough. I continued to fret and worry at it like a scabrous wound.

'Whattya thinking about, lover boy?' Helen asked. She leaned back into me.

I turned my attention to her, to us, recalling her visit to the bookshop yesterday.

'I was wondering whether you had decided to go to Turkey?' I asked resignedly.

'Do you not want me to go?' Why was she asking me a question that she already knew the answer to?

'Does it make any difference what I want?' I asked.

'Of course it makes a difference,' she said.

'Then, no, I don't want you to go.' She spooned water onto my knees with a cup she used to rinse her hair with.

'But you tell me it's important for your PhD, so you should go.'

'What are you worried about, *ma belle*?'

I started to wash her stomach and flat chest. 'Zorba is my worry,' I said over her shoulder. 'It's the two of you in Turkey together that I worry about – lift your arms please.'

'You don't trust me then.'

I soaped her stubbly armpits. 'Him I don't trust. You …' I rinsed her off with the cup. I wanted to tell her that she felt worthless, and that being with a man made her feel wanted and needed. But I wasn't even sure if that was true.

'Me, I'm just weak,' she said. She laughed and turned around. 'It's my turn to wash you now.' She hadn't told me if she was going to Turkey or not but I didn't push it. I let myself be washed and went back to fretting over my pursuers.

TWENTY-EIGHT

In Paris, North African immigrants lived in sprawling suburbs, servicing, behind the scenes, the romantic Parisian vision portrayed in films and travel brochures. Of course affluent Arabs lived in Paris too, many Lebanese had second homes there, but they didn't live in the same neighbourhoods as their fellow migrant workers, and they frequented cafés and restaurants where they spoke French. West Berlin had Kreuzberg, where the Turks, Kurds and Arabs lived next door to anarchists and bohemians. When in Berlin, I would sometimes go to Kreuzberg just to hear the voices and smell the cooking to get a sense of home, a hint and flavour of the camp. I didn't know anyone living there, of course, but I felt comfortable, relaxed even, just wandering about, soaking up the atmosphere. To do the same in London meant going to the southern end of Edgware Road and wandering into some of the food shops bringing a taste of home to those living in the area, but it wasn't the same as Kreuzberg or certain parts of Paris.

The high-profile Arab community in London was a moneyed one that lived in some of the most exclusive property areas of the city. The poorer Arabs, like the Moroccans and some Palestinians, co-habited with other immigrants in

East London, and, like their Parisian counterparts, made sure the hotels and clubs ran smoothly for their well-to-do brethren who came from the Gulf to shop, gamble and do business. A sense of affluence existed in Edgware that could be seen in the cars driven and the clothes and sunglasses worn, which made it a world away from Kreuzberg and Clichy-sous-Bois.

After leaving Helen to meet her friend Maria, I stood in a snack bar run by Lebanese twins on the Edgware Road. Although she had asked me to go along I wasn't keen, or in the mood, to meet anyone new. I was savouring a grilled chicken pitta covered in garlic sauce. I watched a group of middle-aged men sitting at a table smoking and, as Jack would say, putting the world to rights. Their accents made them Iraqis; they could have been in a street café in Baghdad were it not for the fact that they were exiled in London to escape Saddam Hussein's torturers.

The owners of the café tried to strike up a conversation but I wasn't having any of it; I was still worried about my encounter with the competition the day before. According to Abu Leila, the Arab community was riddled with informers and he was forever lecturing me on the dangers of trusting anyone. I suppose I probably shouldn't have come down here.

'Sometimes you will be drawn to your own, but remember that they are the prime target for the enemy,' Abu Leila had said. According to him, people thought they were working for some Arab state when they were feeding intelligence back to the Israelis. 'The competition are experts at this sort of dissemblance, Michel. They get people to think they are helping the cause when in fact they are doing the opposite.'

So there I was, drawn to my own yet unable to have a proper conversation. I was an outsider. They were a foreign people to which I no longer belonged, from a land from which I had been exiled. Exiled by Abu Leila. The truth is that the Arabs are a diverse people, both ethnically and geographically. True, we are united in many things, like our famed ability to welcome complete strangers into our homes and give them the last of our food. And there is a common language, at least in formal Arabic, a legacy of the Islamic empire – colloquial Arabic is another matter – and a common religion, if you discounted us Christians and a handful of Jews. But we are always lumped together, and sometimes, when it suits us, we pretend we are one people. There are other, more bloody, divisions within the Arab world, to do with religious factions, tribe, money, class and politics. I watched a Mercedes-load of young men in sunglasses cruise past, blaring Arabic pop music from open windows. Back in Beirut Mama would have been cleaning their rooms while they were out, making them tea when they were home.

I finished my sandwich and left, playing the innocent the rest of the afternoon, wandering around like a tourist and deliberately not taking any counter-surveillance measures. I went to the cinema, and even into the National Gallery, before heading towards University College and the student union building where I was to meet Helen.

Gower Street is a dirty line of buildings blackened by years of bus fumes. Walking down it from Euston Square underground station, I passed the entrance to Russia House (MI5 headquarters, according to Vasily, who said they had their own door that led straight into the tube at Euston Square). Ramzi's hospital was down a street on the other side of the road and Helen's college just further down on the left. I walked past it, turned a corner and went into Waterstone's, where I had bought my new copy of Primo Levi. I had plenty of time before I was to meet Helen and I wanted to make sure I didn't tie my followers to her.

I spent an hour in the bookshop, looking out of the windows onto the street, browsing books in the art section, then moving to electronic engineering to see if familiar faces followed me around – the likelihood of someone else being interested in both art and electronic engineering seemed slim. Eventually I convinced myself that I was alone.

Leaving the bookshop, I crossed the road to the student union building. I hung around the empty lobby and watched for Helen through the dirty glass doors. I saw her and her tutor walking towards the building together and my chest seized up: so much for her being with Maria. They were deep in conversation and he was gesticulating as he talked. Why can't we Mediterraneans keep our hands still? Helen was nodding her head, dressed in sandals and a summer dress. He was holding her attention, judging by her expression. They stopped on the other side of the road and she gestured to where I was. I thought I'd been spotted but she was just pointing to the building. Zorba started to say something but she shook her head and frowned. He took her hands in his and I like to think that she tried to shake them free.

She said something to him and he shrugged and held out his palms in surrender. She laughed and they hugged each other, longer than I found comfortable. She had to pull away from him because he wasn't letting her go, and I was about to go outside when they separated. He was laughing as she wagged a finger at him.

She crossed the road to come into the building while Zorba stood there watching her. I went down the hall towards the toilets before she came in, then doubled back so that she didn't know that I had seen her with him.

'Michel! You're early.' She grabbed my hands harder than necessary.

'Shall we go?' I said, gesturing to the door. Zorba's bulk was still visible through the glass behind her.

'Why don't we get a drink here first? I'm gasping.'

'I thought you hated the bar here?' But she was already heading for the stairs. I looked back through the doors, but the fucker was gone.

TWENTY-NINE

Abu Leila's voice came down the phone in reassuring cadences, even in his bad German.

'Don't worry about it, Michel, we carry on as planned.'

I was in a call box near Archway underground station, a short bus journey from Tufnell Park. Abu Leila was referring to the Cambridge meeting. I reminded him that venues and accommodation were all sorted.

'When is the first board meeting?' I asked.

'We'll discuss that face to face. Let's meet in Paris next Tuesday.' Meeting in Paris next Tuesday meant meeting in Berlin the day after tomorrow.

'That's fine, I'll get back to you when I have a flight booked,' I said, which meant I would ring him when I was in Berlin. 'What about the competition?' I asked. 'They're showing great interest in the business at the moment.'

'Don't worry about them. They have probably lost interest. Just bring the product samples. Bring them to Paris.' He paused and I heard him light up – I could almost smell the tobacco. 'Are you in London?'

I hesitated. Why was he asking me a question he knew I wouldn't answer?

He didn't wait for an answer, however, and asked, 'Have you looked at the samples?'

'No, of course not,' I said, surprised that he needed to ask. 'Why would I?'

'It is important that you bring them to me as you found them.'

To avoid detection I decided to stay in Tufnell Park until I travelled to Berlin, on the basis that the competition, if they were still on my tail, wouldn't be looking for me there. I figured that Abu Leila's reassurances that they had lost interest were just that, reassurances, and I thought it irresponsible of him to make them. It was possible, although unlikely, that they knew they had missed their chance and gone home. I walked home from the phone box, choosing to reflect on Helen instead of the conversation I'd had with Abu Leila, which left me feeling uneasy.

Last night and this morning Helen and I had spent in Tufnell Park, either making love (although that's not what she called it) or talking. That was when I had confronted her about being with Zorba, after giving her what I thought was enough time to bring it up on her own. She said that she'd bumped into him after seeing Maria and it was hardly worth mentioning. Why, she explained (after making clear that she was under no obligation to explain anything), would she have asked me along if she was planning to see Niki? I had no answer to that, and she didn't give me a chance to think of one, distracting me with a pre-breakfast 'treat' in her bed. Afterwards, though, when she had gone to the toilet, I came up with at least three alternative scenarios which involved her changing her mind about seeing Maria when I'd said I wouldn't be going with her. Two of these scenarios involved her having sex with Zorba (once in his office), while the third involved them arranging to meet in Turkey for a holiday together. This last one gave me the most heartache and was given added credence when she told me, in our by now ritual post-sex bath, that she would be going to Turkey after all. It was only for a week, and Zorba wouldn't be going, as he would be on holiday with his wife in Greece. It was after this news that I got out of the bath and went for a walk to call Abu Leila.

As I neared home I thought it might be prudent to test the emergency entrance to the house. I also decided to tell Helen my true feelings for her. I turned off Fortress Road onto the street that connected to mine. Halfway before my street I stopped to tie my shoelace and, when I was sure no one else could see me, ducked into a narrow passage that ran along the bottom of my garden. At one time there must have been gates to the gardens either side, to allow access to them, but over the years these had been fenced over, or, like the one leading to my house, been padlocked on the house side. Except that some time ago I had picked the rusty padlock, leaving it unlocked and in situ, so that from the house it still looked locked. The path ran through to another street that came off Fortress Road but was so clogged with overflowing bushes and trees, as well as debris thrown from gardens, that you couldn't actually see all the way down it. This meant once you were on the path you couldn't be seen from the streets at either end.

The garden to my house was a neglected, overgrown rectangle into which nobody ever set foot. The owner didn't maintain it, using it to dump unwanted furniture and rusting appliances. It was a discarded cooker, with weeds sprouting from underneath, that served as one of my caches. I removed a dirty plastic packet from a cavity in its back. Inside was a thin leather case. Inside that, the steel flat-lock picks and the torque wrenches were in pristine condition, like dental instruments.

Once I had the back door open (twenty-five seconds; Vasily would be proud) I kept it from closing with a piece of cardboard and replaced the picking set in its hiding place. Back inside, I was on the ground floor next to the stairs, the front door being at the opposite end of the hall. I closed the back door behind me, went up to my floor and tapped on Helen's door. My nerves jangled; I knew what I wanted to say to her but just not how I would go about it.

She opened the door, newspaper in one hand. 'Are you still sulking, *ma belle*?'

'I don't want to fight with you,' I said.

She smiled and started to undo the buttons on her jeans. 'Good – shall we use your room or mine? Your mattress is firmer.'

I shook my head. 'No, not that – I just want to talk.'

'I'm only joking, silly.' She opened her door wide and let me in, patting my behind as I passed her. I felt belittled by this action. I sat in her armchair and she sat cross-legged on her bed, spreading out the newspaper in front of her as if to read it. 'OK, Mr Serious, tell me off then, but I'd really prefer some punishment.'

'Everything is about sex with you,' I said.

She looked surprised. This wasn't how I'd planned to tell her how I felt, to try to explain my jealousy.

'I think you take things a little too seriously, Michel.' She looked over to the window, then back at me. 'Sometimes, I have to say, you are a little too intense. It could scare a girl off.'

It was my turn to be surprised. We sat in silence for a bit, all thoughts of my saying anything now gone.

'So when are you going to Turkey?' I asked. I hadn't thought to ask in the bath, being more upset at the fact that she had left it so long before telling me than that she was actually going – I had already resigned myself to that. She licked her finger before turning a sheet of newspaper.

'Saturday,' she said, without looking up. How was she going to arrange a visa that quickly? I watched her holding her hair back from her face with one hand so she could read the paper, her lips slightly pursed in concentration. With her other hand she fiddled with a thin gold chain around her neck.

At this moment I was certain that I loved her. At this moment I also knew she had been planning to go to Turkey all along and that all these arrangements would have been made some time before; no one just flies off to look at burial sites in Turkey without arranging it with the authorities. Zorba was probably not going to Greece with his wife at all. All this went on in my head, of course, but I didn't see the point in saying any of it out loud. Instead I slumped down in the chair. Besides, I was going to Berlin tomorrow, and had to think of a way to explain my absence just two days before she was off to Turkey.

THIRTY

Of course I lied to Helen. My uncle, the distant relative I'd told her lived in Berlin, had taken ill. I had no problem lying to her since she was, no doubt, lying to me. I assumed that she was going to Turkey with her tutor and, had I thought it would do anything other than end our fledgling relationship, would have found proof and confronted her with the evidence. Her outward brashness hid something, I believed; I would catch it periodically in her eyes, when she relaxed her guard. I didn't know what it was, something to do with her father, I supposed, but it made me feel protective of her. Of course I didn't think her tutor cared about any of this and I believed, despite having no evidence to prove it, that he was taking advantage of her.

I disembarked at Tegel after a sweaty landing and checked into a budget hotel, favoured by backpacking students, near Checkpoint Charlie. You had to share toilets, but it was anonymous and had a quick turnover of guests. Once I'd stowed my bag in my room I looked like everyone else, in my worn Levis and T-shirt, as they gathered outside consulting guidebooks. I rang Abu Leila in East Berlin and he told me he would come over in the morning, we would meet at the KaDeWe.

'I need cigarettes,' he said. 'I can't get Turkish cigarettes here – the East Germans make their cigarettes with cow shit.' He told me to bring the envelope with me. I checked for it in my jacket and wondered why he was coming over to the West, but it was not the sort of thing you could ask him, like the many other things I couldn't ask. I'd have thought it was safer for him in the East; West Berlin was crawling with agents from every country. But then East Berlin was crawling with Stasi, so you had to take your pick.

It was dusk as I walked through Kreuzberg and towards the river and Hallesches Tor, where many people were congregating. They were all coming out of the U-Bahn station, exiting on the south side of the river. I followed the crowd and crossed the bridge towards the park, where there was some kind of fair going on. Shawarma and doner kebab stalls were plentiful, and there was *tabla* playing, Egyptian belly dancing, people selling halva, falafel, Turkish Delight. A man in full Bedouin dress was leading a magnificent white stallion, giving children rides. Off to one side, a group of people were roasting a whole sheep on a spit. There were also Caribbean rum stalls, salsa dancing groups, tacos with refried beans and cocktails with umbrellas. Anarchists were smoking hashish, old Turkish men were smoking *nargileh*s. This was a gathering of communities celebrating their culture through food, drink, song and dance. This was a carnival of exiles giving thanks to West Berlin for being a refuge. There were information stalls with pamphlets and posters.

About the Communist Party of Iraq, about the plight of the Kurds, the genocide of the Armenians, a stall celebrating the recent withdrawal of the Soviets from Afghanistan and supporting the Mujahideen – how Vasily would have cussed. Vegetarians promoted the virtues of pulses and vegetables, waving away the smoke of barbecuing chicken with their leaflets. Someone gave me a pamphlet telling me how the Romanian people were suffering under Nicolae Ceausescu, and I looked for Antanasia, my old university girlfriend, on their stall, but of course she wasn't there.

Then I came upon a stall that had the Palestinian flag draped over it. It was staffed by four German students who wore *keffiyeh*s like the *fedayeen* had when they'd left Beirut in 1982, just weeks before the massacre. One of them, a thin pale woman, thrust a pamphlet under my nose. On the cover was a picture of bodies in the street after the massacre in my camp, bloated and obscene. I had seen these photos before, I had some of them in my safety deposit box. I had even seen the beginning of some film footage that I hadn't been able to watch all the way through for fear I'd see the people I had left lying there. The pale girl was saying something to me in German.

'The perpetrators have never been brought to justice for this crime – have you heard of it?' I nodded numbly, looking at the leaflet. She continued, 'Many people were killed, many disappeared. The Israelis, under the command of the Zionist general, Sharon, surrounded the camp and fired flares over it all night, to help the people who did this.' I remembered the flares; I had stood outside our house watching them turn night into day. Mama had called me in to our last supper, my father and uncles looking serious, my mother looking tired but forcing herself to be cheerful.

'Will you sign our petition?' the girl was asking. She thrust something under my nose. I studied it but could not figure out what the petition was for. Was it to bring Sharon to justice? Was it to charge the killers? Different strains of music were fighting for my attention, different smells, different languages. People were shouting and laughing. I looked at the picture of the dead bodies again; they were on the main Sabra Street. I had walked down that street many times, to my UNRWA school, to the dirt patch that served as a football pitch. I was jostled back to the present by two drunk young Turks, who pushed by arm in arm, looking back at me and giggling. The girl in the *keffiyeh* was talking again, shrugging and looking at her colleagues. It appeared that I was shaking my head; I would not sign anything, no petition could fix this. She was trying to take the clipboard back but I couldn't let go without explaining.

'I'm tracking the killers down,' I told them in German. 'I already know some of their leaders' names.' Try as I might, I couldn't keep the clipboard steady in my hand. 'When I find them I'm going to bring them to justice.' Now I couldn't keep my voice steady either. 'I'm going to kill them. I know how to do it – I've been trained.'

I let out a bark of a laugh, feeling a strange detachment from myself as if I had escaped my own body. I let go of the clipboard and handed her the leaflet. She grinned stupidly and the others were quiet behind the stall. I smiled, but they didn't smile back. One of the young men spoke.

'Go on now, we don't want any loonies here.'

I didn't understand who he was talking to; I looked around to see who he was talking to.

'Go on, fuck off, dopehead.' I looked around again but saw no one else at the stall.

I walked back through the fair and left the noise and the colour and the smells. I ended up back in my hotel. In my small room, I took three codeine and went to bed, despite feeling hungry. It was half past five. At six o'clock I got up and took a fourth tablet.

THIRTY-ONE

I woke with a hole in my stomach; I hadn't eaten since lunchtime yesterday. I was half-asleep still, in a post-codeine stupor. I had overslept and had no time for breakfast before my *tref* with Abu Leila. I taped the fraying envelope to the middle of yesterday's *Der Spiegel* newspaper, puzzling, as I went through my pre-meeting shake-off routine, over my outburst at the stall yesterday, and feeling embarrassed by it. It had come from nowhere. I wasn't going to kill anyone, so why had I said those things? Things I locked away in my safety deposit box and in my head. It was as if they had just leaked out. I put it down to tiredness and stress and concentrated on the practicalities of my *tref*.

Abu Leila and I had agreed to meet in the KaDeWe department store, a huge building on the Ku'Damm. It was similar in scale to the Harrods store in London. On the top floor was a food emporium that featured many stalls, like an upscale indoor street market. Instead of Bratwurst, doners and the chips with curry sauce that you might find at any street *Imbiss*, they sold caviar, oysters and steak tartare. You could find hundreds of types of sausage here, a hundred varieties of beer, a hundred different breads and, more importantly, in the tobacco section, every brand of cigarette made in the world, judging by the range on offer. I found Abu Leila sitting at a Turkish-themed stall drinking coffee. He was the only person there, and was chatting in Turkish to the man behind the counter, sharing some joke. When I sat down Abu Leila nodded and the Turk, dressed in black with a full-length white apron and a red fez on his head, poured me a Turkish coffee. He raised the coffee pot high above the small cup so that it was filled with a long stream. He then disappeared to the other side of the kiosk and started to polish the spotless counter. I needed something to eat but didn't want to ask for it now that he had gone.

'I didn't know you spoke Turkish,' I said to Abu Leila. He had three twelve-pack cartons of Turkish cigarettes on the counter beside his coffee; he had done his shopping. Grey bags hung under his eyes. I put *Der Spiegel* on the counter between us but he ignored it.

'How are things with you?' he asked, breaking open one of the cartons and taking out a new flat packet. I told him I was fine – I did not mention my strange episode yesterday at the fair, nothing would be served by it, it was an aberration. I was glad when we started to talk business; the fake Turkish surroundings were reminding me that Helen would soon be in Turkey with Zorba. I briefed Abu Leila about the Cambridge house, told him that if I was to be responsible for security then I needed to lay down some rules. He lit up and blew out some smoke.

'OK, tell me what you need.'

So I told him what I needed: that no one would leave the house except with my permission, that no wives or mistresses should be contacted, or worse, brought to Cambridge.

'One of the party is a woman,' he broke in. 'I assume she would be subject to the same rules?'

'Of course,' I said, annoyed at the interruption. I continued that coming by air from Amsterdam was possible, with a private charter.

He interrupted again: 'I'm not keen on using Schiphol; the competition has a big station in the El Al airport facility.'

'I'm sure there are other airports one can fly from ...' I trailed off. It struck me that he didn't look that interested in what I had to say about security arrangements. I was disappointed with his attitude, as he was always telling me that PLO officials never paid enough attention to security and I had gone to a lot of effort to put the whole thing together. I decided to persevere.

'There is another thing,' I said. 'It would be good for me to have help with this – when people arrive, I mean. I can't cover all the angles on my own. I need someone at the station, at the house. I need a car and a driver—'

Abu Leila raised his hand. 'No way can all that happen, Michel. This needs to stay small. I can't trust anyone else with this. You'll have to do the best you can do.' That, as Jack would say, took the wind out of my sails. To make things worse he asked me to write down the address of the house, which I did, and he put the piece of paper in his wallet without reading it.

'Tell me about Ramzi, and' – patting the newspaper with the envelope in it – 'the story of this.' The kiosk man came over and gave Abu Leila a refill, fawning over him as if he was a regular. I asked him for a not very Turkish pretzel. When he'd gone, Abu Leila turned to me expectantly. I briefed him as best I could, recalling word for word my conversation with Ramzi, as I would have put it in my report had I been able to complete it. When I was finished, Abu Leila looked at me, then took off his glasses to clean them with the napkin that was under his coffee cup. I nibbled at my pretzel.

'You have given a good account as always, Michel.' He put his glasses back on.

'Doesn't this change the Cambridge meeting in any way?' I asked.

Abu Leila shrugged. 'I'm not sure. It depends. Tell me about the driver.'

'The driver?'

'You said Ramzi told you a new driver brought them from Ramallah to the crossing. Did he describe him?' I put my pretzel down and described him as Ramzi had: a thin, balding Palestinian with a small scar that prevented hair growth on his chin. When I was done, Abu Leila looked into his cup and I had no clue as to whether I'd portrayed someone he knew or not. Then he drained his coffee and left money on the counter before picking up the newspaper. He stared at me in a way I had not experienced before. It felt uncomfortable, like I was being studied under a microscope. I had the sensation that he looked like someone different, someone I didn't know, like when I caught glimpses of Helen looking much older.

'Did you open the envelope?' That took me aback; it was the second time he'd asked this question. But he continued to stare at me, not changing his expression.

'Of course not,' I said, blushing and looking away, knowing

it was a weakness even as I did so. 'I would never do such a thing.'

His face regained its usual smile and he stood up, clapping me on the back. 'Of course you wouldn't. Let us walk down the Ku'Damm and look at the women in their summer dresses.'

'Are you sure that's a good idea?' I asked. We never walked together down the street; our meetings were all in safe houses, restaurants, cafés and museums, and we always left separately.

'If your time is up, Michel, your time is up, it is God's will.' I was confounded at his unlikely fatalism, it was a negation of everything I had been taught. I was going to argue but then he said, 'We'll just walk up to the Kranzler. We need to talk about your future, Michel, and I want to do it in a real café,' waving at the Turkish stall, 'not a fake.'

THIRTY-TWO

Once outside the KaDeWe we wandered up the Ku'Damm in the direction of the Europa Centre and the Kranzler Café. It was hot after the artificially cooled air of the department store. Abu Leila was smiling to himself. He held up his purchase of Turkish cigarettes, as if to explain his delight. I desperately wanted to stop and do some counter-surveillance, to pop into a shop with a big window and check out the people on the street to see whether I recognised anyone from the KaDeWe. Two German boys, ten or eleven years old, ran past us shrieking and shouting. We heard their parents call after them from behind us. The boys were whining for ice cream. Abu Leila laughed, saying, 'A spell in Gaza would do them good, Michel. To appreciate what they have, yes?' He said something else but I couldn't hear him over the sound of tourists and traffic. A motorcycle was revving nearby. I had to ask him to repeat himself and leaned in to him so I could hear his answer.

'I said that I think I will have to move from the GDR soon. Their ideology is built on absolutes, and absolutes can't bend when the wind of change blows, they just snap.'

'Where would you go then?' I asked.

He shrugged, as if the question hadn't occurred to him.

'It is your future I am more worried about, Michel.' We slowed down for an elderly woman in a red top walking in front of us, and I started to ask Abu Leila what he meant when the woman stumbled onto her knees. I instinctively bent forward to help her up, but then she fell forward again, her face hitting the pavement with a nauseous slap. She was lying motionless on the ground. Her underskirts were showing. I got down beside her and pulled her dress down over her legs. Then, while on my knees, I saw dark blood spreading on the pavement from under her body. I looked back up at Abu Leila, who was mouthing something that I couldn't hear over the sound of an idling motorbike that had stopped nearby. He was holding out the copy of *Der Spiegel* to me. I saw someone in black leathers and a motorcycle helmet with a tinted visor step up behind him and point something at the back of his head. People were scattering in wordless panic. I reached up to warn him or to pull him down or something, but Abu Leila jerked and looked surprised then dropped to his knees. The newspaper fell and the cartons of cigarettes scattered onto the pavement, the open one spilling its contents. I worried that the packets would fall into the blood pooling on the pavement. The man in leathers took another step towards us and pointed again and Abu Leila nodded at me. His right eye exploded in a red mess onto the inside of his glasses. I tried to hold him up as he collapsed across the woman on the ground. The man in leathers was now properly visible to me: he was holding an automatic with a silencer. I tried to identify the model. A small wisp of blue smoke eased out of its long muzzle. Behind him another man, again in black leathers, sat astride a black 750cc Honda, its engine throbbing as it waited by the side of the road. The driver's head was turned to us, but, like his companion, no face was visible beneath the dark visor of his helmet. The man with the pistol looked at me, at least I think he did, it was impossible to see what he was looking at, he may have been checking Abu Leila for life or looking at the things on the pavement. He stepped forward and shot again. I flinched and Abu Leila twitched in my arms. Someone screamed. The rider shouted, '*Yalla*!', sounded his horn and revved the engine. The killer put the weapon inside his leather jacket, then turned and ran back to the bike, swinging himself onto the back and wrapping his arms around the driver's midriff. The engine screamed horribly as the bike accelerated violently into the traffic, its front wheel leaving the ground momentarily. You could hear the bike for a long time in the distance.

A crowd had started to gather. I looked down to see the back of Abu Leila's head, or what was left of it, and I was frozen, unable to function. He was growing heavy in my arms. A logical, KGB-trained part of my brain was telling me to get out of there. A fifteen-year-old part of me was making me stay put, to get underneath him and hold my breath, to play dead. The crowd grew bigger but kept a safe distance. I let Abu Leila sink down on top of the old woman. Still on my knees, I started to pick up the packets of Turkish cigarettes, then remembered the copy of *Der Spiegel*. I found it, still folded, a couple of metres away. No one came forward to help, I heard no 'Let me through, I'm a doctor.' But a man called hysterically for the police and an ambulance, both at this stage redundant. Then a woman screamed, and I couldn't understand the point of it, but it helped me to get up, helped me walk away from the man who had been my mentor and surrogate father. A father superior in many ways to my own poor uneducated dead father, also shot in the head.

Out-of-focus people were muttering and pointing and I could hear the sound of a siren because the Germans lose no time in ringing the authorities about the smallest thing. But this was not a small thing, and I pushed through half-hearted attempts to stop me leaving and broke into a run until I reached the entrance of Kurfürstendamm U-Bahn station, where I took the stairs three at a time and boarded the first northbound train.

I stood near the doors, ready to jump off at every stop if necessary. Everyone who got on looked at me and took a step backwards. It was as if I carried the violence of what had happened with me. Was I being paranoid? It was only when the train was going through a tunnel that I saw, in my reflection in the glass of the door, dark stains on my face. I put a hand up and transferred blood to my fingers. Was it my own? I felt my head and body for possible holes or nicks, but concluded that the blood was Abu Leila's and wiped it off with tissues with a trembling hand. Stupidly, I hadn't gone through his pockets to remove anything incriminating. But at least I'd had the presence of mind to pick up the copy of *Der Spiegel* with the envelope inside. I started thinking that I should be going to my hotel to get my bag – I had my passport on me – but I wasn't sure whether this was a good idea or not. I weighed up leaving the trail of an unpaid hotel bill, a plane ticket and an overnight bag (including a packet of codeine) against going back to pick them up, thereby remaining longer than necessary in West Berlin. It was a matter of hours, if not minutes, I reasoned, before the police had a description of me from the many witnesses, and it would soon be circulated to every official at every exit from West Berlin.

I got off at the end of the line and took a taxi straight to Tegel Airport, driven by a mercifully unsociable German who took the Autobahn agonisingly slowly. A motorcycle passed us, and I sank into my seat, feeling stupid for being a slow-moving target on an open road. I cleaned myself up some more, picking small bits of dried bloody matter from my clothes, one of which was a hair attached to a tiny piece of skin.

An hour later, after vomiting and cleaning up in the airport bathroom, I sat in a rumbling British Airways plane as it taxied onto the runway that would lead it into the sky towards London.

It was the first time I had looked forward to take-off.

THIRTY-THREE

I made my way to King's Cross without much thought for anything except getting to my room. I took the escalator from the underground two moving steps at a time. From the main-line train station I walked onto the street and stepped straight onto an open bus without even having to break my stride. It was getting dark when I got off the bus near Tufnell Park tube station, something I never did – usually getting out earlier at Kentish Town and walking. Inside the front door I stood for a moment, breathing hard in the darkening hall, listening to the sounds of the house. Helen would not be home as she was going to Turkey the next day and had planned to stay at her mother's flat because it was nearer the airport, and besides, I was meant to be away. I got to my floor without seeing anyone, listened at her door but heard nothing, and listened at my own before opening it.

In my room I sat on the bed with the sodium glow of a street light coming in through the window and tried to filter the torrent of thoughts I'd suffered since leaving Abu Leila lying on the Ku'Damm in West Berlin, not four hours before. I couldn't get a purchase on my thoughts; they were like black slippery eels in a tank. I dealt with them one by one. I put myself in the shoes of the West German police: I had left my bag in a Berlin hotel, and had left Berlin within an hour of Abu Leila's death, buying a ticket with cash at the British Airways desk at Tegel. My bag, now sitting for the second night in a room booked only for one, had a British Airways return ticket for tonight in the name of Michel Anton. Records at Tegel would show that Michel Anton had actually left earlier in the day, soon after Abu Leila had been shot. Checks would soon show the frequency of my visits to West Berlin, and a routine inquiry with the Swiss would expose the fact that Michel Anton no longer existed but had died aged two. All this meant that Michel Anton from Geneva could be no more. Because they would connect the forged passport with a murdered Middle-Eastern-looking man they would refer the matter to the Bundesnachrichtendienst, the federal intelligence service, who would no doubt make contact with their UK counterparts, since that is where I had gone. The bag in the hotel also contained an open pack of codeine tablets which had a batch number on it. They would try to track these to a prescription at a pharmacy but would soon realise that they had been stolen. It was unlikely that my dealer could be tracked down, although he could provide no information about me even if he was; he knew me as Roberto, not Michel.

I went through these and other matters: like that *yalla* shouted by the bike rider. An Arabic urge to 'come on', 'move it', 'let's go'. Who were they? I tried to make sense of these threads, but I grew weary and took just two codeine from a new pack, bolting the door and lying down with my jacket and shoes still on. One of the slippery eels in my head kept reappearing as I disposed of the others one by one, although this became more difficult as the codeine took effect. It was a big one though, this eel, one that was uglier and more difficult to get hold of than any of the others. Even as more of the codeine metabolised into morphine I couldn't expel it. I would have taken more codeine, but a corner of my brain nagged at me to remain in control. An hour later I was rocking my head, so I got up quickly and for the first time put on the lights. I made coffee and drank it, but the caffeine fought for head space with the morphine, and I veered between a calm and an anxious place. Stupidly I'd left the curtains open and went to close them; I was getting sloppy, and sloppy was dangerous.

At midnight I was pacing up and down, still in my jacket – I could feel the bulk of the envelope rescued from Abu Leila sticking into my ribs. What to do with it? Who to give it to? I paced up and down some more, until I turned the light out and went into the hall. I listened at Helen's door, although I knew she wasn't there. I went down to the garden and fetched the lock-picking set from the abandoned cooker.

Her curtains were open and the light from the street lamps filled her room with the same unpleasant yellow as mine. I kept the lights off and lay on her bed and smelled her pillow; it was the herbal smell of her shampoo. I breathed in and I breathed out. Sometimes I could hear a car or a bus on the high street. I heard a car door close, but gently, as if they didn't want to wake anyone up. Considerate, I thought. I was beginning to relax in Helen's room. Did Abu Leila have a family that needed to be notified? What had happened to his body, was it already being cut up in an autopsy? What was it he was going to tell me about my future? To my surprise I started to cry. I buried my face in Helen's pillow to muffle the noise. I cried like I was fifteen and had lost my family all over again. After a couple of minutes I stopped and sat up – I wasn't crying for Abu Leila, I was crying for myself. It was loathsome self-pity.

I wiped my eyes. Something bothered me about the sounds I'd heard outside. I wondered why, following the closure of a car door, a car engine hadn't started; nor had I heard it drive up and park beforehand. I heard a creaking on the stairs. A soft step, the groan of a floorboard, then silence. It couldn't be Zorba. I took soft steps of my own to Helen's door and I heard the slip of metal on metal, a slow keying of a lock, or maybe the racking of pins, not on Helen's lock but on mine next door. Then I heard my door click open and probably two people go in, judging by the time it took for the door to close behind them. My heart sounded, and I crept back to the bed and listened at the wall.

They were quiet, professional; they didn't speak or make much noise. Maybe a squeak of a drawer, a pressing of bed springs, nothing that you would hear if you hadn't got your ear pressed against the wall. They spent fifteen minutes searching for something in there, then the noises stopped and I heard them leave, gently closing the door behind them. I went back to Helen's door, terrified that they would try to come into her room. I desperately looked for a bolt, but none had been fitted: stupid, stupid Helen. What about all the stuff under the bath, what if they searched the bathroom? But then I heard that creak on the stairs again and the front door clicking shut. I hadn't heard them come in but they had probably wedged it open, and besides, I had been blubbing like a baby. At the window I saw two men dressed in dark clothes walk down the road. They stopped by a car with a silhouette in the driver's seat, and one of them opened the door. The courtesy light didn't come on as the door opened, because people on a night-time stake-out always disable it. The other man walked on and he was betrayed by the slope of his shoulders as he went. I watched him until he disappeared around the corner. It was the pale-faced man I had last seen outside Foyles.

THIRTY-FOUR

The car was still there half an hour later. A dirty Golf, although I couldn't discern the colour under the yellow street light. I could make out the number plate; if they believed they hadn't been seen they would still use it. It scared me, knowing that they had come into my room when they thought I'd be in it. They must have followed me here, since I'd stupidly done no proper counter-surveillance from King's Cross and nobody knew where I lived – not even Abu Leila, and SOAS had only a PO box in their records. They'd entered my room when they thought I was asleep, no doubt detecting which room I was in when I'd put the light on without closing the curtains. I was a victim of my own ineptitude. They must have thought I'd disappeared and perhaps were hoping I'd return. This meant that they might know about the back entrance, since my friend who had gone around the corner would have found the path running down behind the gardens by now. No doubt he was watching where it came onto the street, with someone at the other end. I took them to be the competition: Mossad agents wanting the envelope. I desperately wanted to get out.

It was starting to get light when I went into the bathroom. I didn't go into my room, assuming they had placed something in it that would tell them if I did: either a microphone or a motion detector, something connected to the door, maybe. I unscrewed the panel on the side of the bath. I emptied the zip-lock case onto the floor, taking an inventory: the *Le Monde* article, one Greek passport, my Lebanese passport and £3,500. My Swiss passport and the fat envelope were still in my jacket. My first priority would be to go and empty my safety deposit box.

I left the house through the back door and went through the garden to the gate at the end. I listened for a bit, then opened it slowly. I heard nothing, so I went into the alley. I could have gone either way and come out on one of the roads leading from mine to Fortress Road, but I had to assume that both would be covered. I would go straight through instead. I climbed the fence opposite and walked up the tended garden to the back of the house. The lights were off, which hopefully meant they were still asleep. If I'd wished for a side alley that led to Fortress Road I was disappointed – all the houses on the road were terraced; I would have to go through the house. I still had my set of picks on me after using them on Helen's door. I got through the back door and closed it quietly behind me. It was nearly half past five, and some people get up that early. I was in the kitchen – a family room with an enormous refrigerator covered with children's drawings and magnetic letters. It was very quiet, until the refrigerator came to life with a shudder and started grumbling. I moved slowly into the hall, thankful for the wall-to-wall carpet, and studied the front door: bolted from the inside. The front door they bolt, but not the more vulnerable back one. The staircase was opposite the front door, and I looked up it to see darkness at the top.

Two bolts were on the door, top and bottom, and I pulled the top one slowly through its eye, pressing the door to reduce the friction and noise. I had it undone when a noise made me jump.

'Who are you?' A small child, a girl, sat half-way up the stairs, a blanket in her hands. She wasn't upset or frightened, more curious than anything. She held the blanket up to her cheek and rubbed it between her fingers.

'I'm nobody. I'm just leaving,' I said softly, and put my finger to my lips, giving her a smile. I undid the bottom bolt more quickly than the top, then opened the door. Coats were on pegs by the door, and I chose a raincoat, along with a cap; any disguise at this stage would be useful. I waved at the girl and stepped onto the street, closing the door gently behind me.

I crossed the empty road and turned right, walking towards Kentish Town – I figured they would have someone outside Tufnell Park since it was the nearest station. I pulled the cap over my eyes as I passed the junction to the street with the alley on it. If they had anyone waiting for me, that was one of the places they would be. Within ten minutes I was on the platform at Kentish Town, and within fifteen I was on the first train heading into central London.

I was hit by a memory of Abu Leila. We were in West Berlin, at a small restaurant that did a Moroccan lamb and date tagine he was fond of. Abu Leila had just told me that I belonged to a big family. At first I thought he was talking about my dead family, which, relatively speaking, wasn't that big.

'We are a family of uprooted gypsies, outsiders wherever we go. And although we wander alone, this inability to fit in, to be accepted, is what binds us together.' He was drinking from a litre-sized *stein* of beer and there was a glisten in his eyes – it wasn't often I saw him drink. 'We are roaming warriors, Michel, lost in a world that cares only about its immediate needs.' He had gone on in this vein for a few minutes, then he'd said something that distracted me from my food. 'One day you may find yourself looking for these fellow travellers, but they will not be where you think they are. Sometimes when travellers congregate in a place they call home and settle down they lose their identity, they become something different, something soulless.'

'What do you mean?' I'd asked. Was he talking about Palestinians in general, or people like him and me, invisible even to those Palestinians openly engaged in the struggle for a homeland?

'I'm talking about a soulmate, my son. A soulmate could be an unlikely person that you may not at first recognise as a soulmate. A true soulmate may not be of your world.'

He'd lost me, he seemed to be talking about more than one thing, and I didn't press it; a litre of beer does not sit well with a burdened man, and Abu Leila had never been a drinker. A smoker, yes, but not one to wallow in alcohol-induced self-pity. That was the first time it had occurred to me that he might actually be a lonely man. Now he was dead.

I stayed on the Northern Line until Stockwell, and went back north again on the Victoria Line to Green Park, then southbound on the Piccadilly Line to Knightsbridge, where I got off. The people on the trains had started out as black and Asian, people on their way back from night shifts or doing early cleaning shifts. They slumped in their seats and slept, and had I not been on full alert I would have joined them. The numbers and ethnic mix increased at each change until, by the time I emerged above ground opposite Harrods, it was rush hour and the train was full.

Although employees were entering Harrods, it wasn't yet open to customers, so I sat in a small café on a side street. It was full of breakfasting taxi drivers and the smell reminded me that I hadn't eaten anything except a pretzel since yesterday morning. I ordered a bacon sandwich and a mug of tea. I needed to let someone know about Abu Leila. People must be wondering what had happened to him. Arrangements would need to be made, networks dismantled, the envelope given to someone. The only thing I could think to do was to contact the PLO in London and let them have the envelope. Since it was somewhere I avoided, I didn't know who to speak to, but I knew there would be a security officer, someone who would know what to do, who to tell.

What I also hoped, as I drained my tea, was that the same person would tell me who I should now report to, what I should do next, and how best I could use my experience and training for the good of the cause. There was the small matter of making contact. Phoning them was out of the question, and besides, I didn't have a name. Somehow I would need to get a letter to them.

I looked around at the breakfasting taxi drivers.

THIRTY-FIVE

Standing in the drinks section of the food hall at Harrods I checked my watch. It was two minutes to twelve and the place was busy with tourists. I carried a Harrods carrier bag full of passports, a large amount of money in various currencies, forged documents, packs of codeine and the file of papers and reports on the massacre – the whole contents of my safety deposit box. The well-worn envelope sat in my inside jacket pocket, digging into my armpit every time I moved.

I had chosen a young taxi driver sitting on his own to deliver the note to the PLO mission, offering him £100 and strict instructions to hand-deliver it to someone inside. He'd jumped at the chance. The mission was a short taxi ride from Harrods – I knew where it was after using it for trade-craft practice when I'd first arrived in London, spotting the surveillance who were watching the place. I hoped the note had been passed to whoever was responsible for security. All I'd written was, 'I worked for Abu Leila and was with him when he was martyred in Berlin. I have his personal effects. I will be in Harrods drinks department at 12 p.m. You will know me by what I carry.' It was the first time I'd written in Arabic since leaving Lebanon.

I was having second thoughts. I clutched the plastic bag and the carton of Turkish cigarettes I'd just bought, wondering whether I should leave – but where would I go? I was tired, too tired to think straight. Would anyone come? Perhaps they thought it some hoax or trap; they might even have called MI5, who would take their concerns seriously after Berlin. Hopefully though, I'd given them little time to organise anything. I stared at a bottle of Johnny Walker. I heard Arabic at my ear.

'The cigarettes are a nice touch, Michel.' I hadn't put my name in the note. I turned to see a thin balding man with a kindly face and the wary eyes of someone trained to notice things. He had a twenty-four-hour growth of stubble except for where there was a small white scar on his chin. Exactly as Ramzi had described him: the taxi driver who had taken them back to the bridge from Ramallah. He gave nothing away in his expression, but experience was furrowed in his face. Not just age, but things seen and done. 'It is Michel, no?'

I nodded, checking the busy store behind him.

'I'm Khalil. Don't worry, I'm here alone, for sure. Like you, I know how to be careful. You have something for me, something of Abu Leila's?'

'I didn't know where else to go,' I said. 'I wanted to report what happened – I felt it to be my duty.'

The man who called himself Khalil took some cigarettes from his raincoat, remembered where he was and put them back again. He was studying me for something. His eyes flicked to the Harrods bag. I grasped it with both hands. This was not how I had imagined things would go. Why wasn't he asking me the details of what had happened in Berlin?

'I would like to talk about our mutual friend, I most certainly would, but not here. Let's go somewhere more private, where we can sit down.' The last thing I wanted was to go somewhere private. Who was this man anyway?

'He knew the Old Man,' I said, my voice cracking.

Khalil smiled sadly. 'Believe me, Michel, when I tell you that he was no friend of the Old Man.'

I didn't understand.

'This was a mistake,' I said, but didn't move. If only he'd say to me, 'We'll look after you, everything will be all right,' I'd go with him. But he simply stood there scrutinising me. I could now see the potential violence in him; I'd seen a friendly face because I needed to.

'What do you have in the bag?' he asked.

'My life,' I said. 'But I've brought it to the wrong place.'

'Do you have the envelope?'

'How—'

'It's best for you if you give me the envelope, for sure. Have you opened it?'

I shook my head and started to walk past him.

'You are in danger if you keep it …'

A threat or a warning? I couldn't tell. 'I don't have it with me,' I said, sticking the Turkish cigarettes in his hand. He started to say something but I continued into the air-conditioned cool of the main food hall, then through the exit onto a bright and hot Brompton Road.

I stood on the pavement outside like an idiot, disturbing

the flow of shoppers. I couldn't decide what to do next. Decide isn't the right word: to decide means having options to choose from, and I didn't have options, except to go either left or right.

Standing outside the meeting place was stupid. This Khalil would have brought someone with him, despite what he said. I had to move. With some effort I started to walk, and gradually, with every step, it got easier. I couldn't say whether I went right or left, but it didn't matter. I felt nauseous – Abu Leila 'was no friend of the Old Man' – what did that mean? The man who called out, the man on the motorbike, he'd called out in Arabic – what did that mean? Khalil was the driver who'd insisted Ramzi take the envelope across. But he was no driver. My eyes were stinging as I walked and walked and those eels were in my head again, slipping around in the murk as I trod the pavement. And that big fucker was there, pushing itself forward and cannibalising the others until I could no longer hold it back with practicalities, because I had run out of practicalities.

Things calmed down when I had done walking. I was back in Foyles, because for some reason I felt safe in a bookshop. I didn't know what the people on my tail wanted from me, beyond the envelope, but they wouldn't try anything in public, unless it was killing, in which case nowhere was safe, although the street would be their favoured place to allow an easy getaway, like in Berlin. In all my training I'd never heard of anyone who had been assassinated in a bookshop: hotel rooms, the street, at home, all likely venues, but never a bookshop. In the toilets I locked myself in a cubicle. I sat on the toilet and took out the battered envelope. Perhaps this was the time to open it. Abu Leila was dead, it wouldn't matter if I opened it. But something was holding me back, something I couldn't put my finger on, something beyond my duty as a foot soldier not to interfere in what didn't concern me. But then I didn't even know whose foot soldier I was any more. Someone entered the toilets so I quickly put the envelope away and left.

I remembered that I did have somewhere to go, of course, temporarily anyway. I had the house in Cambridge, the house that Abu Leila wanted for the Palestinian contingent of his rival talks. I hadn't told anyone about the house. I could get the key off Rachel, the letting agent. The truth was that Rachel was the only civilian I could turn to, since Helen would be on her way to Turkey by now. I had her business card in my wallet still, with her home number written on the back. I also had money, plenty of money, and it would help me get about and remain undetected until I sorted myself out.

A bookshop also happens to be a good place to check for surveillance, and by now I was no longer bothering to hide the fact that I was running, which gave me more options. I doubted whether the people in London were the same as the people in West Berlin, but they were just doubts, based on a shouted word and what Khalil had said. The Israelis had recruited Arabs before, without them even knowing they were working for Mossad. Dissembling, Abu Leila had called it. But then Abu Leila was 'no friend of the Old Man', and he had been organising rival talks. Those eels were swimming in my head again. I spent a couple of hours in

Foyles, browsing everything from poetry to military history, but I couldn't see my pale, slopey-shouldered friend, nor was the Golf visible when I cut through the backstreets to King's Cross Station, stopping only to buy some clothes and an overnight case to put the Harrods bag in.

I rang Rachel at her office from King's Cross. She was still there, according to the receptionist, and for a moment I panicked when she asked who she should say was calling, because I'd forgotten what name I'd used – but then it came to me: Roberto Levi. Rachel sounded truly pleased to hear from me. No, I didn't need to come to the office for the keys, she would gladly meet me at the station and drive me to the house. When I hung up I finally came face to face with the black thought swimming in my head, holding onto it and seeing it for what it was: the dark awareness that I was absolutely and irretrievably on my own.

THIRTY-SIX

Rachel's BMW was waiting at the curb when I came out of Cambridge railway station. She wasn't wearing the suit that revealed her legs but instead wore a pristine tracksuit that suggested some physical activity was planned. Her hair was tied back less severely than before, and dark roots had started to grow through. She asked me to excuse her outfit, she was off to the gym, but was more than happy to drop me off at the house. I sank gratefully into the leather and closed my eyes on the short trip to the house, as she chatted about boring things, happy to carry on with me throwing in the odd grunt. I opened my eyes as she pulled in to the drive and it was still light. She handed me the house keys.

'When are the rest of your party arriving?' she asked.

'I'll be on my own for several days,' I said. 'Is there somewhere nearby I can get food?' I hadn't eaten since my greasy breakfast this morning.

She shook her head. 'Not at this time of the day. I could come by and pick you up after the gym,' she said. 'We could go out and eat. If you want to, of course?' She puckered her lips.

'I'm too tired.' And it was true, I was too exhausted to spend an evening of pretence with her.

'Of course, I can see that. I'm sorry.' She smiled. 'Listen, why don't I bring you something back later, a takeaway or something?' She was eager to please, and I was very hungry and in need of company, so I agreed with her suggestion of Chinese.

The house was bigger than I remembered. I made sure all the doors were locked and, after drawing the curtains, lay on the thick carpet in the front room. I wanted to take some codeine, but Rachel would be back in a couple of hours with food and I needed my wits about me when I was with her. I closed my eyes. A vision of Mama came to me, her hands, soft and prematurely wrinkled from continual washing, tucking me in. Then she disappeared, but I heard her screams, screams of dismay and horror at what she had just witnessed. I had only seen the beginning of it when we were lined up, before being knocked down by my father as the shots rang out. I'd heard one of the men, the man in charge, order someone to shut her up, and her voice was muffled as she was dragged into the house. But I had just lain there then as I was lying here now, as I had yesterday when Abu Leila was shot. I had done nothing.

I was woken by the unfamiliar doorbell. I went upstairs and looked out of the window of the dark bedroom. Rachel's BMW was in the drive. I scanned the street but couldn't see much of it from the window because of the trees. I went down and opened the door.

'You look like you've just woken up.' She pushed past me in a green dress, carrying a paper bag of food and her gym bag. I could hear her in the kitchen as I bolted the door. 'You haven't warmed any plates. Why are men so useless?' she said with a laugh. She was still flushed from her workout and shiny from the shower. She had little make-up on; it was a nice contrast to her professional get-up. In her summer dress and flat sandals she reminded me of Helen, and where she lacked Helen's grace and litheness, she made up for it in cleavage. We ate at the breakfast bar, and Rachel opened a bottle of wine. I told her the bad news.

'Teetotal, eh?' She poured herself a large glass, leaving me to wonder how she would drive home. 'I wish I could be teetotal.'

It soon became clear that Rachel had no intention of going home. After dinner she poured herself another drink and took the bottle to the living room, kicking off her sandals along the way.

'Isn't the carpet great? I think there's a decent hi-fi in here, Roberto.' Roberto went to look for it and found, hidden behind a sliding panel, a collection of records, mostly jazz, and a sophisticated sound system. Helen would love this, I thought, but Rachel hated jazz and so Roberto found something else to put on, some mindless popular music he found on the radio, and sat down opposite Rachel, who was sprawled on the big sofa – except she couldn't sprawl like Helen could because she didn't have the legs for it.

She started to tell me how she had spent last summer on a kibbutz in Tiberius and asked whether I had been to one. I shook my head; I wouldn't be allowed near one, I thought. Had I been to Israel then, or thought about making *aliya*, she asked. I shook my head, although Mama's village Lubya used to be in what Rachel called Tiberius, near what was called the Sea of Galilee. She spoke at length of her positive experiences, and not once did she mention the Palestinians or Arabs, or make reference to any problems there. Maybe, in her mind, there weren't any. Maybe she felt it rude to mention them, since I was, after all, a client, and one must not mix politics with business. The more she drank, the more she spoke and giggled. The more she drank, the more blurred she looked. She asked me a few questions, but I let Roberto lie with practised ease. Roberto, despite my exhaustion, was on form, a master of sleight of speech and verbal mirrors, bouncing back her questions with feigned interest in her. I wanted to tell her about my grandparents' home in Lubya, as had been told to me, but instead Roberto spoke of an imaginary family of Italian Jews from Turin, culled from my reading of Primo Levi's potted biography; for Roberto had started to believe that he was related to Primo. Rachel made no such connection because she did not, by her own admission, read books, preferring, she said, popular magazines and sentimental films.

'And the newspapers, Roberto, so full of doom and gloom – I never read them,' she slurred. Both Roberto and I agreed with her. I, because newspapers were full of omissions and lies; Roberto, because he was as shallow as Rachel and would say anything to ingratiate himself. Roberto and Rachel wanted to be liked; they didn't like confrontation or the unpleasantness real feelings could arouse. I wanted Rachel to leave, because she wasn't Helen, and I felt comfortable with Helen. Rachel was nebulous and lacking to me, but Roberto found her fascinating. Roberto, to his credit, knew that we both needed her; she was our link to the outside world. He was right, we did need her, but he wanted to take it further, he wanted more; he wanted to get to know her between her short legs.

Soon, Roberto had been invited onto the sofa and was nuzzling at Rachel's neck. I, however, pawed at her breasts, because she knew nothing about anything. Roberto pulled off her hairband and admired her dyed, brittle hair. I laughed inwardly at her dark roots and impatiently pulled down the straps of her dress because she thought a kibbutz was a fun place to spend the summer. Roberto kissed her bare shoulders while I pulled up her dress and put my hand between her sweaty thighs. I was rough because she had not visited Lubya, where Mama's family came from, even though there would be nothing to see because it had been razed to the ground after everyone had been driven out in 1948. She made a groaning noise, and silky-spoken Roberto persuaded her to remove her bra.

'Gently, Roberto, gently,' she said, to the wrong person, and Roberto apologised on my behalf, but I pulled and snatched at her underwear until it was around her ankles. Roberto wanted to get on his knees and kiss her between her thighs, but I said she didn't need it or deserve it and wanted to get straight to it. We argued about it until Rachel took things into her own hands and all I could see was the top of her head, and so studied her darkening roots. Roberto and I both enjoyed what she was doing – she did it with some enthusiasm – until her mouth was unexpectedly and efficiently replaced with a condom, conjured from I don't know where. Then she was on her back on the thick carpet, and both Roberto and I had our way, although Roberto wanted to take it nice and easy but I saw it as an opportunity to teach her a lesson. I thought I'd got my way over Roberto but she kept urging me on; faster and harder.

Afterwards, I went to the bathroom and flushed the sagging condom down the toilet, followed quickly by my Chinese meal, most of it undigested. I heard Rachel flush the toilet upstairs and followed the noise. When I got up there she was in the big bed in the master bedroom with its en-suite bathroom. I brushed my teeth, took some codeine and slipped in beside her, resting on her welcome bosom.

'You were like an animal, Roberto,' she whispered, twiddling with my hair. She was right, I was an animal: a dog maybe, or a pig.

'I'm tired,' I said. She turned out the lights and I moved to my pillow. She leaned over me in the dark, smelling of wine, her breasts resting heavily on my back.

'If you want to do it again, just wake me,' she whispered. But I'd just taken four codeine and so it wasn't going to happen.

THIRTY-SEVEN

Mama hadn't spoken often of her parents' house in Lubya, west of Tiberius, and even less of her parents. From what Uncle Elias had said – my only uncle on her side of the family – they felt that she'd married beneath her. Uncle Elias intimated, out of earshot of Mama, that my father's family had not done well, even before the 1948 exodus, and that Mama's parents had despaired when their only daughter had left the relative comfort of an apartment in Jordan and gone to live in a refugee camp in Beirut. So Mama, out of respect for my father, never talked about them. She did describe the house though, and whenever I admired the big houses and apartments she went to clean, she always said they were nothing compared to her parents' house: the lemon trees in the back garden, the fig tree at the front, the wooden shutters closed against the heat in the afternoon, the view over the olive grove they owned. These were all descriptions from when Mama was a girl, of course, and were whimsical and nostalgic and set against the dirty reality of the camp. She would laugh and say, 'Imagine it, Michel, we used to have people come to clean for us!' But it was a laugh tinged with bitterness. I discovered from later research that the house had been razed to the ground along with the whole village. Afterwards, the rubble was planted over with pine; so there had been no going back for my grandparents. They died in Jordan. I never met them, as they never came to Lebanon to see us.

Rachel came back to the house for three nights. She wanted to go out to eat but I said I was too tired in the evenings and had a lot of work to do during the day. I told her I was preparing the ground for the negotiations and meetings with various technology companies, putting together portfolios and the like. She believed all of this, and believed that I was out during the day, when in fact I never left the house. After that first night we talked little. I gave her money to bring food back each evening and we watched tennis on television or listened to silly pop records and she drank lots of wine and we had sex, and afterwards she read women's magazines while I stared at the ceiling and avoided thinking about what to do next because I hadn't a clue. Before she slept, Rachel applied a greasy lotion to her face that she said would stop her getting wrinkles when she was older. She stayed until I could bear her cheery little face and eager-to-please manner no longer.

On the fourth night, after we had finished eating, I was about to tell her that she couldn't stay any more (with the excuse that the rest of my party were arriving), when she said she wanted to talk. She made it sound serious. We were sitting at the breakfast bar over our half-empty foil containers of Indian takeaway. She'd hardly touched her wine. I prayed she wasn't going to make some declaration of love.

'I can't stay the night, Roberto,' she said, worry on her face. 'In fact, I can't stay here any more.'

I was filled with a relief which I did my best to hide. 'Why not?' I asked, supposing that I ought to show some interest in her reasons in case my ambivalence became apparent. 'Is something wrong?'

She put a manicured hand on mine. 'No, you're a sweet man and everything, but my boyfriend is coming up to Cambridge for a few days tomorrow, before we go on holiday to Spain.' The shock she could see on my face was genuine. 'I'm sorry, Roberto, if I've hurt your feelings. This was nice while it lasted but it was never going to be a long-term thing. You must have known that.' But of course: her absence of curiosity in me was an indication of her lack of real interest. She had used me just as well as I had used her.

'Do you have to go tonight?' I asked, and meant it – the sudden realisation that I was being rejected was unpleasant, especially when it meant having to spend the night on my own.

'Don't make things awkward, Roberto,' she said, in an excessively concerned voice. She took her hand off mine and gave me a sad look. 'It was fun – let's just leave it at that.' She said she would still be available professionally, regarding the house, and added, 'You mustn't feel awkward about calling, Roberto.' And she insisted on giving me a hug, which I had to stoop for.

When she was gone I cleared up and had a bath, but then the bath reminded me of Helen and I became heavy-hearted so I got out. I did sleep well on my own though, and could at least put Roberto Levi to sleep as well, which was a relief. But I couldn't stay holed up in that house forever, sitting all day in front of the TV watching tennis and soap operas, however comforting this arrangement felt for Roberto.

The next morning I left the house first thing, wandering down the tree-lined road until I found a phone box. It was my first time out of the house, and I carried all my belongings with me in my bag, just in case.

After getting the number from directory enquiries, I rang Helen's department at University College and, after some to-ing and fro-ing, got through to someone who knew who she was. By my calculations she should be back from Turkey, although I had no idea whether she would be at the college. But I didn't know where else to ring her; there was no telephone at the Tufnell Park house. I asked the male voice whether Helen had returned from her site visit to Turkey. He thought she was due back today but wasn't coming into the department until tomorrow. I persuaded the voice to write down a message for her, saying that Michel had called and would call back tomorrow. Before the voice hung up something made me ask whether Professor Niki had returned from his holiday in Greece.

'Er, I don't think he went to Greece,' the male voice said. 'I think he was at the same site in Turkey as Helen and the others.'

I had no room for anger or jealousy (after all, wasn't it what I'd expected?) but I still felt a pang of disappointment, despite not being in a position to be righteous. I hung up and dialled the speaking clock.

I walked further on, past houses as big as the one I was staying in, but the more I walked, the smaller they got, until they were all conjoined in one terrace like the streets in Tufnell Park. I happened upon a main road with a row of shops, one of which was a post office. I picked out a postcard, a picture of one of the Cambridge colleges, and addressed it to Helen at our Tufnell Park address. I wrote: 'I miss you and would like to see you as soon as possible. I'll ring you at your office.' I signed it '*Ton belle*' and posted it first class. In the Italian delicatessen next to the post office I bought olives and bread and cheese and pasta and Italian sausage. I walked back to the big house – no fig or lemon tree here – thinking that I would go into Cambridge proper tomorrow. I spent the rest of the day eating and watching television, happy to have the place to myself, but not so happy at having so much time to think. I toyed again with the idea of opening the envelope, but I took codeine instead, as it seemed the easier thing to do. I spent the night in fitful worry, despite the codeine, which didn't seem to take. At one point I went and stood in the front garden, watching the street for an hour, standing perfectly still in the dark shadow of a tree. Nothing came of this foolishness so I went back inside, falling asleep towards dawn.

THIRTY-EIGHT

I passed some kids on roller skates doing figures of eight in the road on my way to the phone box to ring Helen at the college again. It was midday. I stood with my bag between my feet and fed a lot of money into the phone while I was passed from extension to extension. At last Helen's voice came on the line. I was so relieved I couldn't speak.

'Michel, is that you?' Her voice was hushed; people were talking in the background.

'You're back,' I said.

'Yes, well done, I'm back. Came back last night, got your postcard this morning. Are you in Cambridge? What are you doing up there, are you all right?'

'Yes and no.'

'What does that mean? Do you know your room's been trashed? The landlord is pissed off, whoever did it stripped everything. Hang on a minute ...' Her voice became muffled; it sounded like she'd put her hand over the mouthpiece to speak with someone else in the room. The people who'd searched my room while I was there hadn't made enough noise to trash it. Had they come back or was it different people? I fed another ten pence into the phone box. She came back on the line and I didn't know what to say.

'Are you still there?' she asked.

'Yes.'

'Are you coming to London?'

I watched the kids on roller skates. So little traffic came through that they could play without much interruption. 'No, I can't. You come to Cambridge. Please.'

'What's wrong, Michel, why all the mystery?'

'Come to Cambridge. Come today.'

'I have to write up the site visit, that's why I'm in the department.' But she was thinking about it, I could tell.

'Bring it up here, you can write it up here.'

She was silent, and I could hear people talking in the background at her end. I thought she was talking to someone else again but then I could hear her breathing. I watched the roller-skating kids move off the road to let a dirty red Golf go past. A dirty red Golf with the same number plate as the one I'd seen from Helen's window in Tufnell Park. It was driving away from me up the road towards the house, it had passed the phone box without my noticing it. Helen was talking.

'But I'm going to my mother's place on Monday. Do you still want to come, by the way?' Of course, her mother's place in Scotland, remote and by the sea.

'Yes, I do. Definitely, more than ever.'

'Have you started drinking, Michel?'

'Helen, listen to me. Can we go today? I'll meet you down there, just tell me we can go today.' I knew I was sounding desperate.

'You're beginning to scare me a little, Michel.' From her tone I could tell I was losing her.

She had to know the truth. She deserved to know it – some of it, anyway.

'I'm in trouble, Helen, and I can't go back to my room.' She went quiet again and someone laughed in the background. I wondered if it was Professor Zorba. She muttered something about not being unpacked or packed and something about her mother still being in Scotland. I watched the Golf slow down and go around a corner beyond the house. Another car, a Renault 4, interrupted the roller skaters and did a three-point turn. It parked facing away from the house towards me and no one got out of the car. It was too far away for me to see who was in it. I turned my back on it, glad that I'd brought my bag of money and documents out with me.

'Helen?'

'Yes, I'm here.'

'Will you help me?'

She sighed. 'We would go from Euston. Can you come back today?'

'Yes, I can be there this afternoon.'

'OK, ring me when you're in London. I'll get the train times and pick up my bag from the house.' I was concerned about her picking her bag up from the house but didn't want to worry her unnecessarily; anyway, if they'd moved up to Cambridge, then maybe, just maybe, they'd given up on Tufnell Park. In my heart of operational hearts I knew that they would still have someone there, even if it was just one person. I'd have to worry about that, and how they'd tracked me to Cambridge, later. Helen gave me a more direct number to call her on and we agreed a time after which I could ring.

'Helen.'

'Yes?'

'Don't tell anyone where you're going, OK?' Again the breathing and the other voices in the background.

'You have a lot of bloody explaining to do when we meet.' She hung up.

'*Je t'aime*,' I said, to the dial tone.

Perhaps I shouldn't have sent the postcard, although how they could have pinpointed the house from a Cambridge postmark was beyond me and my training. Besides, they couldn't have got up to Cambridge so quickly. I also assumed that Helen's departmental phone must be clean; there was no way, given that I seemed to have tracked her down to a common room or somewhere, that they could have the whole switchboard covered. They could have bugged the phone box I was in, but they'd have had to have known I was here in the first place. I thought about dismantling the receiver but was conscious of the Renault behind me; I'd been in the phone box long enough. I dialled the speaking clock. At the sound of the tone it was 12.16. I dug around in the bag for the baseball cap I'd stolen from the house in Tufnell Park, pulled the peak down hard and walked away.

I stopped at several points to see if anyone was following, going through a couple of parks and catching a bus into town. I walked to the station using backstreets, praying the station wasn't being watched, although one reason I'd chosen Cambridge was the ease with which it could be watched. On a fast train to King's Cross I gave things more thought. Perhaps it was Rachel, perhaps she had found my behaviour odd and reported me to someone. But then she'd been there every night for three days and they'd had plenty of opportunity to act. Act how, to do what, to get the envelope? Rachel had ignored many opportunities to take it. It was only as we were pulling in to King's Cross that it came to me. I had neglected an essential fact, and I hung my head in shame: I was not the only one who knew of the house in Cambridge; I had given Abu Leila the address the morning he was killed, written it down on a piece of paper for him which he'd put in his wallet – the wallet that I'd left in his pocket when I'd abandoned him on the Ku'Damm pavement. I cursed myself again for not clearing his pockets. No doubt then that German, and perhaps British, intelligence knew of the house, which could explain how the competition knew about it too.

At King's Cross I went down into the underground station and found a pay phone that was on its own. This time I got straight through to Helen, who answered on the second ring.

'Where have you been? There's a train in forty-five minutes.' She sounded breathless. I told her I would meet her on the train.

'Why not at the station?'

'On the train,' I said. 'Don't hang around for me, just buy yourself a ticket and get on the train.' I hung up as she started to argue.

I took the underground to Warren Street, then doubled back to Euston, where I came up the escalators and went immediately to the ticket office. It was fifteen minutes since I'd hung up on Helen. I stood in one queue then moved to another, just to throw anyone who might have jumped in behind me to try and overhear my transaction. I bought two first-class, one-way tickets to Glasgow, paying in cash. I left the ticket office and found a good vantage point – wedged between a pillar and a flower stall – from which to observe the doors through which I knew Helen would enter the station. From here I could see anyone who might have followed her from Tufnell Park.

The train was due to leave in thirty minutes.

THIRTY-NINE

From my hiding position I could see Helen approaching the entrance to the station through the large glass doors. There she was, in jeans and white T-shirt, Indian shawl around her shoulders, long legs, hair loosely tied, her runaway father's wristwatch glinting in the sun. I had never before felt so happy to see someone. She was striding with purpose, a large kit bag slung over one shoulder. I pulled my cap down and waited for her to come through the doors, then saw, some twenty metres behind her, Professor Zorba. There he was, slicked-back hair, crumpled linen suit, bulging midriff, a newspaper in one hand. He was obviously following her; dodging behind pillars and stopping and starting like a bad parody of a private detective. The sight of him made my jaw tighten and my vision blur in anger.

Helen pushed through the doors, heading for the ticket office, passing just five metres away from me but so focused that she would not have seen me had I waved. It took all my willpower to avoid rushing out and hugging her. I concentrated on Zorba, who was approaching the doors. As he neared them I took off my jacket and swung my bag over my shoulder. I made sure that Helen was facing the counter, then ran forward and pushed the big glass door open hard as he approached it. It caught him full on the chest with the big metal door handle. The wind left him like a deflating set of bagpipes and he dropped to the pavement.

'Oh my God. I'm sorry. Are you OK?' I said, quickly bending down and applying a thumb to his windpipe, my hand covered by my jacket, the Stasi Beeskow training at last paying off. Unable to take in a badly needed breath, he started to panic and I let go for a second. 'I think he's OK,' I said to a concerned bystander. 'He just needs to catch his breath.' Most people were too busy catching trains to stop. Besides, once they saw someone else looking after a fallen stranger, it absolved them of the need to do anything themselves.

I checked on Helen: she was at the counter. I pulled Zorba to his feet and half-dragged, half-pushed him over to a wall out of her view, where I held him up and reapplied pressure to his neck.

'I want you to listen to me, *malakas*,' I said into his hairy ear. 'I want you to leave Helen alone. It's finished between you and her. Go back to your wife.' I released the pressure and he took a deep breath, coughing and spluttering. 'If I see you near her again I'll fuck you upside down, do you understand me?' I said. He nodded, clutching at his neck, his eyes welling up. He was pathetic, and part of me wanted him dead. I hated him. Hated that he had lain on top of Helen, maybe even used the scarves on her as I had. I would easily have killed him if I thought I could get away with it. As a matter of fact, I could have got away with it, even with all these people walking past, so that wasn't what stopped me.

I let go of him and he slumped half-way down the wall. I had to go, the train left in ten minutes. I couldn't see the ticket office from where I was; hopefully Helen had already boarded the train. I started to leave when Zorba grabbed my sleeve and looked up at me. He rasped words out from his damaged throat.

'I hope she leaves you,' he said, with a little smile. He put his hand to his throat. 'It will be more painful than this.'

He was tougher than I thought, I give him that. I left him bent over with his hands on his knees, dry-retching onto his suede shoes.

With Zorba indisposed, I went into the main hall and looked for the Glasgow platform: number five. I stood with my back to the entrance to platform four, checking my watch against the station clock. Five minutes. I scanned the main hall, no longer caring whether I was being obvious or not; by now they would know that I was carrying out overt counter-surveillance. Try as I might, I could spot no one suspicious, although it wasn't an ideal place to spot them, and my dealings with Zorba may have caused them to pull back. It wouldn't do any harm for them to think I'd lost the plot. I moved to another platform entrance and did it again, then wandered onto platform three and watched people board a train. I checked the platform clock: three minutes. I went back into the main hall and walked slowly back towards platform five, stopping, looking up at the board and putting my bag down as if I had all the time in the world. I watched platform five through the entrance, looking for the guard to see what he was doing. A teenager with a rucksack ran onto the platform and got onto the train. No one else was embarking, and the guard put a whistle to his lips in readiness, looking at his watch, moving next to the barrier so he could close it before he blew his whistle. I bent on one knee and retied an already tied shoelace. While still on my knee I grabbed my bag handle, then stood up and walked briskly to the platform, all in one movement. The guard was starting to close the barrier as I went through. I made the first door of the train just as he blew the second of two long whistles. I got on and slammed the door shut, which coincided with the train jerking to life. My hands were shaking. I pulled down the door window and looked back at the departing barrier as the train started to pull out; I was definitely the last one on.

As the train ran out of platform, I saw two people standing behind the barrier. They looked very small at this distance and could have been absolutely anyone. If it was them, I didn't care. They hadn't tied me to Helen, that was the important thing.

FORTY

I didn't know where to start with Helen: with the fact that I knew Zorba had been with her in Turkey, or the fact that I had just assaulted him, or the fact that I was an undercover PLO agent whose handler had been shot in the back of the head by persons unknown and was being followed by other persons unknown, possibly Israeli agents, who wanted an envelope that was sticking into my ribs? I wasn't even sure where Helen stood on the Palestine issue; many people were ambivalent about the whole thing, believing at best that it was a two-sided problem with both sides equally to blame. At worst, they thought the Palestinians were terrorists who had no claim to anything, and that villages like Mama's never existed to start with. Should I tell her that I had nobody to report to and nowhere to go? Or should I start from the beginning, with my upbringing, the camp, that I was not who I told her I was? Could I even begin to tell her about that terrible day?

All this churned in my head as I tracked Helen down on the train. The tickets were all allocated to specific seats, and she was wedged in the window seat by an overweight middle-aged man who had no doubt thanked the gods when he'd discovered who he was seated next to. She was staring out of the window, trying to avoid physical contact with the man, who overflowed from his seat. He was intent on verbal intercourse with her and I interrupted him in mid-sentence.

'Let her out, will you, she's with me.' He looked up at me in annoyance. Helen's face broke into a relieved smile. Stupidly, the man started to protest, as if there was something to argue about. I cut him off. 'I'm not in the mood, believe me I'm not – I've had a difficult day, so just get out of your seat so she can get past.' I pulled Helen's bag down from the overhead luggage rack.

'Where are we going?' she asked, when she had squeezed past the man.

'Somewhere more comfortable.'

Something had changed between us. We did not embrace or kiss. I still had Rachel on my skin and Zorba in my mind. She was full of questions and no doubt Zorba was still fresh on her skin. We collapsed into our first-class seats, Helen at the window. A steward took our orders for tea, coffee and sandwiches. We had a couple of seats on their own so we had the illusion of solitude, although there were people in the seats in front of us so real conversation was going to be difficult. I needed to know where we stood, so I kicked off in a low voice.

'Did you tell anyone you were going to Scotland?' I asked.

'No. But it was really no secret that I was going next week,' she said.

'Does anyone know where it is?'

'Most people know where Scotland is, Michel.' She wasn't going to make this easy, and I couldn't blame her.

'I mean your mother's place, does anyone know where it is?'

'Apart from my mother? No.'

I took a deep breath through my nostrils and exhaled through my mouth. 'What about your tutor?'

'Niki? I think he knows where it is, I've spoken about it, obviously. But no, he's never been there, which I think is what you're really asking.' Did that mean I was the first to be asked there? If I could believe her, of course; after Turkey, who knew what was true. 'By the way, shouldn't I be the one asking questions?' she asked. She was right, but I didn't know where to start. I pointed to the seats in front and put a finger to my ear to indicate that we could be overheard.

'Have you got a pen and paper?' I asked. I had to get her bag down to retrieve a notepad, and then the coffee and food arrived. When we were settled back in our seats I told her to write her questions down. We didn't touch the sandwiches except to determine that they were limp. She looked out of the window and so did I, switching between the view (a blur that was the outskirts of London) and her left ear, which had the small mole that I had taken for a piercing when I had first invited her into my room. She tapped the pen on the pad as she thought – I was thinking that I'd have to get rid of it afterwards; the idea of anything being written down made me break out in a sweat.

She wrote slowly on the pad and showed it to me: 'What's going on?' it said, in elegant handwriting.

'You need to be more specific,' I said.

She pulled a face and thought, then wrote again. 'Who trashed your room?'

I took the pen and pad and wrote, 'Israeli agents – Mossad, I think.'

'Really?' she said out loud, with a mix of incredulity and worry.

'I think so. I can't be sure. I'd have to speak to them to find out, but I'm not that keen.'

She didn't smile.

'But what were they doing in your room?'

I hesitated, but decided it had to be done, and it was easier done writing it down than saying it. 'Because I work for the PLO and have something they want.'

She frowned and took the pen. 'But you told me you were Lebanese???' The question marks were super-sized.

I took the pen. I was drenched in sweat and it wasn't the heat.

'No, I'm Palestinian, but I was born in Lebanon.' Then I wrote, 'This is very difficult for me.'

'It's no fucking picnic for me,' she said loudly.

'I'm sorry,' I said, keeping my voice low.

She took the pen and wrote quickly, tossing the pad into my lap. I picked it up. The elegant script had turned into a scrawl.

'FUCK YOU. Arsehole,' it read. She turned to the window. We watched the outside go by for a while. It was as if the train was standing still and the whole world was hurtling past us. I started to feel dizzy with it and had to actively correct the illusion. She picked up the pad and wrote for a while. When she was done, she passed it to me without looking at me. I took it and read: 'You tricked me into getting on the train. You knew that if we'd had this conversation beforehand I'd be on this train alone. You lied to me, and have lied to me all along.' I shook my head but she snatched the pad back and wrote, 'By the way, are you a terrorist?'

'No, I'm not,' I said. I wrote on the pad quickly, trying to match the speed I wanted to speak it, 'I am not a terrorist. I had to lie to you – it was the only way if I was to carry on being with you, WHICH I WANT TO DO. I didn't lie about anything that matters, like how I feel. This is the truth. It's all that matters now, the rest of it we can sort out.'

She took the pad and read it. I watched her but gained no clues as to her reaction. She reached out for the pen and I placed it in her hand. She wrote, more slowly this time, tilting the pad so I could see it.

'How do I know that you're not just using me because you're in trouble?' I read. She looked at me, moving her face up close to mine with the question formed in her eyes.

'You don't,' I said. 'But I'm not.'

FORTY-ONE

To my relief we didn't dawdle at Glasgow Central. It was straight out of the station to the car in which Helen's mother Sarah was sitting at the wheel, smoking. Because she had double-parked we set off immediately, and introductions were done as she drove us west out of Glasgow. She was a poet, Helen had told me on the train, as light relief from our other discussions, which we'd agreed to postpone until we had more privacy. I told her that everyone thought they were a poet. No, said Helen, she was published and well reviewed. Sarah was an attractive-looking woman – more so in some ways than Helen. She had her hair much longer, but it had gone completely grey and looked as though she hadn't combed or washed it for several days, giving her a wild look. She caught my eye in the rear-view mirror and smiled. The warmth of it dissipated my pent-up anxiety of the last few days, as if I'd been given permission to feel tired. I wondered why Helen's father would leave such a woman.

We drove west for an hour, until we reached the shore, and stopped at a small ferry terminal. Out on the loch ('It's not called a lake, Michel') I could see the ferry, a small blob that appeared to grow bigger while remaining in the same spot. The Scots pronounced the 'ch' in loch as Arabs pronounced the 'kh' in Khoury. I left Helen and Sarah chatting, and stretched my legs while checking for people from the train and memorising car models and number plates and faces; anyone following us would have to catch the same ferry.

Looking at the mountains on the other side of the loch reminded me that I had never been in the countryside before. I had always left one city only to land in another, spending the distance in between airborne. From Beirut to Nicosia, from Nicosia to Berlin, both East and West. From Berlin to Moscow, then back to Berlin. From Berlin to London, with trips to Paris, Geneva, Milan, Oslo, Athens and other cities in Europe, sometimes not even leaving the airport. I had been to Beeskow outside Berlin to learn how to defend myself with my bare hands, but except for that I had never been outside a major urban setting. I had never been on a boat either. Helen and I went to the front ('It's called the bow, Michel'), although this bow was flat and the water had a hard time pushing past the steel face that when let down became a car ramp. We tentatively held hands, both feeling our way.

'The bow is usually pointy, Michel.'

Irritated, I told her that I had seen boats before, and came from a sea-faring people.

She laughed and squeezed my hand. It was the first time she had laughed since we had left London, and it was good to hear. On the other side of the loch Sarah drove until we passed just trees and rock. The road rose and became narrow and steep and we had to stop to let the occasional car coming the other way pass by. Obviously, I was going to be reliant on Helen and her mother to get around since I couldn't drive. The only public transport, according to Helen, was a daily bus to and from the nearest town, which itself was several kilometres from their house. Thirty minutes later we were going down instead of up, and I could see incredible views of the water through the gaps in the trees. Then we were on narrow roads again and it was getting dark. Helen and Sarah had gone quiet, Sarah occasionally opening her window to smoke. I dozed in the back.

When we stopped, I learned that night-time in the country is not like night-time in the city; it is completely dark. It would have been impossible to see at all if not for the light given off by the stars. And the sky was full of stars, too many for me to take in at once. I craned my neck to see them, and the more I looked the more were revealed. I heard a rhythmic roar in the background; it came and went, like someone repeatedly dragging something over gravel.

'Michel,' it was Sarah's low, cigarette-damaged voice, 'help me with this shopping. Helen's fallen asleep.'

Inside the house, I helped unload groceries in the small kitchen. Sarah put a large pan of water on the stove.

'Put some lights on, Michel.'

I obeyed, going into the front room and putting on a floor lamp. There were no harsh overhead lights, everything was indirectly and softly lit, every bulb subdued with a dark shade. It smelled both of stale cigarette smoke and the inside of a Greek Orthodox church. It was like a bigger version of Helen's room in Tufnell Park. Throws and cushions were everywhere. One wall was covered in a mess of books. French windows opened onto a wooden deck – I unlocked them and stepped outside for some clean air. And what air it was. I was hit by the salty smell of the sea. The source of the roaring became apparent; the house was practically on the beach. Although I couldn't see it clearly, the sea was ebbing and flowing in the distance, and I could just make out the white line where the water kept breaking on the shore. Sarah joined me on the deck, holding two big glasses of red wine. She gave me one and I took it, not wanting to break the spell. We stood together, listening to the water, looking out over the dark beach. She had put a shawl around her shoulders, and she stood close enough for it to touch my arm.

'Should we wake Helen?' I asked.

'You'll like it here, it's my refuge from reality,' she said, ignoring my question. She lit a cigarette. 'I hope you'll be able to rest for a few days; there are very few people around so you'll get plenty of privacy.' I wondered how much Helen had told her. We stood for a while, the glass growing heavy in my hand. I could smell the tannins coming off the wine. I was acutely aware of Sarah beside me. I felt safe. Then Helen's sleepy voice called from inside the house.

'There you are,' Helen said, stepping onto the deck. I felt guilty and stepped away from Sarah, as if I had been caught doing something improper. 'Mother, we haven't been here two minutes and you're already corrupting him.' They both laughed at some private joke, and Helen took the wine glass from me. 'I told you, he doesn't drink.' I gave them a stupid grin.

We ate pasta by candlelight in the small kitchen. Helen

and her mother finished the bottle of wine between them and opened a second. I observed the similarities in the two women's facial expressions, the way they pushed back their hair, how they favoured one side of their mouth for smiling. I detected an edginess between them, a tension apparent in the comments passed off as jokes and in the forced jollity of Helen's tone – her face had set in a permanent grin. I assumed this was to do with their shared history. It came to me as I watched them that Helen's father could have been driven away rather than pulled away. Sarah appeared to be such a strong woman, and that didn't sit well with some men. I caught her once or twice studying me over the candles as Helen talked of her thesis and her trip to Turkey, and the lambency of the light and her unkempt grey hair made her look like a white witch. When I came back into the kitchen after using the toilet they were having a whispered argument which stopped as soon as they saw me.

'Mother and daughter stuff, Michel, terribly boring,' Sarah said, getting up and clearing the plates. I hoped that Helen wasn't confiding too much in her mother, but I gained no clues from either of their expressions.

After dinner Helen and I went out onto the deck and down some wooden steps onto the beach. She took her sandals off and flung them back onto the deck.

'The tide is out,' she said, and ran off ahead of me into the darkness.

'Helen,' I whispered, inexplicably worried about shouting in the dark wilderness. I ran after her until her footprints were no longer visible. I could only see a few metres ahead of me. I had moved away from the sea and was rising onto softer sand mixed with grass. It grew in clumps with spiky tips and I lost her trail. I caught a glimpse of white ahead. I headed towards it, cursing the grass, wondering how she had come through here barefoot, not realising that it was easier than in shoes.

I came across her lying spread-eagled on the sand, looking up at the sky. She was naked.

'I'm glad it's you,' she said. 'For a second I thought it might be that well-hung brute of a butcher's son again – he wanders about these dunes at night and it's difficult to fight him off.'

'Again?' I looked around, as if he might be hiding in the grass. She laughed, but it wasn't her usual laugh.

'You're so easy to tease, *ma belle*. Come here and get naked.'

I sat near her on the sand. 'You're drunk,' I said.

'I think I might be entitled, don't you? My boyfriend could be a terrorist.'

'I'm not a terrorist,' I said, but I was pleased with the term boyfriend.

'But that's exactly what you'd say if you were one.' She moved her arms and legs in arcs, making smoothed segments of sand underneath them and a ridge of it between her thighs. 'Do you want to fuck under the stars?'

I would never get used to her crudeness. I shook my head, I needed to sleep; and besides, I could never do it out here.

'It's my mother, isn't it?' She looked up at the stars. 'You'd prefer it if she was out here.' I kept my mouth shut and stood up. I knew better than to argue with a drunk woman, especially about her mother. 'I bet you like older women – all that sagging flesh. You Mediterranean boys are all attached to your mothers.' I thought of Mama and worked my jaw. Then I thought of Zorba, old enough to be Helen's father. I wanted to say something hurtful about his sagging flesh, but I couldn't bring myself to. Maybe if I drank I could – alcohol seemed to make hurting other people much easier.

'I'm going to bed,' I said.

'I think I'll wait for the butcher boy and his sausage.' She giggled. I moved into the darkness, hopefully in the direction I'd come from.

'Michel! Wait, please,' she said, sounding less brash. I stopped and looked around. She was struggling into her dress, pulling it down over her head, and I felt a surge of desire that I hadn't felt when she was lying with her legs apart on the sand. She tugged the dress over her hips and walked up to me, stuffing her white panties into my pocket. We walked along for a bit before she put her arm through mine.

FORTY-TWO

When I woke I was on my own, and it took me a moment to remember where I was. Then I heard the sea sucking at the sand and shingle. The open window opposite the bed framed a uniformly blue sky. I could also hear swooping bird cries, and the distant shrieking and shouting of children. The other single bed was unmade but empty. Helen and I were sleeping in this room and her mother was in the double bedroom next door, although I hadn't seen Helen last night, having left them talking when we'd got back from the beach. It was eleven o'clock.

I went to the source of all this light and sound and looked out over a crescent-shaped sandy beach. Judging from a map I'd looked at last night, I was looking at it from the southern tip of the crescent, and a rocky slope rose gradually at the other, some two kilometres away. I could see no other houses, but a dozen people were on the beach, far enough away that I could only make out their sex by their swimwear. A group of smaller figures huddled over the sand, the source of the shouts and laughter. I could roughly work out from the deck below me where Helen and I had ended up last night. I got dressed and went downstairs. Helen had left a note on the kitchen table: 'Have taken Mum to Glasgow. She's going to

London. Back this afternoon. Love Helen.' I was surprised that Sarah was leaving so soon, particularly since she'd driven all the way into Glasgow the day before to pick us up. Did something happen between them last night?

After I had fried some eggs, wandered around the house (two rooms and a kitchen downstairs, two and a bathroom upstairs), lain on Helen's mother's bed, looked in all the drawers and cupboards, examined the books (mostly poetry) and found an attic hatch behind which to hide my documents and money (keeping the envelope on me), I stepped onto the deck with some old binoculars I found and sat in a faded deckchair.

I could watch the beach from here, the binoculars brought everyone into detailed focus. I looked for individual men or couples fully dressed, people with radios or headphones or binoculars of their own. I scoured the dunes, then went upstairs and scoured them from the window before going back outside. I could see two middle-aged men sitting at the north end of the beach in shorts and T-shirts and sunglasses. I didn't know if it was the usual thing in Scotland for men of this age to go to the beach on their own. But then two women emerged from the dunes carrying baskets and a beach umbrella, joining the men and gesticulating, perhaps protesting at having to carry everything. The men laughed and one of them got up and put up the umbrella. Otherwise there were three families and a teenage couple, further down the beach, entwined around each other. It was the two couples together I decided to keep an eye on.

I would have expected more people to be on the beach in this weather but Sarah had mentioned that it was difficult to get to; you couldn't park nearby, which put most people off.

I removed my shoes and socks, spread my toes. This end of the beach, where the house was built, was more rocky and shingly, unlike the widest middle part and northern tip, which were yellow with sand. Across the water was a large land mass that rose high into the clouds from the water. I alternately watched some boats and the foursome with the binoculars until my eyes grew tired and I put the binoculars down.

When I woke the sun was low and Helen was sitting in a chair beside me. She was holding a perspiring glass of white wine, half empty. On the small table between us was my codeine sulphate. Not a single packet, but all six packs that I had rescued from my safety deposit box. I glanced at her, but she was looking out at the beach, now empty apart from a family who were packing up. I must have taken the codeine out of my bag in the bathroom before I'd hidden the documents and money in the attic and forgotten to put it back. One pack I might have explained away, but not six.

'I see you've managed to take your shoes off – that's progress, Michel, it really is.' I wasn't sure what she meant.

'What happened to your mother?' I asked, to buy myself time.

'She went home, that's what happened.' A follow-up question would be a waste of time.

'What happens now?' I asked. She took a long breath through flared nostrils and picked up a packet of the codeine, shaking it gently. I was just grateful that she hadn't flushed it down the toilet. I was starting to sweat, and it wasn't the Scottish summer.

'Codeine sulphate is a painkiller, I've looked it up,' she stated. I nodded. She looked at me and I looked at the beach. 'You can only get it on prescription.' I nodded again. 'You must be in a lot of pain to need so much,' she said, without irony. I was trying to tell whether the tide was going out. 'Do you take it all the time?'

'Only when I can't sleep,' I said.

'Can you get to sleep without it?'

'Yes of course. Sometimes I get headaches, that's all.'

She tossed the codeine back onto the table but it slid onto the deck. She sipped her wine. I had to restrain myself from picking the packet up. 'Sorry, I thought we'd moved on from lying,' she said.

I closed my eyes for a few seconds then turned to look at her. 'OK then. I take it every night because I cannot sleep without it. I've been taking it for several years. It clears my head of … well, everything.'

'In that case maybe I should try it. I could really do with clearing my head,' she said. There was a time when I would have liked nothing better, but that was when the morphine was running through my brain, not when I was clear-headed.

'It's not a good idea,' I said. 'Especially not with alcohol …'

'No, not now, later, when you usually take it, before we go to bed. I want to know what it does for you.' She leaned forward and flung the rest of her wine out of the glass onto the sand. Then she stood up and stretched. 'First, though, we must clean the beach.'

Cleaning the beach meant walking the length of it with a large plastic bag and a long-handled grabber that allowed Helen to pick things up without bending down. It was for the detritus of the day-trippers: empty Coke cans, dirty tissues, chocolate bar wrappers, plastic bags, even a used condom (no doubt from the teenage couple I'd seen earlier).

'They have no respect for this place,' said Helen. 'They think they can just leave their shit everywhere.' I walked barefoot on the sand, picking up things weathered by the sea and left by the tide. Flotsam and jetsam, according to Helen, rubbish thrown overboard, sometimes floating all the way in from the Atlantic. My favourite things were bits of wood worn smooth and bleached by years of exposure. I collected an armful of these and carried them back to the house.

'Can I make a fire?' I asked.

She laughed, and it was good to hear the spontaneous, unaffected nature of it. 'Yes, you can make a fire. I'll make some supper.'

We ate in front of the small fireplace in the living room – you cannot be outside in Scotland at dusk because of the little insects that eat you alive. Helen didn't drink any alcohol.

'Does the codeine make you horny?' she asked, when we were done eating.

'No, it just makes you feel warm and fuzzy.'

'Then let's fuck before we go upstairs, I think there are some scarves somewhere.'

'No scarves,' I said. 'Let's just make love.' So we made love, with the curtains open to the night, in front of my small fire, without scarves or other aids, and it was like that first time in Tufnell Park, after the jazz club. We had overlap, and we finished in the same place at the same time.

Afterwards, we watched the fire until it died and it started to get cold; we were still naked. She went upstairs to get a blanket.

'Do you still need the tablets, even after what we have just done?'

I nodded, embarrassed, but tired of lying. She prepared a tray with two glasses of water, the packet of codeine and some incense, then put it on the bottom of the stairs. She came over and pulled me up. She pulled the blanket off me onto the floor and took my hands.

'If I do this with you, then it will be the last time we do it. We do it together, but from tomorrow you start to wean yourself off. I'll do it with you, one tablet less each day until you don't need them any more.' She shook my hands violently as if to shake off my torpor. 'Do we have a deal? We'll get rid of the pain some other way.' I wasn't sure I could do it. I felt exposed, not just naked. I fidgeted and looked around the room, anywhere but into her eyes or at her body. 'You have to promise me, otherwise you can take the tray and go to bed on your own – tonight, tomorrow and every night.' I looked down at the space between our bare feet.

'Look at me, *ma belle* – we'll get through this together.'

I followed her as she carried the tray up to her mother's room, where she had changed the bedding. She lit some candles and the incense stick. We sat on the bed with the tray between us. She opened the packet.

'How many?' I hid my face in my hands.

'I've been taking three, sometimes four,' I said into my palms.

She said nothing, clicking out eight little white, perfectly formed capsules. We took one each and drank some water, then another, until they were all gone. I told her we should lie down.

We started off lying face to face, then lay on our backs, holding hands. Outside, the surf pushed in and pulled out. Each time, it pulled out a bit further and longer until I worried about it not coming back in again. It was pulling me with it but I held onto Helen and it was OK. Then the ebb and flow became synchronised with her breathing and it slowed right down, which meant that she was controlling the sea.

FORTY-THREE

Helen was subdued in the morning, waking up after some difficulty, and only when I had taken her breakfast in bed. She ate it with a distant look in her eyes that worried me; I shouldn't have let her take four tablets at once, not the first time.

'You don't have to take them again,' I said.

'I'll take them as long as you're still taking them,' she said, but then spent most of the morning in bed. I watched the beach with the binoculars and popped up to see her every now and then.

'You're like a jack-in-the-box,' she said, on my fourth visit. 'Run me a bath.' I sat by the bath as she soaked, washed her back, read some poetry to her, passed her the pumice stone, washed her front.

'What do they want with you?' she asked. 'These Mossad people.'

'I'm not sure,' I said. I told her about the envelope coming from the West Bank, Abu Leila's shooting, going back to Tufnell Park, entering her room, hearing people in mine, meeting Khalil and ending up in Cambridge. I expected her to fly off the handle, as Jack would have put it, but she was remarkably sanguine.

'Lucky for you that you were creeping around my room. Did you try on my underwear?'

'I wasn't creeping. I missed you, that's all. I couldn't sleep.'

'I'm teasing you, silly. Why Cambridge, of all places?'

So I told her about the Cambridge meeting that Abu Leila had set up, the house I had rented. She nodded at my explanation and relaxed into the bath. I didn't mention Rachel; I didn't see the point. Rachel was no competition to Helen. I told myself that to balance this omission I wouldn't mention my knowing that Zorba had been with her in Turkey. In time she would learn what I had done to him at the station, but for now I would live in the moment.

'Do you think he was killed because of this meeting?'

'I'm not sure, I think that's how they found the house, but to be honest I don't even know who killed him.' I could see her mulling it over; I'd already told her that the meeting hadn't been sanctioned by Arafat.

'You mean it was Palestinians, not Israelis, that killed him?'

I shrugged non-committally. I had admitted the possibility to myself, but couldn't do so to someone else. I didn't mention that the killers hadn't been after the envelope. She squinted at me, as if trying to get me in focus.

'You're very calm for someone who was shot at,' she said.

'It wasn't me that was shot at,' I said. It seemed so long ago now, even though it was just seven days earlier.

'So what's in the envelope?' she asked, after some moments' silence.

'I don't know.'

'What do you mean you don't know?' She looked incredulous. 'You're carrying this thing around that people have come several thousand miles to recover and you don't even know what's in it?' I said nothing. What would she say if I told her it had been smuggled out by a heavily pregnant woman? 'Aren't you even curious?'

I told her I wasn't, that it wasn't mine to open.

She shook her head in disbelief. 'What are you going to do with it then?'

'I don't know,' I said, and I honestly didn't.

'But that's ridiculous,' she said, sitting up and in the process sluicing water over the edge of the bath. 'It might tell you why Abu Leila was killed, or even who killed him.'

How to explain to this English rose my growing fear of what I might find inside, even though I knew I would have to face it at some point? I couldn't properly articulate it but my fears were tied up with the fact that opening it meant breaking Abu Leila's trust, and not opening it was the only act of loyalty that still remained to me, a demonstration of allegiance to the dead man who was not my father. And breaking his trust could only mean a terrible punishment in the form of the truth, and the truth was something he had taught me should be avoided. Helen was staring at me in expectation.

'I can't explain it,' I said. 'I'd have to explain everything.'

She stood up and let the water drip away. 'Then that is what you will have to do,' she said. 'But now you must dry me.'

So every day of our detoxification I told Helen a new thing, a new bit of my story, a new truth, usually as we cleaned the beach in the evening or sat on the deck, or inside when it rained, as it did often here, even in August. I worked backwards: telling her the things I did for Abu Leila, the trips I had taken, the people I had met, the unknown messages I had passed, the money I had laundered. On the second or third night – I can't remember – I brought down all my passports and identification documents from my bag and laid them neatly out on the kitchen table. My hands shook as I called her into the kitchen. She sat down and studied the neatly arranged patchwork of my life.

'Are any of these real?' she asked.

I picked up the Lebanese passport. 'This is, in the sense that it isn't a forgery – but it's not me, I'm not Lebanese.'

She took it from me and opened it. 'Michel Khoury,' she read, then flicked through it. 'Your student visa runs out in a couple of weeks.' She put it down. She read through the other documents. 'Tell me something – is Michel your real name?'

'Yes. Yes, it's my real name.'

She picked up a UK driving licence – a driving licence for someone who couldn't drive. She put it down and picked up another document, a French *carte de séjour*, then a British National Insurance card, a German *Personalausweis*, an Italian *carta d'identità*.

'You like the name Roberto, huh?' My face burned, but thankfully she wasn't looking.

'It's just a name,' I said. I gathered up the documents,

bundled them together, and went to take them back upstairs. I got as far as the kitchen door.

'Michel.'

I looked back at her.

'Thank you.'

The day after showing her the documents we were walking the beach, picking up rubbish under a patchy sky. One minute the sun would emerge victorious, only to withdraw again after a new ambush by the dark clouds. I had my jacket on, with the envelope inside it.

I told Helen about Abu Leila, my time at university in Berlin, in Cyprus with Jack. All this stuff poured out of me.

At some point she interrupted me. 'I don't like the sound of this Abu Leila,' she said.

I thought I'd misheard.

'He was a good man,' I said.

She picked up a half-eaten sandwich covered in sand with her grabber and placed it in her plastic bag. 'I didn't say he wasn't – I just think he took advantage of your situation really.' She stopped picking up rubbish and looked at me. 'If you think about it, he used you for his own purposes.'

'Rubbish. He helped me,' I said. 'He sent me to a good school and to university. He educated me. He was like a father to me.'

'He did it for a reason, Michel. Not because he was fond of you. He needed you to follow a certain path, his path.'

I dropped my gathered sticks and stomped on past her down the tide mark, blind with anger. I reached the tip of the crescent and strode up a path in the rise, climbing for a long while before sitting in the long grass. The wind came in gusts off the sea and knocked the grass flat. I could see Helen walking back along the line where the sand became dunes, a small figure, no bigger than my thumbnail. I remembered a conversation in Berlin where Abu Leila himself had told me that 'my purpose was now being played out' in London. I remembered him telling me, in Cyprus, that I would be going to Berlin, telling me that I should study German at The English School in Nicosia, that I would go to Moscow, that I would do this, do that. I tried to think of a time when he had asked me whether I'd wanted to do any of these things, but I struggled to think of one. But then wasn't I a soldier of sorts, even though I had no uniform? Wasn't I part of a grander plan that called for sacrifice and putting your own interests last? Hadn't we shaken hands in Beirut all those years ago? I'd known nothing else, no other life, after all. Where would I have been without Abu Leila? Nowhere, I would have answered, were he still alive. But I dared to allow myself to imagine an alternative path I might have taken. Perhaps I would have stayed with my foster family, perhaps I would have gone on to study to be a doctor like Ramzi, set up a practice in Beirut, maybe even in the camp, looking after my people. These thoughts felt like a betrayal of everything Abu Leila had done for me.

Down on the beach I saw a man step out of the dunes several metres in front of Helen; she would have to acknowledge his presence either by stopping or avoiding him. From this distance it looked like he was looking out to sea. She walked in front of him and stopped. He was talking to her. She nodded and pointed out over the grey water. His shape or posture didn't ring any bells with me; it was not my slopey-shouldered friend, although I wished I had the binoculars with me. They talked for a minute, then Helen walked on and the man watched her walk away. He stood there until she reached the house, then turned and walked back into the dunes. I could see him for a while until the path disappeared into the trees.

Back at the house I found Helen in the kitchen peeling potatoes.

'Are you OK?' she asked.

I nodded.

'I'm sorry if I upset you.'

I told her it was nothing, that I'd overreacted.

'Who was that man on the beach?' I asked.

'What, are you spying on *me* now?' As if I spied on everyone else.

'No, of course not. My question is whether you know him.'

She shook her head. 'Do I have to report to you every time I talk to a strange man?'

I kept my voice even; had she not listened to anything I'd told her? 'Yes, you do – at the moment I think it would be a good idea,' I said.

She put the peeler down and looked up. 'Oh my God, do you think they might have followed us up here?'

'Only if they've connected us in some way.' I thought of Zorba retching on his shoes outside Euston. If they had picked me up at Euston after following Helen there from Tufnell Park, or indeed followed me from Cambridge

Station, they might have seen me attack him. No doubt he'd have been happy to direct them here. It was the only way they could have found me – I'd been detected as a result of my own jealous rage.

'Should we call the police?'

I repressed an urge to laugh. 'And tell them what, exactly?' She made a small pyramid out of the potato peel.

I sat down opposite her. 'Tell me about the man,' I said.

FORTY-FOUR

On the final day of Helen's home-concocted codeine withdrawal plan we sat outside a place advertised as a café by day and a bistro by night. Tonight we were to have no codeine, and we'd just been shopping for food and treats to take home. I drank a bitter lemon, Helen drank wine, making the one glass last. We were in the small village nearest the house, a ten-minute drive. We watched holidaymakers straggle back from the beach in a long weary line that ended in the town's only hotel. The sun hung low and the damned midges gathered, looking for exposed flesh. Two women in bikinis came towards us, and clearly they were mother and teenage daughter. They had sarongs wrapped around their waists to cover their thighs. The daughter glanced at us as she approached, still at an age where she was self-conscious about her developing womanhood. The mother too looked at us, or rather at me, protective of her daughter, assessing my threat as a sexual predator. I looked away, embarrassed. Helen nudged me and moved her head closer to mine.

'Does Michel wish Helen had tits like that?' she asked. She was serious.

I laughed and shook my head, unsure whether she was referring to mother or daughter. 'I think Michel has his hands full with Helen as she is,' I said. 'Any more and he wouldn't be able to handle her.'

Helen stuck her lower lip out as the women passed. 'Still, Helen sometimes wishes that she was endowed with more.'

Last night I'd had a blow-by-blow account of her encounter with the man on the beach. Helen described him as being in his forties, fit and good-looking 'in a swarthy kind of way', although I wasn't sure if that was just to rile me. She had recounted their conversation, adding needless and stupid descriptions in an attempt to ridicule the exercise and make me jealous.

According to her, he had a slight accent, 'More than you do,' she'd said. 'And no, he didn't look Jewish.' I'd said nothing because I hadn't asked; I knew she was trying to get a rise out of me. Anyway, I knew from experience that it was stupid to rely on looks to make such a judgement. And besides, his being Jewish or not told me nothing. I was left with an uneasy feeling about the encounter though, and Helen had agreed to let me know if anyone else approached her or if she saw him again.

To my relief we left the café and walked back to the car; I hated sitting out with people about, I was reminded of how much observing and memorising of faces I usually had to do, something I'd had a break from at the house, apart from the obsessive beach-watching. Helen had something planned for when we got home, some more burning of incense, some ceremonial destruction of the remaining tablets. It was just symbolic, I told her, but she said that was precisely what I needed.

'People have had rituals since they started sitting around fires, Michel, with good reason. Trust me, I'm doing a PhD in rituals.'

So I trusted her. We went back to the house before it got dark – to comb the beach for rubbish left by the day-trippers. I kept to the tide mark, picking up the things washed in by the sea: a long bleached bone, a bottle with no message in it, several bits of frayed blue nylon rope that would take a thousand years to degrade, an old flip-flop worn thin by the sun and sea.

In the house I lit a fire and Helen went into the kitchen, returning with a tray on which sat a plate holding the remaining pills. Next to it was a mortar and pestle, similar to one used by Mama to grind garlic with salt. I laughed at Helen, but she just smiled and handed me the pestle. I put three of the tablets in the wooden bowl, like tiny, perfectly formed cloves of garlic, and tapped them lightly with the pestle. They split into fragments.

'We need them turned into powder, Michel, not smaller pills.' I ground them down, adding three more. I hoped she would leave the room so I could pocket some of the tablets for emergencies, but she stood opposite me throughout, until every last tablet was pulverised.

Then we went to the fire, and I wanted to sniff or lick some of the powder before the inevitable, but it was a fleeting, if strong, desire.

'Say goodbye to the pills, *ma belle*.'

I poured the powder onto the fire and it burned with a bright orange flame, sending white smoke up the chimney.

The mortar felt like I'd emptied it of lead, not powder. I also felt a lightness in my chest, a clearing in my head. 'There's more to burn,' I said.

Helen looked surprised. 'You have more pills?'

'No, not pills.' I ran upstairs to the bedroom and pulled a chair to the middle of the room. In the ceiling was the hatch into the roof and I pushed it open and felt about for my Harrods bag, which wasn't where I thought I'd left it. But then I found it and pulled it down. Inside were the passports and papers and money and newspaper cuttings and reports, and I took it all, leaving the money, which I put back, and went downstairs. I checked for the envelope, which I had carried on my person at all times since leaving Tufnell Park.

As Helen watched, I put everything, apart from the Lebanese passport, in one pile. I picked up the Swiss passport and put it on top of the Lebanese passport – might I still need it? The truth was I just felt vulnerable without it, and besides, since Berlin it was no longer usable. If I was going to do this then I would do it properly. I put it on the fire. Helen squeezed my hand as we watched it burn. It curled and crackled in the flame. I put the Greek passport on next; it burned with a blue flame. They, and other documents, all burned in different colours that we were convinced reflected their respective national flags but in reality were all the same blues and oranges and greens.

When some false company notepaper and business cards and fake utility bills had gone, we were just left with my macabre mementoes of the massacre. The cuttings and copies of reports: a European Union report, the official

PLO account, the Israeli Report of the Commission of Inquiry into the events at the refugee camps in Beirut – the so-called 'Kahan' Report, a UN effort running to 300 pages. Everyone had investigated, questioned, taken evidence, examined the photos, watched the TV footage and written a report to tell everyone else how terrible it was. No one, not one cocaine-addled whisky-soaked Maronite Phalangist, not one obese cynical Zionist general, not one conniving pseudo-fascist puppet warlord had been brought to justice. Who would bring them to justice? Who would do it? The PLO? According to Abu Leila, they were more interested in making deals in Norway with the people who had let it happen. The Arab nations? A craven, rhetoric-filled group that were either beholden to the West, to whom they sold oil, or too busy suppressing their own people. The Lebanese government? There's a funny thing – the very people that had carried out the massacre were now ministers in the government. Their leader, the man who stood on the Israeli command centre roof overlooking the flare-lit camp, was minister for tourism, according to the clipping I'd found in *Le Monde*. And the West? The West wrung its liberal hands, but to them it was a small thing in a big picture, something that did not concern them directly, something that Third World people did to each other.

Helen put her hand on my arm.

'You're shaking,' she said. I gathered the newspaper cuttings and the reports and placed them in her hands.

'This is when my parents were murdered,' I said. 'This is when all of my family were murdered.'

Then I went outside.

FORTY-FIVE

The darkness enveloped me like a cold blanket. I walked on the sand, listening to the water reach up the beach then drain away. It washed at my thoughts and sucked the bad ones out. Washed and sucked, washed and sucked. Helen was reading the cuttings in the house. She had been for a while. I could see the light coming through the windows in the distance. Soon she would know everything, almost everything, the context of that day at least. She'd caught me off guard, asking about the name Roberto. I would have to explain all that to her, although I didn't understand it myself. I walked up to the dunes through the soft sand and sat down in the long grass facing the sea. It was as if I could hear voices in the surf, whispering and talking. Then the voices seemed to get stronger.

They weren't imagined at all, they were real.

I lay down in the grass; no one should be here at this time of night. I crawled in the direction of the voices, the noise I made covered by the surf. The voices grew distinct but I couldn't make out the words. I crawled a bit closer, breathing in sand. I could hear Hebrew. I froze, sharp grass stabbing my face. Another voice answered and I cursed Abu Leila's memory for not allowing me to learn the language.

Without lifting my head I could make out three shadows in the dark, crouched down in a circle. They were looking at something on the ground between them, a sheet of paper or a map illuminated by a small torch. I couldn't deal with three of them on my own, and no doubt at least one other was waiting in a car somewhere. I crawled slowly backwards through the grass until they were out of sight, then, hunched down, ran along the line where the beach met the dunes until I came to the house.

I looked through the French windows and saw Helen blowing her nose. I went inside and closed all the curtains.

'We have to go,' I said. She started to say something, but a length of snot came out of her nose. She laughed at this and I smiled, giving her my handkerchief. I threw the cuttings on the dwindling fire, giving it a final surge of flame that reached up the chimney. You could still see the pictures though; even the text was still readable on the burnt newspaper. The words existed in a delicate state of clarity that was only destroyed when I poked at the grey fragments and they disintegrated. 'We have to leave, they're here, they've found us.'

'What do we do?' she said, calm as anything.

We went upstairs. I told Helen to leave the lights off. We packed our things, taking our time because, as I reassured Helen, they would do nothing until they thought we were asleep, because they just wanted the envelope, although I had no reason to believe that. I was frightened because we were in the middle of nowhere and they could do anything. Why couldn't I have just left Zorba alone?

I asked Helen how she felt about driving us out.

'What other way is there?' she asked.

Then I realised what I was asking. 'You don't have to come,' I said. 'They're not here for you.'

'If you think I'm staying here on my own you're fucking mad. Besides, have you learnt to drive overnight?'

I carried the bags down to the car. I opened the car door, quickly disabling the courtesy light, and put the bags on the back seat, then went back into the house. Helen was in the front room, peering at the books on the shelves.

'You can't appeal to their good nature by reciting poetry,' I said. 'I doubt they're the kind of men who read it. We must go.'

'But you are, Michel. You're the kind of man who reads poetry.' She pulled a thin book from the shelf and put it in her handbag, looking around the room for any forgotten items.

'Wait in the car and I'll be there in a minute,' I said. 'Don't put the car lights on or start the engine or close the car door.' I went upstairs and took the holdall with the money from the attic hatch. I got down the stairs in three steps.

Helen was in the driver's seat, her door ajar. I got into the passenger seat, leaving the door open.

'OK. Start the engine.' She turned the key but nothing happened, not even a starter motor. She tried again three times – it was dead.

'It won't start,' she said. Of course it wouldn't start, these people were professionals and had been at the house already. Helen looked panicked, so I kept my voice level, although my stomach was churning. They had probably been inside as well, looking for the envelope. I could feel it next to my chest like a slab of iron; sitting there since Berlin. They would have disabled the car after we'd come back from town, probably when we were on the beach picking up rubbish. I was panicking now. Think like Vasily, I told myself. You can't have a crisis if you have a plan.

'Where do they park, the day-trippers that come down to the beach?' I asked.

'About a mile and a half up the road; we pass it when we come to the house.' I remembered a wide bit of the road where I had seen several cars parked on the verge. That's where the path started down to the beach, about twenty minutes' walk. I retrieved the bags from the back seat and got out of the car. I spoke quietly, as I wasn't sure how far away they were.

'Is there another way up there, apart from the road and beach path?'

'You would have to go through the wood, but there's no path and in the dark …'

'Through here?' I pointed to the trees by the drive. She nodded. We pushed through the brambles, glad of our jeans. Something hooted in the trees. I picked up a stick to push back the brambles, holding them aside to let Helen pass. After ten minutes we stopped to get our bearings and breath, down on our haunches.

'Michel?' she whispered.

'What is it?'

'This is real, isn't it?'

'It doesn't get more real,' I said. I listened to the unfamiliar noises of the wood, trying to discern anything manmade.

'Michel?'

'Yes.'

'Whatever it was that happened to your family, did you see it?'

I couldn't see her face in the dark, which meant she couldn't see mine. 'Yes,' I said.

She put her hand to my face and held it there for a few seconds. I kissed her palm. 'We'd better keep moving.'

A few minutes later we came onto the beach path some fifty metres from the road. The path rose up from the beach, now in the far distance, not visible from where we were. I told Helen to wait in the wood, told her that I would be back soon enough.

'Where are you going?' she whispered.

'To get a car.'

You couldn't see the road from the path. I walked in the shadow of the trees until it was visible, then stepped into the wood. The Renault 4 was there, facing away from the house, but no other car. This didn't mean that the Golf wasn't nearby. My Russian with the toy cars would tell me that it would be somewhere down the road beyond the house, facing the other way. They would have radios, communicating by clicks if nothing else. I moved closer through the trees. My heart jumped. In the driver's seat I could see my slopey-shouldered friend who I had first spotted in the canteen at UCH. I needed to get him out of the car without him alerting his colleagues. On the other hand I didn't have much time, they may well have visited the house and already be on their way back up the path.

But no, they would have called the car back to the house. We might have enough of a headstart to get clear, provided Helen's driving didn't suffer under the pressure she must be under. She'd been remarkably calm so far, considering what I'd thrown at her. I worried that she was still in shock and that she would imminently crack in some way.

I wasn't sure whether I should kill the agent or just incapacitate him. If it took the former to do the latter then that is what I'd have to do. Method became my concern; he was possibly armed. He wouldn't be expecting me, so I had surprise on my side. Of course all this thinking was just a way of putting off the inevitable. I was at a point on the path where I had to step onto it and commit myself. I found a heavy stick that fitted my palm nicely and was about to move when the car door opened and he got out. I stepped back and froze behind a tree. He came around the back of the car and approached me, undoing his flies. He stood against a tall pine two trees away and the night air was filled with the sound of his urine splashing against dry leaves. I could smell it. I stepped out. He turned towards me, but was more concerned with doing up his flies than defending himself. I hit him square across the temple before he even managed to get his hands up.

FORTY-SIX

I had to hit him again, as he collapsed to one knee, because he tried to get up. This time he slumped onto his front, his hands trapped beneath him. I turned him over and dragged him by his arms into the trees so that Helen wouldn't see him, then searched him for a radio. I found it in an inside pocket and turned it off, throwing it into the woods. He also had a Canadian passport on him, which I pocketed. I removed his belt and tied his hands behind him, just in case he regained consciousness soon. His undone trousers had been yanked down when I'd dragged him so I pulled them off and threw them into the woods. Then I went to get Helen.

She took the wheel of the Renault and complained that the gear stick came out of the dashboard. I couldn't help so I left her to it. We trundled off. I looked in the glove compartment. I saw no clue as to the identity of the driver, but I doubted whether he was Canadian. I checked the passport, which had an unmemorable name that I forgot as soon as I read it.

'Where are we going?' Helen asked.

'When does the first ferry to the mainland leave?' I asked. It was after midnight.

'Five in the morning, I think.'

'Then I don't know,' I said. The Renault's headlights lit up the hedges and stone walls as we made our way along the narrow road.

'I know where we can go,' she said. She turned left and we climbed a winding road, then we dropped and climbed again and she drove slowly through a sleeping hamlet and down a dirt road for five minutes. The Renault did not have the suspension for it – it vibrated and rattled; I imagined nuts and bolts falling off it like in a cartoon. Then she pulled off onto a tarmac road that was blocked by a barrier. She told me to get out and open it, which I did, letting her through before closing it. A big sign warned trespassers of the dangers of entering. She drove past me and the headlights picked out some run-down buildings, not ruins in the ancient sense but relatively new buildings that had been abandoned and neglected. She drove the Renault between two of them and killed the engine. I caught up with her as she got out of the car.

'What is this place?'

She explained that we were in an abandoned village that was built in the fifties to house the expected population boom due to the growing oil industry.

'Turned out it was all happening on the other side of Scotland,' she said. 'I used to come up here with the butcher's boy sometimes.' It was too dark to tell if she was teasing. 'There's a small ferry terminal in the village we've just been through, it goes west rather than east towards Glasgow, but I thought that would be a good thing.' She peered at me in the dark. 'Have I done good?'

'You've done good.' I hugged her. We stood like that for a moment. Then she broke free and told me to follow her.

We moved between the houses and went through a doorway with no door. The front wall of the building was missing, revealing a wide view of a loch. We were high up, with an excellent panorama of the starlit water.

'We can see when the ferry leaves the other side. We'll have plenty of time to get down to the port,' she said. She told me that once over the water we could drive north and connect with the mainland, then head back east. 'I'm assuming you'll want to get back to civilisation?'

'I do feel more in control where there's public transport,' I said. We dragged an old sofa over to face the view and sat down.

'Let's rest,' she said. 'We can hear and see any cars for miles.' We put on extra clothes against the cold. She lay down with her head on my lap. 'People come up here to neck,' she said.

'Neck?'

'Kiss and grope,' she said.

'Ah yes, the irresistible butcher boy.'

She laughed and squirmed on the sofa, trying to find a comfortable position on the semi-exposed springs. I laughed too, but felt jealous of this butcher boy.

'What's the plan, Michel?'

'To get through the night, and to catch the ferry,' I said. I had no real plan beyond making sure Helen was safe. A car noise echoed off the hills and we saw lights several kilometres away light up the road below. They disappeared over the hill and it went quiet.

'My family were shot,' I said, looking out at the black water. She started to raise her head but I gently held it down. 'No, please stay there, don't look at me. Don't say anything.' She relaxed and I stroked her hair, traced the outline of her ear. 'We were having dinner on the second night of the massacre you read about, and some men came into the house, smashed the door off its hinges. The funny thing is we would have opened it if they'd knocked, because we didn't know what was going on at the time, the scale of it anyway.' I could envisage that last meal, a meal I hadn't eaten since. I could taste the fried onions. 'We were taken outside and lined up against the wall. All the men, that is, and me. Mama, my mother, was held back. They made her watch when they started to shoot us – she had to watch it.' I stopped to regain control of my voice; I could feel it slipping away from me. I traced Helen's jawline with my finger, pushed her hair behind her ear. 'My father knocked me down, when the shooting started, and fell on top of me, or maybe he threw himself on me, I don't know, but it's how I survived.' The clouds parted and the moon emerged, just a half-moon, but bright enough to light up the other side of the loch. 'I could feel him breathing for a while, and I could hear Mama screaming. I should have moved, done something, I don't know.' Helen shook her head on my lap. My thigh grew damp and I looked down to see tears dripping from her eyes straight onto my jeans. I stroked her forehead. 'One man was in charge, who gave the orders. He told them to shut my mother up.' I took in some air because I'd forgotten to breathe, and Helen took my hand from her face and clutched it hard to her chest. 'They took her inside the house,' I said.

That was it. I couldn't tell Helen any more. I could remember the rest in vivid detail, because I'd heard it all going on. I knew exactly what had happened to Mama. After some time it had gone quiet, my father had grown heavier, then stopped breathing. I couldn't tell Helen any more of it; I didn't want to poison her ears. Instead I said, 'This man, the officer who gave orders, they called him Roberto.'

'Roberto. Yes of course,' she said. 'Roberto,' she repeated, as if it was an unfamiliar or foreign word. She patted my hand. I think she understood something that I couldn't articulate. Soon her grip relaxed and she fell asleep. It grew cold and my leg went to sleep but I didn't want to wake her.

The moon moved across the loch and I tracked its path when it was revealed by the clouds. Things became clearer. The sky turned grey and a mist layered the still water, like a thick but incredibly light blanket. A small boat went right to left, out to sea, ploughing a v-shaped furrow. Helen stirred and turned onto her back, looking up at me. My legs had gone to sleep. Her eyes were bleary, and the corner of her mouth was crusty with dried spittle.

'It's not your fault, you know,' she said, in a voice croaky with sleep. 'You did the right thing that day. It was what your mother would have wanted you to do. You do know that, don't you?'

I nodded. She was right, but I had needed someone to tell me. I wiped the corner of her mouth.

She smiled. I could hear a thrumming coming off the hills on the other side of the loch. She touched my face.

'The ferry's coming,' she said.

FORTY-SEVEN

Helen drove north for a couple of hours after crossing the loch – we'd been the only ones on the ferry apart from a couple of locals and a post van. She grasped the wheel with white knuckles, leaning forward in the seat, peering through the rain-smeared windscreen. The rain droned on the roof, occasionally sending me to sleep until we braked or turned and I would wake up. Helen would apologise for these interruptions and I would drop off again.

At lunchtime we stopped for breakfast at a roadside place used by truck drivers, filling ourselves with hot tea, fried eggs and sausages.

'Did you miss the tablets last night?' she asked.

'If I have the same distractions we had last night every night then I won't need them at all,' I told her.

She laughed and mopped her plate, then drained her tea. 'Michel, where are we going?'

'Glasgow, then London. Back to civilisation, as you call it.' After lunch Helen drove on, this time east. She was starting to sag in her seat. We were on main roads now. Rejuvenated by dozing and food, I formulated a plan, a plan based on the constraints I was under. I had burned most of my options back at the cottage, only my Lebanese passport remained, with a student visa that ran out in a couple of weeks. It was true that I had lots of money, and I could hole up somewhere, buy documents, a weapon even. But I was worried about Helen and whether I had exposed her to danger. Then there was the matter of the envelope digging into my ribs. I looked at her, but she was intent on the road, pale with fatigue. On the outskirts of Glasgow I saw a shopping centre. I told her to stop there.

We needed new clothes to disguise ourselves. I particularly wanted Helen to look different, as one of the agents had spoken to her up close and they possibly had photos of us. I gave her money and told her to buy things she wouldn't usually wear. We split up, and I bought new shoes and an expensive suit that I wore out of the shop. In the changing room I took the envelope out of my old jacket and weighed it in my hands. It was frayed and sweat-stained, with one corner worn away. I put it in my new jacket. In a newsagent I bought a *Daily Telegraph* and an oversized card – it had a drawing of a small bear with a plaster on its forehead, and inside was written in cursive script, 'Get well soon!' In the toilets I wrote, in Arabic, 'He who has health has hope; and he who has hope has everything,' stuffed twenty $1,000 bills inside the card, then wrote Ramzi's name and work address at UCH on the front, marking it personal and confidential. Hopefully they would use the money for their medical charity. They would probably realise who it was from, but I hoped they would still accept it for what it was. I posted the card outside, then went to the coffee shop, where I'd agreed to meet Helen.

Over coffee I opened the newspaper (more to hide behind than anything) and inside was a small piece about Abu Leila, although it didn't mention him by name. It said the reason for the shooting on the Ku'Damm was still unknown and that the man was still unidentified. The German police said they had no leads but were ruling nothing out, including a terrorist link. It was a hundred words of lather, except for a sentence about the old woman who was killed, who turned out not to be so old but just disabled, a professor of physics visiting from Frankfurt. I could see no mention of Mossad or the PLO, or that Abu Leila had had someone with him. Had the murder happened behind closed doors then it probably wouldn't have reached the press, or would have been suppressed for security reasons. But because it had happened in broad daylight in front of so many people it was difficult to hide. I was in no doubt that the killers wanted it known that they had struck, to send a message to others, perhaps those who were planning to attend the Cambridge meeting.

Helen arrived wearing a knee-length skirt and a fitted top, carrying lots of bags. I'd never seen her in a skirt before. I suggested she do something with her hair.

'Don't you like my hair then?' she said in mock distress.

'It's one of the first things that attracted me to you,' I said.

'Really?' She sounded dubious. 'So it was nothing to do with the fact that I wasn't wearing anything but a towel?'

'Were you not? I didn't notice.'

I was rewarded with a punch on the arm. She tied her

hair back as best she could and put a baseball cap on, pulling the short tail over the strap at the back. We spent half an hour dithering over sunglasses, then went to buy two small cases.

'Why don't we just share one suitcase?' she asked.

'It's just better to have two,' I replied, explaining that we might have to split up to avoid detection.

We transferred our belongings to the new cases in the Renault, which I'd decided we should leave behind; we'd spent more time in it than common sense dictated. It made us, as Jack would have said, stick out like a sore thumb. The competition would have reported it stolen, just so the police could do their work for them: all they would have to do was monitor police radio to determine where it was spotted.

'We'll get a taxi from here,' I told Helen.

'To the station?'

'No, to the airport.'

In the taxi Helen rummaged in her new handbag and removed a tattered book. She blushed. 'It's for you.' The love poems of Kahlil Gibran, a well-worn edition. 'I noticed you had a copy in Tufnell Park. I thought you might like another, since you can't go back there. It's not in Arabic, of course, but my mother doesn't really read Arabic, which is why she has this one, so if you could make do with an English edition until—'

I kissed her for the first time in too long. It lingered and her lips were like warm butter. We held hands until we arrived at the departures building at Glasgow Airport.

I paid the driver and we put on our sunglasses. Inside, the place was busy with holidaymakers.

I took Helen's hand and led her to a table near a lone public phone box. I went to the phone and memorised the number written under the handset. I sat down opposite Helen and scanned the area as best I could. I wanted to kiss her again but I needed to stay strong, stay cool and professional. Instead of kissing her I took off my sunglasses, then hers. I held her hands, stroking the smooth skin with my thumbs.

'I'm going to check out flights and buy tickets,' I said. 'Then I'm going to ring you on the phone box behind me when I've sorted everything out. If it's busy I'll ring back three minutes later.'

'Can't I come with you?'

I maintained eye contact and shook my head. 'They'll be looking for us together. It's safer if we split up and meet on the plane. If anyone comes to talk to you then tell me when I ring.' Strands of her hair had escaped her small ponytail so I tucked them under the cap. 'If I don't phone in the next hour, then I want you to go to a police station, preferably a big one.'

'I thought you said the police would be of no help?' she said.

'You want to ask to speak to a Special Branch officer. Be insistent that it's someone from Special Branch, tell them you have information about foreign agents on British soil.' Special Branch officers were the eyes and ears of MI5 on the ground. Vasily said that MI5 was filled with university-graduate desk analysts, and that Special Branch were the people who did the legwork. I wrote down the licence plate numbers and descriptions of the Golf and the Renault. Under the table I put the piece of paper with the car numbers on it inside the Canadian passport I'd taken from the agent. I then slipped the passport into the middle of the *Daily Telegraph*, which I told her to put in her bag.

'When you have the attention of a Special Branch officer, tell him you have information relating to Israeli agents who are active in the UK. Give him the piece of paper with the licence plate numbers and the Canadian passport. Tell him the truth about everything, about me, everything I've told you.'

She nodded. I was hoping MI5 wouldn't be happy that Mossad agents were running around on their turf. Nor would the Canadians be pleased if they were using forged or stolen Canadian passports. At the very least it would cause logistical problems for them. Maybe, if I was lucky, a minor diplomatic incident.

I fiddled with the big watch on her wrist.

'Helen?' my voice was close to breaking. It leaked out of me, this softness, and I had to plug the leak. I surveyed the area for faces, checked for people standing on their own, talking into their sleeves or collars, listening to headphones, reading newspapers. I started to feel more in control.

'*Ma belle?*'

I stared at the second hand on her watch then looked up. 'You should know that I hate flying,' I said.

She put her hands on my cheeks and squeezed slightly. 'Don't worry, I'll hold your hand,' she said.

'You're an angel.'

'Yes I am. Don't you bloody forget it.'

'I won't.'

I smiled, picked up my case and got up and walked away without looking back.

FORTY-EIGHT

I was surprised at where you could fly to from Glasgow. Flights left every couple of hours to London. There were flights to Paris, to Athens, to Rome. I could go to Paris, get new documents from my painter–forger woman, then go back to London. But then I remembered that I couldn't go to Paris as I no longer had my Swiss passport and I'd need a visa. I daydreamed about other destinations on the flight board that I could go to with Helen, all of them inaccessible to me. My options were limited.

I bought two one-way tickets to Heathrow from a Britannia Airways counter, and left one there for Helen to pick up. The flight left in forty minutes and I wanted to leave ringing her until it was called, so I wandered around, bought a *Glasgow Herald* and some Sellotape, all the while struggling with the longing to go back to Helen. In a toilet cubicle I taped what money I had left into the middle section of the newspaper, then folded it in three. With any luck it would be the last time I'd have to carry money or documents like this. I put the newspaper in my bag and took the worn envelope out of my jacket pocket and held it up, shook it, felt it. Now was not the time to open it. Soon, but not now.

As soon as the first call for the London flight came I rang

the phone box next to Helen. My heart was pumping extra hard. She picked up on the third ring.

'Michel?'

'Helen, I've booked—'

'Michel, he's here. The man from the beach, I've seen him.'

'Has he seen you?'

'No, I don't think so. He came through the entrance with a couple of other men and they went straight up to departures.'

'You did well to spot them,' I said. They're close, I thought, but didn't look around. I gave Helen the flight number and told her where I'd left her ticket. 'I'll watch you go through passport control and make sure you're OK.' She didn't say anything. I could hear the second call for the flight being announced where Helen was as well as around me. It was a strange sensation, as if there was a parallel world on the other side of the line, but I attributed it to codeine withdrawal symptoms.

'Helen?'

'You're not coming with me, are you, *ma belle*?' Her voice was flat. She was right, although I had at least hoped to tell her face to face. Now that they were in the airport I couldn't risk it. 'Don't do this to me, Michel. Don't be another man who fucks off. Don't do it.'

I shook my head until I remembered that she couldn't see me.

'I'm putting you in danger, I can't stay here, can't even be seen with you.' I looked out of the kiosk but couldn't see them.

'Don't pretend this is about me, that you're so fucking noble.' Her sobs came down the phone. It had the odd effect of making me feel strong. I needed to be stronger than she was; we couldn't both fall apart at the same time. I pushed another coin into the slot and waited for her to speak. She blew her nose.

'Where will you go?' she asked.

'I don't know. I just know I can't stay in England any more.' I sounded cold and distant, even to myself. I heard her sniff and blow her nose again.

'You bastard,' she said, less strangled, and I could visualise her face setting into its hard mask. 'I knew it when I saw you walk off with your case. All that fucking crap about needing two cases – you planned this all along.'

The truth was I hadn't, not consciously anyway, but I didn't say anything.

'I'll get in touch with you when I've sorted myself out,' I said. 'I just need to sort all this out.' I waved my hand as if to capture what 'all this' was.

'You'll get in touch with me? Jesus, you sound like I've just fucking auditioned and you have to consider whether I was any good.'

'That's not what I meant,' I said. A pause, then her voice came over clear and strong.

'OK, listen Michel. Get yourself sorted out. Deal with what happened with your family – I don't know, maybe you should have a memorial service or something, get a tombstone erected, get it out of your system.' She stopped and let out a long sigh. Her voice softened. 'Grieve for them properly.' I looked down at my shoes, brand new this morning, to go with my suit; your shoes should always match your clothes. The shoes had little perforations in the top; I had no idea what they were for. I had a strange awareness of myself, as if I was someone else waiting to use the phone, looking in, and I hated what I saw: my shoes, my suit, even my face.

'Are you still there, Michel?' she asked, exasperated.

'Yes. Yes I am.'

'Have a good life, *ma belle*.' She slammed the phone down and I was left with a buzzing in my ear. I depressed and released the hook switch and, out of habit, dialled the speaking clock.

From a vantage point I watched Helen pick up her ticket from the Britannia Airways desk. I wanted to see her go through security so I'd know she was safe; I didn't think they would concern themselves with her once we split up. If I was expecting her to look out for me, I was disappointed. Even at this distance I could see her face was expressionless and her movements mechanical, as if sedated. It didn't look like anyone was watching her, which was the key thing, the thing I focused on. She walked through the barrier and glanced back once, but she didn't see me. Then she was gone. Her disappearance from view caused a constriction in my chest and a burning in my eyes.

I didn't have much time. At a British Airways counter I consulted on flights. After a discussion with the man behind the desk, I paid cash for a one-way ticket, travelling with British Airways to Athens, then, after a couple of hours' transit, with Olympic Airways to Beirut. I had an hour before the flight. I looked for the busiest and most public coffee shop and sat down at a small table in the middle.

I took the envelope from inside my jacket and put it on the table. I sipped my coffee. I slit the frayed envelope open at the top with a teaspoon, taking my time. A clammy hand clutched mine. By my side stood the slopey-shouldered man, breathing hard. He sat down opposite, keeping his hand on mine and his grey-blue eyes locked on me. He had two scabbing contusions on his forehead where I'd hit him last night and his pale freckled skin was glossy with sweat. His eyes flicked to the envelope.

'Maybe you'll regret doing that,' he said. 'Although I'm surprised you haven't already looked.' He sounded well spoken, with a careful enunciation, but with a slight accent, maybe Dutch. I was aware of someone else at my shoulder; I looked round to see a muscular man with a crew-cut, his right hand inside his cagoule. A smaller guy, obviously a graduate of the same training school, stood behind him at the entrance to the coffee shop, he could have been the guy who'd spoken to Helen on the beach. These men were not the people who had followed me to Foyles. Sure, they were on the same side, led by the man sitting opposite me, but following people was not their business. I figured they wouldn't try anything with all these people around us. If they'd wanted to kill me, they would have done it at the house, where they'd missed their chance. I looked at the man opposite, noticing that some of the freckles were actually midge bites.

'I want to see what all the trouble was about,' I said.

He studied my face and made a decision. 'OK, you have a

right to see it, even if you can't keep it.' He slowly removed his hand and glanced at the man at my shoulder, who sat down beside me, dragging his chair up against mine.

From the envelope I pulled out three or four pages folded in three. I straightened them out on the table. The first was in Hebrew. A smiling headshot of a young Abu Leila was in the top right-hand corner. It looked like a form of some kind, the spaces filled in by hand. I could at least read a date: 20/11/1945. A date of birth? I looked at the second sheet. Another photocopied form, but in colour, and another date, this time December 1982. An older Abu Leila, looking intently at the camera, epaulettes on his shoulders. Epaulettes denoting a major. A major in the Israeli army. I went cold. Know your enemy, he'd said. A large blue diagonal stamp cut across the form, at the top of which was a crest with a *menorah* on either side with olive branches meeting at some Hebrew beneath. No, you can't learn Hebrew, he'd said. I looked up at the pale-faced man who was smiling at me, but the smile wasn't reflected in his eyes. I looked down at the third sheet: a picture of Abu Leila being pinned with a medal, just one other man in a suit present. I felt sick. I looked at the papers again, but they had blurred.

The pale-faced man snatched the sheets from my hand. Everything beyond the table became indistinct, the sounds muted. I tried to stand up but the big man gripped my forearm with iron fingers. The pale face said, 'Where are you going, cockroach?'

'I'm going home,' I said.

'Home?'

'Beirut,' I said.

'OK, cockroach. We can find you there if we need to squash you.' I shook off the grip on my arm, picked up my bag and stood up. The flight to Athens was being called. I brushed past the smaller crew-cut at the café entrance and walked steadily to the departure gate without looking back.

FORTY-NINE

The ragtag group of ten- to twelve-year-old students in my weekly French class would probably never have an opportunity to use the language, but I was motivated by the hope that at least one of them might find it helpful in breaking from the confines of the refugee camp that I had left over ten years ago.

One cold and damp November afternoon, a few days after the fall of the Berlin Wall, two weeks after Canada publicly asked Israel to explain the fraudulent use of its passports and three months after being back in Beirut, I left the UN-run school and went to the small grocery store nearby, where I bought tinned beans, cheese, eggs and tomatoes, and as I stepped back onto the muddy street a voice beside me said, 'It's not Harrods, for sure.' I turned to see Khalil, the thin balding man I'd met in Harrods. He was in a black coat worn at the elbows and carried an ancient Samsonite briefcase. The scar on his chin looked whiter than I remembered, or maybe the stubble was longer.

'It has everything I need,' I told him.

'Good to see you again, Michel.' He shook my hand firmly. 'I would like to have that conversation about Abu Leila now.'

I shrugged, checking the street for his backup. The dark weather had cleared the boggy street of most people. He leaned in, smelling of fresh cigarette smoke. 'You can be sure I'm alone. You have finished teaching for the afternoon, I think.'

It was a visit I had been waiting for, hoping for, even, although, since I was associated with Abu Leila, I was half-expecting there to be no conversation, just three or four shots to the head. I made a joke to that effect as we walked to my rented apartment. Khalil looked genuinely hurt at the suggestion.

'We are not animals,' he said.

My place was on the top floor of a seven-storey building on the outskirts of the camp. It had a balcony big enough for one person to stand on. The rent was low because of the eagle-eye view of the camp where I worked. Sometimes I stood there early in the morning watching it come to life. Sometimes I stood there long before dawn.

Khalil looked out of the balcony door and said, 'You can keep an eye on things from up here, for sure.'

I took his coat and he sat on my only armchair, coughing phlegm into a handkerchief and taking out some cigarettes and a gold lighter.

'What about Abu Leila?' I asked, thinking of him kneeling before me in Berlin, his glasses bloodied and shattered.

Khalil wiped his small mouth. 'What about him?'

'You said that you weren't animals. He was shot on the street like an animal.'

Khalil snorted. 'Did you see what was in the envelope from the West Bank?'

I nodded. Why bother pretending otherwise?

'He was responsible for the death of at least five operatives in the Territories and the arrest and torture of many more. He gave away many secrets, the most damaging being political. Is that reason enough?' He coughed again into his handkerchief and I had no answer, just questions.

'How do you know what was in the envelope?' I asked.

He stopped coughing and raised his watering eyes to me, dabbing at them with his handkerchief in a disarmingly feminine manner.

'Because, my son, I put it there.'

Khalil paid three long visits to my small apartment, and on the first made it clear that he needed to know everything.

'Everything?' I asked, thinking of Helen and me making love in Tufnell Park and Scotland. He stopped looking for things in his open briefcase and looked at me over the lid instead.

'Let me tell you, Michel, that some were of the opinion that I should bring you to Damascus to have this discussion, let us say, under less pleasant circumstances, and keep you there until we were satisfied. I told them it would be counter-productive.' He cleared his throat. 'I wasn't wrong, was I?'

'I'll answer any questions you have,' I reassured him. I just wouldn't volunteer anything, I thought.

He stayed for hours at a time, and wrote down every detail in a black notebook. Every so often he would take out a grainy photograph from his battered case and show it to me. It would always be of Abu Leila with some individual or in a group, taken from a distance, and Khalil would want to know if I had ever seen the other people in Berlin. Recounting the complete pointlessness of my life, describing the empty shell that had been created by seeing the contents of the envelope, was unpleasant. Although I had gone through it all in my head since being back, often standing on my balcony in the dark, speaking it out loud made it real, brought the sham into keen relief. I was embarrassed in the telling of it, more than anything, like someone who has been the butt of a cruel practical joke.

At the end of his second visit Khalil said, 'You were just a pawn in Abu Leila's dangerous game of chess, Michel.'

What is it with professional liars and chess? I thought of Abu Leila's first visit to the apartment not three kilometres from where we were sitting, and his chess analogy. I hated him now, of course, even though I wanted to believe that everything he had told me was still true.

It was only on the third and final visit that Khalil asked me about the envelope I had opened in Glasgow.

'Did Abu Leila look inside it? Before he was executed?' he asked. He was intent on my answer. I recalled our last meeting in the KaDeWe, our walk down the Ku'Damm – the envelope was still sealed and inside the newspaper when I had taken it from next to his lifeless body. Khalil was visibly disappointed at this information. I understood that Khalil had meant Abu Leila to see the contents before his execution, and for it to be found on his body – that was its purpose; a death sentence for him, and to let Mossad know that the PLO knew. But neither Mossad nor Khalil, for different reasons, wanted anyone else to know. It was a setback for Mossad, who thrived on appearing infallible, and embarrassing for the PLO, given Abu Leila's seniority and length of service. All of which explained why Khalil had wanted the envelope back, and why the Israelis had come after it. 'And how was he on that day?' Khalil was asking.

'What?'

'Abu Leila, how was his demeanour?'

'He wanted to go to the Kranzler Café. He'd just bought cigarettes at KaDeWe.' I didn't tell him that he was about to discuss my future.

'I told him that smoking would kill him, for sure,' Khalil said, without a smile. Of course Khalil must have known that Abu Leila would be on the street, they must have been watching us in the KaDeWe. How stupid was I?

'What was his real name?' I asked.

He fiddled with his gold lighter. 'Amir Serfati. He was a Moroccan Jew, what they call a Mizrahi. His parents emigrated to Israel in '54.'

I rubbed my temples. I recalled the Moroccan novels he had given me, the Moroccan food he liked, his talk of Arab Jews being the original Jews.

Khalil smiled. 'What? Did you think he was Palestinian?' He lit a cigarette and blew out smoke in a thin stream. 'He was organising the meeting in Cambridge to coax out those people interested in this silly idea of one state.'

'Coax them out?'

'Yes, to get rid of them. The plan was to hit the house in Cambridge. He wanted to deal us a deadly blow.'

I shook my head in disbelief. I said I couldn't imagine the

Israelis carrying out such an operation in the UK, and why on a group of people who were marginal in the PLO?

'You're being obtuse, Michel. You were an important part of the plan, your involvement would have made it look like it was us that had arranged it. You found the place, organised security. Abu Leila would have made sure that information implicating you fell into the hands of British Intelligence, left a few clues to help them along, to make the right connections. Of course he didn't know I was onto him.'

Abu Leila – I couldn't think of him as Amir Serfati – always said the Israelis were good at dissembling. He would have known, since he was the father of all dissemblers. He'd said the meeting was contrary to the Old Man's plans, so it would look like the Old Man had sanctioned the hit. If it was true, it was clever: get rid of the people who are a threat and blame it on their own, using me as the fall guy.

This had been my purpose all along, then, to be a conduit that would lead people to the wrong conclusion. I felt sick.

'But if I'd been arrested I would—'

Khalil cut me off with a laugh, but it wasn't joyous. 'Arrested? If you'd been alive to be arrested. You would have been linked to Abu Leila, which would have pointed to us. He would still be in place and sowing lies and division among us, you would have been branded a traitor.'

I rubbed my whole face, trying to wash it clean. I didn't want to believe that Abu Leila would have allowed me to be sacrificed. Instead I asked, 'So there were no Israeli delegates?'

'Yes, there were, that was the beauty of the plan, for sure.' Khalil grew animated. 'Although the plan was to martyr the Palestinians – and I think you met some of the assassination team in Scotland – Abu Leila's meeting would also have exposed the closet Israelis pursuing this one-state idiocy, even before they left Israel. They have no political future, of course, and have been charged with disloyalty to the state.'

He started coughing again and I went to stand at the balcony doors, looking down at the camp. I could tell roughly where my house used to be, it had been bulldozed flat in the second siege of '88, but by referencing other parts of the camp, like the hospital, I knew where it had stood. Someone had built an unofficial memorial to those that had been killed in '82 but I had yet to visit it. I turned to look at Khalil, who was gathering his things into his case.

'What of the Palestinians who were going to attend, what's happened to them?'

Khalil snapped his case shut.

'They also have no political future. In a way Abu Leila did us a favour, exposing these people; what they were planning undermined the sanctioned contacts.'

'You mean the talks in Oslo?' I said, to shock him. It worked, for he sat up straight and frowned.

'What do you know about Oslo?'

'Abu Leila said they would fuck us at Oslo,' I said.

Khalil winced, picked up his cigarettes and lighter then stood, holding his Samsonite at his side.

'I think we're finished, Michel.'

'Am I in the clear?'

'As far as I'm concerned you were in the clear when I saw you in Harrods. I can't speak for the Jews, of course. I suppose we're both relying on your silence and discretion.' He cocked his head and raised his eyebrows to indicate that it was a question, not just a statement.

'Even if I had any evidence, who would I tell? And who would believe it if I did?' I asked.

He smiled thinly. 'No one,' he said.

FIFTY

A week after Khalil's last visit I went to the main post office in downtown Beirut, still scarred with the acne of many wars. I took a circuitous route, changing buses several times and walking a lot. Not because I thought anyone was still interested in me; I'd spent the week making sure nobody was. It was mainly to work up the nerve to do what I was about to do. It also gave me a chance to reflect on what Khalil had revealed. When I'd walked him to the front door for the last time he'd turned and stopped.

'You know we could use someone with your skills,' he said. I couldn't help laughing, but he'd been serious and frowned at my frivolity. 'So you're happy living here, teaching kids, interpreting for the Western media and charity workers, no money, no prospects?'

I shrugged, trying to remember whether I'd told him about the interpreting, but I hadn't.

'And the cause?' he persisted. 'You could go back to Europe, we could get you a passport.' I imagined flying to London and knocking on Helen's door in Tufnell Park. I doubted she was still there.

'The cause will carry on with or without me.' I gestured

to the balcony door and said, 'Maybe the cause is in the camp, not in Europe.'

'I'm not so sure about that,' he'd said. 'Your beloved camp will be around for some time, that's for sure.'

When he was gone I went to the shelf above the bed in my small bedroom, a bedroom the size of my room in Tufnell Park. Some of these books I'd been made to leave behind when I moved from Beirut the first time, and some were new. I pulled out a slim volume of Kahlil Gibran's poetry and aphorisms in English. It was the edition Helen had given me in Scotland, taken from her mother's untidy shelves. Inside the flap was written – and I only saw this a few weeks after coming home – 'Michel. See page 12. Helen X'.

I let it fall open to page twelve, where a few lines were messily underlined; she must have done it some time between leaving the house in Scotland and taking the taxi to the airport.

It was but yesterday I thought myself a fragment quivering without rhythm in the sphere of life.

Now I know that I am the sphere, and all life in rhythmic fragments moves within me.

Was she referring to herself, to me or to both of us? I think I understood it in relation to myself. Maybe I was finding a way to become myself again, discovering some peace, even a small purpose. I was learning to master my own destiny, not an easy thing to do having been enslaved without realising it.

Many questions remained unanswered, only one of which still haunted me as I made my way to the post office. What was Abu Leila going to say to me just before he was killed? He'd wanted to discuss my future. Was it going to be more dissembling, something to make sure I fulfilled the role that Khalil (another dissembler) said was planned for me? I chose to believe otherwise. I chose to believe that it was going to be something more, that perhaps he was going to warn me. Maybe I was deluding myself but the more probable alternative was too much to bear for the moment.

I waited in line until a counter was free in the post office. Since returning to Beirut, when I'd had time to muse on everything that had happened, go over every detail of my life in the new light of Abu Leila's deception – every conversation, every book he'd given me, every task I'd been asked to perform – I'd regretted spending all that time reading about Jewish history and the Holocaust. I wanted to reject everything to do with him, to purge myself of his influence. But I couldn't really do it, any more than I could purge myself of the day of the killings or of meeting Helen. You couldn't wipe things clean and start again, you had to deal with events, to incorporate them into your being without letting them cripple you.

The truth is that my eyes had been opened by him to things that I probably wouldn't otherwise have become aware of. So thanks to Abu Leila, or Amir Serfati, I had at least come to know my enemy, and to know him first-hand. 'We are a family of uprooted gypsies, outsiders wherever we go,' he'd told me. I'd thought at the time he was referring to Palestinians, but perhaps he'd been referring to Jews.

Maybe, after his pretence at being Palestinian for so long, he'd meant both.

I made it to the front of the queue and was directed to a counter. A pretty headscarfed young woman smiled at me. I told her I wanted to open a new PO box and handed her my Lebanese passport. After she had done the paperwork I asked to send a telegram in English.

'Where to?' the woman asked. Her scarf only half-covered her head, as if she thought, as I did, that it was a shame to completely hide her glossy black hair. I slipped a piece of paper through the gap in the glass; I wanted it to be accurate. I pointed at the paper.

'That's the address,' I said. I had written everything out in capitals. 'The message is below.'

She examined it carefully and said, 'I have a cousin studying in London.'

I smiled at this information. 'Is that so? What's she studying?'

'She wants to become a doctor.' She stuck out the tip of her tongue as she painstakingly wrote Helen's name and the University College address out on the telegram slip, taking her time over the word 'anthropology'. I had no idea if Helen was still at the college, but I was hoping that someone would forward it to her. And even if it was forwarded I had no idea if she would respond, but then you can spend your whole life wondering and waiting.

The woman looked up at me, holding the paper I'd given her. 'Is this all you want to say?'

I nodded. She copied it out slowly and then turned it around and asked me to check it.

I read the message: 'Dearest Helen. Have sorted myself out. Would love to hear from you.'

'That's perfect,' I said. 'Put my PO box as the return address.'

'How do you want to sign it?'

'Just Michel,' I said.

'Dear God,' she said, addressing the heavens, 'you can't send a telegram to a woman without signing off in a manner that shows your intentions.'

She was right. I smiled at her and thought about it.

'OK. Sign it "*Ton beau*",' I said, feeling the embarrassment in my face.

She looked at me and smiled. 'Well, let's hope she thinks so, yes?'

I laughed out loud. Loud enough to attract the attention of everyone in the post office, but I didn't care.

MISCHA HILLER

SABRA ZOO

It is 1982 and Beirut is under siege. Teenager Ivan, parent free for the first time, is interpreting for international volunteers in Sabra refugee camp, getting stoned and working undercover for the PLO. He helps Norwegian physiotherapist Eli treat Youssef, an orphan disabled by a cluster bomb. But events take a nasty turn as Israeli troops surround the camp, separating Ivan from Eli and Youssef, and leaving him to try to salvage something from the chaos.

'A stunning, defiant debut' *Guardian*

'A moving debut ... Hauntingly written, with a wonderful touch for human feelings' *Daily Mail*

'Harrowing and heartfelt but never overwrought. In a few pages, [Hiller] creates a truly terrifying vision of hell' *Independent*

'Hiller's evocation of the war through a teenager's eyes gives this novel both depth and gravitas ... *Sabra Zoo* is a funny novel that reminds us that even the chaos of war can't thwart the complexities of the human spirit and the mysteries of love.' *Literary Review*